Memoirs of a Social Butterfly

The three climbers came over the top of the hill.

The ground was like a wet sponge from all the rain. Harry started to slide; it felt like he was on a waterside. When he stopped, he shouted back to Phil.

'Hey, this's great fun!' He took a few steps onto another slide, but this time he picked up speed.

Ahead, a large rock was in his path. Harry hit the rock sideways. Looking over the rock only a few feet away, the ground dropped down a sheer cliff ... and a hundred-foot drop!

He looked back up the mountain ... He could only see Mike; there was no Phil anywhere. But white as a ghost, Mike was coming down towards him.

'Where was Phil?'

ABOUT THE AUTHOR

Anthony McMahon is new to the writing world. He currently lives in Ireland doing normal 9-5 job but spending as much time as possible in the outdoors, running, hiking surfing and taking pictures. He also creates hand crafted frames for pictures taken.

His stories are character driven and about how real people deal with real situations in real-world situations. Music plays major part, each chapter having a song to capture the essence of the situation.

Playlists of songs used are available on Spotify.

Copyright Anthony McMahon© 2018

The events depicted in this book are fictitious. All persons portrayed are fictitious. Any similarity to any person living or dead is merely coincidental.

Memoirs

of a

Social Butterfly

BY
ANTHONY MCMAHON

Prologue
'California Sun' *The Ramones*

Harry and Phil got off the Greyhound bus at San Francisco's main bus station, heading out onto the main street after picking up their bags. As they looked up and down the street, they could see rainbow flags hanging on both sides as far as they could see. Harry turned to Phil, 'I know this supposed to be the sort gay capital of the US, but this is a bit over the top?'

'Maybe, but hey, it is what it is.' Phil replied shrugging his shoulders.

'Suppose so, right, so where's this hostel then?'

Phil looked at his guide book, then map, 'right it's that way.' He said pointing down the road. 'It's not too far. Hope they have a room for us.'

'It'll be fine if they don't, we'll just find somewhere else. We always find a bed somewhere, don't we?'

'Yeah, I suppose so.'

'Exactly.'

They found the hostel, which was a little further away and up a few more hills than they originally thought. Luckily had two beds in a shared dorm room. They dropped their bags, then headed of out for a wander around. Not far away from the hostel they spotted a pub their guidebook had recommended.

'Quick drink? So we can formulate a plan of action? '

'You read my mind.'

They perched themselves at the bar, ordering drinks form the barman. When they arrived the barman asked, 'So you guys here for the parade or the convention?'

'Huh?' Harry replied looking confused at Phil

'The gay pride parade or the builders' convention?'

'Ah, no we're here for neither.'

'Ah, so your just on vacation then.'

'Exactly, so when are the rest of the Village people having their conventions then?' Phil asked cutting in.

'Phil!' Harry whispered nudging him. 'not the time for jokes like that.' He looked up at the barman who was laughing as he got on with job, serving a few builders who had come in.

They finished their drinks, then decided they would move on. They headed up to Union square where they sat down to try figure out their plan of action for the next few days. Harry turned to Phil, 'you brought us into San Francisco, on gay pride weekend!?'

'How was I to know?'

'Does it not say that in the Lonely Planet guide you always have your head stuck in?'

'Maybe, can't say I noticed it.' He pulled the guide book out, starting to flick through it.

'Didn't notice it, it's like the bloody Paddy's day parade at home!'

'Oh, yeah there it is. Doesn't give a specific date just a general idea.'

'We'll never live this one down. Can imagine the piss taking from the lads?' Harry was looking for something in his bag, 'ah, here it is.' He pulled out a booklet of things to do.

'We don't have to tell them, do we?'

'Man, they'll find out. Someone will know, but this can only mean one thing.' Harry looked up from the booklet, smiling.

'What is it?'

'Strip club.' He was pointing at a page full of adverts for them.

'Ah, I see your logic. Evening sorted so.'

They finished their drinks and headed of for a day's sightseeing on the street cars to the Golden Gate and Alcatraz.

Later in the evening after what felt like a three-day camel ride they finally found the strip with all the bars they were looking for, now which one? Eventually they picked one, paid the entrance fee and headed in. They discovered there was no alcohol being served when they got to the bar, lucky they'd had a few pre-drinks. Finding a table with a view of the stage, they sat down.

'Hey guys, I'm Destiny.' A girl came straight over

'Hi.' They both replied

'How you guys doing tonight? Enjoying your trip?'

'We're great, having a super time.'

'Want me to make it better with a private dance?'

'Em … we're grand for the moment, but if we change our minds we'll let you know.'

'Sure, you'll see me around. Just give us a shout, I'll make it worth your while.' She walked off.

'Hey, it's a bit odd them not serving gargle ain't it?'

'Seems that way, mustn't want lads getting pissed and messy, grabbing at the girls.'

'Makes, sense in a way, I suppose. It would great to go out with her, though.'

'What's that?'

'Just so you could say, I've got date with Destiny.' Phil could only shake his head at Harry.

'Don't use that joke again Harry. It's bad.'

'I thought it was funny. So you gonna get a dance then?'

'Oh, don't know. You?'

'Maybe, if I see someone that takes my fancy.' Just as he said she passed by, Harry nearly dropped his drink. 'Yeah, I'm getting one. Look at her, she's stunning.' She spotted him staring, then headed straight for the table.

'Hey guys, I'm Crystal.'

'Hey, so you gonna dance for me?' Harry thought there was no point in hanging around, he knew what he wanted.

'Your quick off the mark there ain't ya, sunny Jim?'

'What can I say, you're the only one in here I'd have dance for me.'

'Well come on then, I'll give you a good show.' She took him by the hand, leading him into the back. Leaving Phi sitting there on his own, sipping his coke.

'So, you all on your lonesome then?' Another girl approached. *'Oh my god she is lovely.'*

'Em … yeah. My friend just went off with one of your friends.'

'Maybe, you should come back to the magical place they are too?'

She leaned over to take him by the hand, 'Maybe I should.' He stood up to be led away.

When Harry came back out, he saw Phil sitting at a different table, 'So you get a dance then?'

'Yeah, had one. Stunning girl.' Phil smiled back.

'I had two, off the same girl! What'd ya think? She like your accent? Mine loved it, had a great chat with her at the end too. Think she liked me.'

'Harry, don't do this.'

'Do what, she spent ages talking to me.'

'Man, that's her job. That's what they're paid to do. Make you fall for them; they get more money that way. More money out of you.'

'Na, this was different. She even told us the best bar to go to after this to score girls!'

'Man, you're crazy. We heading soon?'

'Yeah, I'm finishing this crazy expensive Coke first. No way I'm leaving it.'

The girl who had been dancing for Harry came over, 'Hey Harry, what you doing sitting over here at the back? I told you to sit up at the front, I'm up on stage next. Wana give my Irish man another dance.' Harry looked at Phil shrugging as she led him towards the stage, 'Come on, you too.' She then said looking back at Phil, who got up to follow. Suddenly they found themselves sitting in the front row. *'Maybe she does like him?'* Phil thought.

Crystal started her dance on stage, everyone in the place was fixated with her dancing, including Harry and Phil. She kept glancing over in Harry's direction, after a few minutes she worked her way across the stage towards the two naive pasty looking Irish lads. Phil nudged Harry and gave him a look as if to say, what's going to happen here? She knelt down in front of Harry looking deep into his eyes, grabbed him by the collar of his shirt and dragged him up onto the stage. Neither Harry or Phil knew what to do. Harry was now lying flat on his back with Crystal straddling him. *'She must really like him,'* Phil thought to himself.

They eventually left and arrived at the club that had been recommended to Harry by Crystal, it was still early so there weren't many people there yet. Harry went to the bar while Phil waited standing at the side of the dance floor.

'So, what's the plan?' Harry asked as he arrived back with the drinks.

'Silly dance time?'

'Bit early for that ain't it?'

'Never too early for silly dance Harry.'

'Alright then. Not on the dance floor though?'

'No, far too early for that, we'll do it just here.' They put their drinks down on a ledge between them and the dance floor.

'So what you going to do then?'

'Oh, I'm going cowboy rounding up the heard.' Harry said.

'Good choice, I'm going fishing.'

They stood on the side facing the dance floor, Harry pretending to ride his horse, throwing his lasso onto the dance floor. Phil was pretending to cast out a fishing rod, reeling it back in.

As Phil was reeling back in he saw a girl moving towards him, *'think I've caught something here,'* he though as she got closer to him, then she summonsed him onto the dance floor with her finger. He looked across at Harry, 'I caught something Harry, I caught something!'

Harry looked back, 'So did I!' The two friends were both being called down onto the dance floor by two girls.

Phil smiled at Harry, 'This is going to be great.'

Phil lay in his bunk looking at his watch, *'four am, good god,'* he thought to himself. *'I'll never get to sleep at this stage.'* He really wanted to punch the bunk above him. The man up there was snoring so loud the whole frame of the bed was shaking. He was carrying an extra bit of weight, which somehow made the snoring deeper and worse. 'Harry?' he whispered across to his friend, who was in a bunk across the room.

'Yeah,' came the reply quite quickly.

'Awake then?'

'Sure how could anyone sleep with the God of thunder above you there?'

'No need to tell me, the whole bed is vibrating.'

'The whole room is vibrating!'

'What we going to do?'

'I saw some sort of sports bar down the road, looked like it was still open when we left them girls earlier.'

'Go for stroll down to see if it is open? Not much else we can do. Need to get outa this room.'

'Let's go, we've nothing to lose.'

They got to the bar and discovered it was indeed still open, so they went in and ordered a beer each. There were three other people in the bar along with the girl who was serving. The back wall of the pub was filled with TV screens and they were showing a football match. Neither had any idea who was playing.

'Two pints of beer please.' Harry asked the girl behind the bar.

'Coming right up.'

'Who's playing?' Phil said quizzically looking at Harry.

'The world cup is on ain't it? Haven't got a clue who's playing. Definitely not one of the big teams like Germany or Brazil.'

Just then the score came up on the screen and the match was between South Korea and Togo. They looked at each other, shrugged their shoulders, then back to the screens trying to figure out what the hell was going on. Neither had ever gotten into supporting football as children, which was a bit strange as where they grew up everyone seemed to support one the big English clubs. Their fathers had tried their best to get them into supporting a team, even buying them jerseys. But, they eventually gave when it was evident they very little interest in the sport.

'Never thought we'd end up sitting in a pub at 5 am watching a world cup match between two random teams.' Harry protested.

'Wasn't high on my list either. But what was the alternative, lie in bed and study the springs in the mattress above?' Phil gave in reply.

'No offence, but neither of you look like you're from either Togo or Korea.' The girl said bringing over their pints.

'Oh no. we're Irish.' Harry protested.

'You don't say. I'd never have guessed!' She replied throwing her eyes to the celling.

'She's joking with you, you moron.' Phil said putting his hand up to his face.

'So what brings you here at this hour? Obviously, it's not to watch the game.'

'Ah, we needed to get away from the god of thunder as quick as possible.'

'The god of thunder?!' asked the girl from behind the bar in surprise.

'Oh, best explain. He's the reason we needed to get out of the dorm so early. We're not raging alcoholics, there's a lad staying in our hostel room and he snores. I mean shake the whole room level snoring and he manages to sleep all the time too. We went in yesterday afternoon there he was snoring, got back at about three am this morning from a bar and he was still waking the dead.'

'Oh dear he sounds like a nightmare.'

'Tell me about it. We've had next to no sleep.'

'I hope he hasn't spoiled your trip to San Francisco?'

'Oh no he hasn't. We've had a great time, haven't we Harry?' Phil gave him a quick nudge.

'It's been a great few days alright. Lovely city, lovely people.' Harry smiled in reply.

'That's great. Glad you're having a good time.' She replied as she headed off down the bar.

They turned back towards the screen. 'Make this a bit interesting, Pick a team?' Phil suggested.

'Okay then, Come on Korea.'

'Right so I'm up for Togo then. Looser buys a pint?'

'You're on.'

They managed to sit through the whole match, mainly by putting small bets on silly things like who would fall over next. How long they would roll about pretending to hurt. They looked around the bar and it was only them and the girl working there.

'Another pint lads?' She the girl behind the bar asked after the full time whistle went.

'Well Philp, I do believe Korea won, so you owe me a pint.'

'Dam. Guess I do. Two more pints please.' She headed off to get them.

'Right so where we going to head next?'

'I'm not sure LA, Vegas?'

The girl came back with the drinks. 'So you boys travelling around California then?'

'Yeah, just trying to decide where to go next.' Phil replied.

'You thought of San Diego?'

'It's a bit far ain't it?'

'No, you can fly down for around a hundred dollars or so.'

'Really? Would you not have to book a flight well in advance though?'

'Oh no. Internal flights are like trains or buses over here. You can just show up and buy a ticket.'

'Really?'

'Yeah. Just jump on the BART over to Oakland airport, jump on a South Western flight and you'll be there in no time.'

They both looked at each other and instantly knew where their next port of call was.

'Say, you don't know anywhere good we can stay down there?' Harry asked.

'Actually yeah I do. Head to Pacific Beach, it's a bit outside the City, sort of near Sea World. It's a great spot full of College kids. See if you can get a bed in the Banana Bungalow. Amazing place, right on the beach.' She pulled out a piece of paper from behind the bar and wrote the details down for them.

'Thanks for that. We'll def drop in. What's the surf like down there?' Harry was now leaning in in expectation, surfing in the Pacific was always something he wanted to do.

'Oh you surf, do you?'

'I try.'

'Surf is great down there, you'll love it.'

'Think I know where we're going next Phil.'

'You don't have to ask me twice. When we heading?'

'Today?'

'Yeah, let's do it. Get away from Thor.'

'Hey, you guys know the best thing about working in the bar at this hour?' The girl cut in.

'Getting to chat to two charming Irish lads.'

She smiled that him and shook her head, 'Yeah, I also get to play whatever music I want.' She was now at the entertainment system, 'you guys ever hear of David Lee Roth?'

'Wasn't he the lead singer with Van Halen at some stage?'

'Yeah he was. Wait until you hear this song. Just love this era of Rock, big hair and spandex. They looked like poodles.' She put on 'Just Like Paradise.' 'I love this song.' She said while disappearing under the bar.

They sat and listened to the whole song. 'It is very eighties, but, I like it.' Phil finally said.

'Yeah I like it too. It could well be another song for our trip play list.'

'Yeah it definitely.'

'Come on drink up, we need to get back and pack.' Harry said sounding excited.

'Hey, hang on a sec there. Hold your horses.'

'You not excited about going for a surf in the Pacific?'

'Obviously, not as much as you.'

Harry downed his pint, 'Hey you had your few days climbing in Yosemite and I had to flute around while you hung off the side of El Capitan. Come on I'll race you back.'

'Harry!'

Harry got up off his seat to leave. Phil downed the rest of his pint and headed towards the door, calling out 'Thanks for all the help.' Along the way.

'Anytime boys. Enjoy the surf and those California Girls.' Came the reply from under the bar.

*****

CHAPTER 1
'A design for life' *The Manic Street Preachers*

Harry opened his eyes and thought, *'Shit, it's bright,'* he was lying on a no uncomfortable sofa still in his clothes from the night before, with what felt like a rug over him. He looked around, through blurry eyes realising he hadn't a clue where on earth he was. Nothing in the room looked familiar to him. He looked at his watch and it was six thirty am. *'Fuck, I've an exam at ten. Fuck, Fuck, FUCK!'* was his next thought. There was no one else in the room, just him there curled up on the sofa on his own, hating his life. *'Ah shit, can I get home have a wash and make this exam? Fuck I need to try; why do I do this to myself? Just one drink Harry, yeah right!'*

Sitting bolt upright, sticking his boots on, he rushed for the front door, making sure he had the holy trinity of wallet, phone and keys on the way. When he got to the door he tried to open it, it was stuck. Trying again this time a little harder, still no luck, the door was properly jammed. *'You've got to be joking!'* Pulling at it again, still no movement on it, again with more force; no way it was opening. Looking around, a little panicked by now, he spotted a window back in the sitting room – this was his way out. Luckily the window was open when he checked, it was going to be a tight squeeze but definitely doable. He got through with a bit of a gangly, awkward landing, but what would you expect of someone in his delicate state?

When outside, he found himself standing in a housing estate, with no idea of how to get to a main road and a taxi home. Looking around he spotted a line of high trees and thought, *'there must be a main road around here somewhere.'* He set off in the direction of the trees, lucky enough it was the boundary of the housing estate; he started his search for a taxi home.

While in the taxi he was trying to piece together the night before, it was just flashes of people's faces and various types of drinks. How did he end up in a house, miles away from home? He had promised himself to take it easy because of the exam. These were after all his 'professional' exams, they were very important to his supposed career. Remembering he had gone for a few drinks after work with his workmates. About seven pm, he received a text from Dervila, he could never say no to her. *'Where was she now?'* he thought. Spending time with her was so much fun, but she really was hard on the wallet, more so on the liver. She would keep him out all night, not that he needed much encouragement; he didn't mind as he had loved every minute of it. The night before was becoming a little clearer now, she must not have been able to wake him and just left him there. Some girlfriend she was.

Home now, just time for a quick nap, wash, then off to do his exam. This was not going to be any fun, at all. A couple of bottles of Lucozade might do the trick here. He closed his eyes; the alarm went off. *'Oh no, that was nowhere near enough sleep, but it would just have to do. Up a quick shower and then off to the exam.'*

When he got to the exam hall, he met Tom from work waiting outside. 'Man you look like shit; what time did ya get home?'

'Oh, about seven am.'

'No way, what were you up to?'

'Ah, you don't want to know. I'm not even too sure myself!'

'You're something else. Look, they're calling us in.'

'How long is it on for?'

'Three hours.'

'No way, how long before you can leave?'

'Pretty sure it's two hours.'

'It's going to be a long two hours.'

'Not just for you. Anyway, good luck – you'll need it.'

'Cheers Tom. Best of luck, too.'

This was going to be the longest two hours of Harry's short life. Sitting in the exam hall he looked around and could see others neatly setting up their desks with different colour pens and rulers, Harry only had two black pens with him and most importantly his two bottles of Lucozade. *'Oh well they'll have to do. Not much I can do about it now is there?'* All he could think of was how quick he could get this out of the way, two bottles were definitely not going to be enough. *'Oh well eyes down, try clear the haze and off we go.'*

When he turned over the page he couldn't recognise the language it was written in. What on earth was going on, it was in hieroglyphics! He really needed to stop drinking!

'Just calm down and it'll be okay, deep breaths, deep breaths.'

After ten minutes staring at the page, it started to make some sense to him. He had wasted most of his twenty-minute preparation time. Now he could start, finish it as best he could in about an hour and a half, then had to sit there for the reaming thirty minutes until he could leave. Watching the clock, he could swear the second hand was flicking between fifty and forty-nine at one stage. Eventually it hit twelve thirty; *'Thank God, I can leave now.'* He was a little disturbed by the not being able to decipher the text on the paper but thought nothing of it. Time to find the nearest pub for a cure and give Dervila a call to see where she had disappeared to the night before.

A few weeks later while sitting at his desk in work, Tom approached, leaning over his work partition.

'Did you know the test results are out today?'

Harry jumped as hadn't noticed Tom approaching, 'Jesus Tom, you scared the shit out of me. No way, what did you get?'

'65%.' Tom seemed quite content with himself.

'Good stuff, at least you passed. Must be happy with that?'

'Yeah, chuffed. You not going to check yours?'

'Oh don't really want to, but best not put it off.'

Harry logged onto the website to get his results; it seemed to take ages with all the passwords. *'Which one did I use for this one, well not that one; maybe this one, ah there it is.'*

'Well how'd you do?' Tom was edging closer, moving around the end of the partition, getting closer to the computer screen.

'Oh this can't be right?' Harry sounded a little confused.

'It's not that bad, is it?' He was nearly on top of him now.

'No; definitely, it says Harry Adams 70%!'

'You've got to be kidding me?' Tom took a step back.

'No, no. It's definitely 70%.'

Tom walked away from the desk shaking his head in disbelief, thinking to himself, *'How does he do it?'*

Harry just leaned back in his chair smiling; another escape from what could have been a disaster. He really didn't fancy having to do a re-sit or having to explain his abject failure to his boss who was already on his case about other things; giving him more ammunition would not help.

*****

CHAPTER 2

The Tide is Out

'You Stole the Sun from Heart' Manic Street Preachers

'Sure this pub will do, it looks old and quiet, off the beaten track.' A kind of old man bar, where you would expect to see men sitting in flat caps, a dog curled up in the corner at a warm fire. Quiet, cosy dark. Somewhere you could escape the hustle and bustle, sit on a high stool at the bar, have a friendly chat with the bar man about something and nothing. One of these trendy pubs with loud music, flooded tourists nattering was the last place he wanted to be, the way he felt. It had been a long hard week.

The bar was indeed old, a real old world bar from a bygone age, before the craziness of the *'Celtic Tiger.'* *'Good, they have coat hooks underneath the bar, that's always a good sign.'*

Harry hung up his coat and sat at the bar sipping his pint. After work drinks were not going to be the same again now he had ditched Dervila. It had taken him a long time, two years in fact, to figure out she was no good for him. Although he did have fun hanging out with her, but the sheer craziness of the situation was starting to take its toll on his body and mind. Leaving work on a Friday, going straight out drinking for the majority of the weekend, with little food or sleep was not good.

Heading into work on a Monday morning, looking like a *'zombie'*, as his boss had put it in a recent review. Feeling better by Wednesday, but then going back out on Friday to do it all over again. It was getting harder and taking longer to recover from these mammoth drinking sessions. How long can someone sustain that kind hectic lifestyle, anyway? Plus, on a recent visit to his doctor, he mentioned not being able to understand a test. When pushed about his social life, Harry was told to calm down in no uncertain terms, try take some time for himself. Was the doctor trying to tell him he was out of control in a nice way? Trying to get him to take up meditation or some hippy dippy shit like that, but that was never going to happen.

Harry knew deep down he had to cut back on the going out, the decision to drop Dervila, to move on was the right thing to do, just still didn't feel like it yet. She wasn't a bad person as such; she had just led him down a bad road. He had fun along the way with her, it just wasn't the way to live his life long term. The way things had ended, still made him feel bad; this pain wouldn't disappear easily.

The bar the door opened swiftly with a shove and a bang, in came a group of people, out for after work drinks. *'Oh great, here we go, they're going to spoil my nice quiet pint,'* he felt himself getting old - decrepit on the spot. Oh well, just finish this pint, move on, find another pub or maybe he'd just head home.

Harry was staring off into space, contemplating what he was going to do with his life. *'I need to find something to do to fill his spare time, maybe I could take up canoeing again?'* He had enjoyed it when he was younger, even still had his kayak sitting out in his parents' back garden. *'It's probably a home to snails and all sorts now, it's been sitting there that long.'* Maybe he could take up something different, join a gym. Sitting in watching TV just wasn't an option, he needed to be out and about. Pity he'd never gotten into football, it seemed to keep all the other lads at work plenty interested, even if they did seem to take it a little too seriously. *'Like you can have any effect on a team playing hundreds of miles away, by wearing your Lucky shirt?'* It had just never held any interest for him; watching any kind of sport hadn't. Checking his phone, although he didn't know why; it's not as if anyone would be calling or texting him. Nothing, that was fine with him really, he just wanted to be on his own.

Taking a sip from his pint, he felt someone bump into his back trying to get to the bar. Great, now he had beer all down his nice white shirt. How rude he thought, he just knew it had to be one of the group that had arrived. He looked around to give them a few choice words only to find this girl standing there. She looked vaguely familiar. He definitely knew her from somewhere, had he meet her on one of his many blurry nights out? She looked directly at him. Instantly he was drawn into the deepest brown eyes he had ever seen, the kind you could get lost in forever. Somehow, she managed to brighten up the dark dreary pub.

'Oh, so sorry. Did I knock your drink?'

'No, its fine,' Harry said, wiping the beer from his mouth and shirt.

'Harry, isn't it?'

Oh now he was in a spot of bother; where on earth did he know her from?

'Yeah... it is. Sorry... I'm at a loss, where do I know you from?'

'It's Grainne, we were in primary school together?'

'Oh, yeah... I've got you now. Been a long time, how you been keeping? What are you up to these days?'

'I'm good thanks, just working around the corner, out for a few drinks with work. You here all on your lonesome?'

'Yeah, playing the total loner this afternoon. Just fancied a quick pint after work, heading home after this.'

There was a spare stool beside her, she pulled it over and sat down.

'Here, hang on for a bit, I'll buy you a pint and we can catch up. It'll be nice to reminisce about school.'

'Oh... go on, can't stay long though.' Harry couldn't say no to those beautiful eyes.

'Same again then?'

'Yeah, cheers. You not going back over to your workmates then? Just going to sit with Oscar the grouch at the bar?'

'Well, they'll be talking about how great they are at this and that. The boys will be trying to get into the girls pants and most of the girls will be more than willing, even though most of them already have boyfriends or girlfriends. Besides, you look like you have an interesting story to tell.'

'Do I look that bad? Well, yeah, it has been a tough couple of weeks. Went from pretty much thinking I had a great life, well-paying job, beautiful girlfriend, to sitting here now on my own, on the verge of being fired with no girlfriend.'

'Jesus, sounds rough. How did it all fall apart? That's if you don't mind me asking.'

'No, it's okay, though it could take a while and I wouldn't want to bother you with my troubles.'

'I've all night, sure you and your mate Phil used to look out for me at school, so I figure the least I owe you is a listening ear.'

'Yeah, I remember that alright, you were a proper little geek. The amount of scrapes we got into over you,' he said laughing. That was the first time Harry had smiled all week, it felt good.

'Well, stop grinning like an idiot and tell me about how you ended up here, Billy no mates spilling pints on yourself!' she said, giving him a nudge on the arm and a smile.

'Hey, I didn't…' He saw her smiling, realised she was joking about spilling his pint. 'Okay, so I had to do an exam for work a couple of weeks ago and like an idiot went out drinking the night before. Met up with Dervila, my now ex-girlfriend, next thing I knew I was waking up in a stranger's house miles away from home. Somehow, I made it to the exam, but I was in proper rag order. Looked at the exam paper – it might as well have been in Greek – couldn't make head nor tail of it. It was like… hieroglyphics. Finally calmed down after about 20 minutes, managed to get through it somehow. Turns out I fluked a pass, but was a bit freaked out by the whole episode. Thought I was going a little mad!

I had my review with my boss last week, he gave me such a rollicking for showing up to work like a zombie Monday through Wednesdays. My excuse of still being able to do my job better than most didn't really wash with him. Suppose he was right, trying to get me to cop on, told me I was bright and could have a big future if I just applied myself. So I had a lot of thinking to do. Came to the conclusion that I'd only really ever seen Dervila at the weekends. She was so outgoing, just always out on the tear, dragging me along. It was great fun with her, but after two years my body, my mind was starting to fall apart. She was none too happy when I told her I was cutting back on drinking and wanted to do a bit more boyfriend girlfriend kind of stuff. So we broke up, it's probably best in the long run for us both. So now here I am sitting in a bar on my own, trying to rebuild my life with a little less partying.'

'So you were a bit of a party animal then?'

'Suppose you could say that. I was going out Friday evenings and not making it home 'til Sunday afternoon most weekends.'

'So you don't see much of Phil then?'

'Jesus, haven't heard his name in a while, but that's a story for another day, he died just over two years ago.'

'Jesus that's awful, were you two still close?'

'Yeah, we were like brothers, always getting in trouble. I really do still miss him. Anyway enough about me, what have you been up to?'

'Jesus, that must have been hard on you. You'll have to tell me about him someday, find out what kind of men my knights in shining armour became. Me, I did the whole university thing, over in the UK. Now I'm back home working in the super, exciting world of insurance.'

'Looks like you've landed on your feet anyway,' Harry said.

'Ah yeah, it was a great experience. I was in London, but glad to be back home though, eating proper food. Yeah, it was one of the first jobs I applied for, so was quite lucky.'

'Out on the lash the whole time over there then?'

'Not really wasn't into that kind of scene, needed to get a part-time job to pay my way and with all the study. Still got out a bit, just wasn't as crazy as some of the others. Not the geek I once was,' she said with a smile.

'Where did you work then?'

'Got a job in the local swimming pool, lucky had my lifeguard qualification and swim teachers going over.'

'So you're a bit of a fish then?'

'Yeah, loved it while in secondary school, even made the national swimming finals a few times. Didn't do much at Uni though, just didn't have the time. Got in with their masters' club a few times, just to make sure I could still swim!'

'Masters?'

'Ah its old fogies swim club.'

'You're not an old fogie yet. So why were you getting in with them?'

'I'm joking, masters is over thirty-five, I think. They're still all quite good, just a group to swim with really. It's not as serious as a swimming club, just a way to keep swimming in a less competitive environment.'

'Ah I get it now. So you doing any swimming now your back home?'

'Yeah, I do a bit with my local masters' club, when I get a chance. I'll bet you have some stories about Phil, I always remember you two off climbing this and that, jumping off bridges into the canal. Two right little adventitious balls of fun, ye were.'

'We joined a local youth club, ended putting all that energy into adventure sports, managed to get jobs out of it too, somehow, working in an adventure centre over in the West. Phil was big into rock climbing, used to drag me along all the time. He was so much better at it than me, would literally drag me up some climbs, shitting myself the entire time. Him laughing and joking; me clinging on for dear life! I was more into canoeing and surfing; you know stuff where you won't fall to an agonising painful death. We shared a room while living over there, you really wouldn't believe some of the stuff we got up to.'

'You really should tell me more, I'd like to hear about the adventures of Harry and Phil.'

Just at that moment a loud shout came from the group Grainne had come in with. 'Grainne, we're going to move on – this place is boring. You coming?'

'Yeah, I'll be over in a minute,'' she said, looking back to Harry. 'He's an awful gobshite at times,' she whispered. 'Here, give me your phone?' She took his phone, quickly typed her number in, 'Text me tomorrow, we'll meet up?'

'Sure now I'll have to, I owe you a drink?'

She walked away to leave with the others, looking back, smiling as she did. Only now he noticed how athletic she was, maybe at least the same height as him. Not sure what had just happened, but he knew made him feel good. How could he feel comfortable around her so quickly, kind of girl he could talk to all day and it would only feel like a couple of minutes. Suddenly he saw a chink of light and was looking forward to tomorrow, text her in the morning and maybe they could meet up later?

Finishing up his pint, now feeling quite content with himself. Funny how a short chat with an old friend could cheer him up no end. It was the first time he had talked about Phil in a while. Maybe since the funeral?

It was always with him, just hadn't felt comfortable enough around anyone else to share it, even Dervila. Maybe, it helped that Grannie had known him, why was it so much different around her? Anyway he thought it was time to head home, he finished the final sip of his pint and left the bar heading for a bus home. As he was walking towards the bus stop his phone rang, it was someone else he recognised, Joe from his canoeing days. He hadn't talked to him in a long while.

'Heya Joe, what's the craic? Long-time, no see.'

'Alright Harry. Jesus it's been ages, what you up to these days?'

'Na, not much at all, got myself a desk job now, working away. Yourself?'

'Yeah, still paddling away. Listen a few of us old timers are heading over west in couple of weeks for the weekend. It's a bit of a reunion of sorts, see what everyone's up to these days. Doing a spot of surfing if ya wanna tag along?'

'Oh I don't know, ain't sat in a boat or on a board in about two years.'

'Ah, it's just like riding a bike, you never lose it. Come on, it's about time you got back into it.'

'Who's headin' over?'

'Well, just me, Dave, Will, Jim and Niamh at the moment.'

'Jesus you still knocking about with them lads? I'd nearly go just to see them. It'd be good to catch up with them.'

'Yeah, there all as bonkers as ever. They'll be stoked to hear your coming. They still talk about you and the crazy shit you used to do. Got yourself a car yet?'

'No, still not got around to it. All my canoeing gear is still at Mam and Dad's, any chance you could pick me up there?'

'Sure I'll give you a shout when I sort out times and what not?'

'Yeah, sure. I'll talk to you in a while.'

Continuing on his way, thinking it would be nice to be back in the outdoors, he realised he had actually missed it. Sitting in his kayak out at sea away from all the noise of the city always made him feel clam. Just him out there in touch with nature. The only noise he could hear was the sound of the surf or sea birds. There was something quite therapeutic about it, he knew it would help him get back in touch with himself. He stuck his earphones I... next to decide who he would listen to on the way home. Flicking through his play lists, *'oh 'The Ramones,' you can never go wrong with them,'* he thought. *'Bonzo goes to Bitburg'* always made him feel better. Sitting on the bus he was thinking how his old life was starting to catch up with him and that might not be such a bad thing.

When he got home he made himself a bite to eat, sat down to watch a spot of TV. *Jesus what shite do they have on TV these days?'* It was utter crap; no wonder he was always out on Friday nights. After a while flicking channels he decided it was time for bed. He lay in bed and put some music on his old vinyl player. *'This is the best way to listen to music,'* he thought to himself.

While laying on his bed staring at the ceiling, all he could think of now was P; damn people for opening up old wounds. Getting up to flip the record over, he spotted the hand written speech he had pinned to his wall. The day of the funeral was running through his mind now. Phil's parents had asked him to name Phil's favourite songs in a few words. He hadn't even owned a suit at the time, having to borrow one of this Dad's, which was ill-fitting.

The song's he'd chosen were: AC/DC: *You Shook me all night long* ; Thin Lizzy: *Cowboy Song* ; Pearl Jam: Wishlist

They were some of Phil's favourite songs.

He thought they best summed him up as a person and would be played at the end of the funeral; it proved to be a very emotional moment for everyone.

He could remember standing at the pulpit, having to put the page down so he could read it, as his hands were shaking so much. As he went to speak he could feel a lump in his throat and tears starting to well in his eyes. The words he said would be etched in his mind forever:

'I've been asked to say a few words about Phil by his Mam and Dad. Phil as you may know, was my best friend in the world. The greatest friend anyone could have. I've known him since we met on the first day of primary school. From there on we always seemed to be getting each other in trouble. From being caught climbing onto the roof of the school, to jumping off bridges into the canal. Sorry Mam. We went through a lot together, from broken limbs to broken hearts. Lost count of the amount of times he helped me get over a girl. He could always make me laugh, he never seemed to be in bad form. He was always banging on about saving the planet, folding crisp packets into little triangles so they wouldn't take up as much room in the bin, even has me still doing it now!

My best memory of him is from when we were kids on a trip over to Clare. On our way back from caving, crossing a field, we were all jumping in puddles. I was a little behind Phil when he jumped into one. He disappeared, the puddle must have been about 8 foot deep! I've never laughed so much in my life. It still didn't dampen his spirits though, surfaced like a drowned rat but was still smiling. We were only laughing about it last week.

One of my last conversations with him was just the other night. He was trying to get me to head up to the Mourne Mountains for a spot of walking and climbing. I was complaining about the length of the walk carrying all that climbing gear; well it is quite heavy. But as he was getting ready for his new job as a mountain guide in the Pyrenees, I decided to go, so I could spend as much time as possible with him.

Well, I suppose he's made the ultimate climb now, hope you made it all the way to the top, buddy.'

23rd September 2005

He had finished off by holding up Phil's phone, asking anyone who had his number to text their goodbyes to him, the phone would be buried with him.

As he looked down he could see people struggling to type and he himself wrote, *'See u in a bit buddy, make sure u keep the rope tight. U hav 2 make sure I make d summit.'*

It was so hard for him to hold back the tears reading it out, he still had the piece of dried up, tear stained paper hanging on the wall over his bed. He hadn't looked at it in a while. Even thinking about it now brought a tear to his eye. Try to think of the good times they had, surely that would help him sleep. He had to try; he closed his eyes and eventually managed to drop off through sheer tiredness.

*****

Chapter 3
Catching the Wave
'The Boys of Summer' Don Henley

Harry opened his eyes to a new day; the sun was gleaming through a gap in the curtains. Time to get up, now what was he going to do with the day? Such an odd feeling to wake up on a Saturday morning hangover free. *'Time to text Grainne? Too early, don't want to seem too keen; maybe after breakfast, hopefully she's free, we can meet up and do something.'* Time for breakfast – bacon and cheese on toast with a cup of coffee would hit the spot. While he was eating he let the excitement get the better of him, sending a text to Grannie.

'Heya, its Harry. How's the head this morn? It was nice talking to u last night.'

He felt butterfly's in his stomach as his finger hovered over the send button, eventually he plucked up the courage to hit send, sat back nervously sipping his coffee, waiting on a response. A few minutes later his phone beeped. *'Man that was quick.'*

'It was lovely to chat 2, wot u up 2 later?'

'Ah not much, wana do something?' His stomach really was doing summersaults into knots at this stage.

'Yeah, meet us outside Bewelys on Grafton St. say bout 1?'

'Kul, c u den?'

Harry was now excited about his afternoon, he just had to think of something to do with her now.

'Shit,' he was a bit out of practice on this. Never had this issue with Dervila, more or less just needed to find the nearest pub. It was time to have a shower and get dressed. What to wear though? It was Saturday so no suit and tie. 'Thank god,' he thought. Jeans, boots and a white polo shirt it was. Some effort, but not too much. 'Is this a date? Na, it's not a date.'

He pulled out his earphones as he approached Bewelys. Grafton street was always packed on a sunny Saturday, stretching up onto his tippy toes to try to see over the crowd and if she was there yet. He was more little nervous now, with the butterflies in his stomach doing somersaults. Hoping he wouldn't be tongue tied when he did see her. He always liked to be early. Good, he couldn't see her, couldn't have her waiting on him now, could he? He found a spot, waited patiently. He gazed around the street was awash with people of all creeds and kinds.

Buskers every couple of yards trying to keep their pitch, from students playing classical music to an old man with a guitar playing the blues and of course the human statues in between. There really was no better place to be on a warm sunny spring day. As he was admiring the man playing the blues he felt a tip on his shoulder, he turned around and there she was. That was twice now she had snuck up on him, he hoped she wouldn't make a habit of this.

'Heya', she said with a lovely big smile. She was even more beautiful in the bright daylight. She was just a little shorter than he was, wearing tight blue jeans with a blue figure-hugging top, hair tied back in a ponytail. She didn't have much makeup on, nor any fake tan.

'You're looking at me with that silly grin again,' she said hitting him in the arm again.

'Ah heya, I was off in my own little world there. You'll have to stop sneaking up on me like that.'

'I did call ya, but you were gazing off into space,' she said.

'Mesmerized by that lad playing the blues over there. So what d'ya wanna do?' Harry enquired.

'Oh yeah he is good. Such a lovely day, we grab a sando and go sit in Stephens green?'

'Yeah, there's a great little deli up there. They do a mean sando.' They started to walk up; she was walking close to him and their arms kept touching as they moved. This was a good sign he thought to himself. They stopped at the deli to grab a quick sandwich and a drink.

'So I would have stayed longer talking to ya last night, but had to go do something,' she said apologising for her slightly abrupt exit the night before.

'That loud lad was a bit of a dick, wasn't he?'

'Funny you should say that; that's what I was doing – dumping him!'

'You were going out with him?! He seemed like a complete asshole.' Harry looked perplexed, how could this be? Such a lovely girl with an asshole like that! *Just the way the world works ain't it?'*

'Well, we weren't going out as such, just hooking up now and again.'

'Friends with benefits?'

'Suppose you could put it that way, weren't really friends though.'

'How did he take it?'

'Not very well, bit of a dent to his ego. Had a bit of a rant and then went off trying to hump every other woman in the room.'

'Trying to make you jealous, no?'

'Just made himself look foolish, got shot down by them all.'

'What on earth were you thinking, going off with a dick like that?'

'I really don't know, a spot of madness maybe?'

They were up at the green by this point. It was full of people as usual on sunny day. Parents with their kids feeding the ducks. Tourists standing looking at maps looking positively lost. Groups of teenagers trying to look as cool as possible, and couples walking around hand in hand.

'Fecking pigeons!' Harry said as he fought his way through a flock some tourists were feeding, 'hate them, bloody flying rats.'

'Bit of a pigeons' phobia there, Harry.' Grainne said teasing him.

'No,' Harry replied realising he hadn't sounded very manly in shuddering away from the flock of pigeons. 'They're just riddled with disease.'

'I'm only kidding with ya. It's packed. Ain't it?'

'Yeah, we stay or head somewhere else.'

'Ivy gardens, might be a bit quieter?'

'Where's that?'

'Just down the road there, off Hardcourt street. No pigeons,' she added, laughing.

'Lead the way so.'

They walked through the green, then on down to the Ivy gardens, where they found a clear area and sat on the grass facing each other, legs crossed, opening their sandwiches.

'So fill me in on College life in the UK,' Harry asked.

'Yeah, the weather was a little better than over here, I had my work in the swimming pool, lifeguarding and teaching swimming to keep me busy. So I wasn't really able to go out too much, had too study to do in my free time. I was paying for my degree so though I should give myself a good shot at it.'

'So you were Pammy on a part time basis then, did ya have a little red swimsuit?' he said laughing, it was his turn to tease a little now.

'Hey, less of the Baywatch jokes, I'm no plastic blonde bimbo in a little red swimsuit. Just shorts and a T-shirt, thank you,' she said with a smile, again tapping him lightly on the knee.

'Ah, ya did ask for it. Speaking of Pammy we did see her in LA a couple of years ago, when we spent a few days there.'

'Just you and Phil? What were you up to over there? So what was she like?' Grainne leaned in looking even more interested.

'Yeah, we headed over together. Sure we only really flew into LA and then back out at the end. Spent a few days on Venice beach, we bumped into her in a bar at Santa Monica, as ya do in LA. We got a photo with her, once we plucked up the courage to go over and ask her. It was terrifying. Shortly after that Phil decided he was going to become a vegan.'

'Oh, she a vegan ain't she? What was he thinking?'

'She is; I think he'd been thinking about it for a while anyway. She sort of gave him the push to do it. Apparently eating beef is very bad for the environment. Cows produce so much methane, which is a greenhouse gas. We also chop down so much forest for them to graze.'

'Oh, yeah I'd heard that. Still wouldn't get me turning vegie. So what did you get up to after your date with Pammy?'

'Oh yeah, we headed up to Yosemite National Park. We met a few Canadian lads we knew for a spot of climbing, they even sorted out a nice river trip for me down the Merced River, just to keep me happy. No way I was doing the climbs they did, they were insane. Imagine camping bolted to the side of a cliff?! Not for me I tell ya, but Phil loved it. We went on to spend a little time in San Francisco, then off to San Diego for a spot of surfing on Pacific Beach.'

'That sounds insane. How long were you there for? Sounds like it was a while.'

'About a month, we had a great time. Met some really cool people. I really think the word awesome is so overused these days, but first day I walked in the valley in Yosemite, it was the correct use of the word. Awesome is probably underselling it to be honest.'

'Sounds amazing, like somewhere I'd like to go.'

'Get your cute little ass over there!' he said with cheeky grin.

'Think I'd need a guide, ya know anyone?'

'Sure I could sort something out for ya. Know a few people over there.'

'Come on, tell me more about Phil. I want to know what kind of a person he became. It's not going to open up old wounds, is it?'

'No, it's probably something I need to do, haven't really talked about him much lately.'

'You really shouldn't bottle things like that up, it'll always surface somehow and possibly not in a good way.'

'Sort of found that out the hard way a few weeks ago.'

'Well, its lucky I'm a good listener then, ain't it?' she said with a warm smile.

'Don't really want our conversations to be all about me.'

'They won't, but you do need to talk it out. Either that or you could end up in therapy and that'll cost you a fair bit. They might be as nice as me either.' She smiled again.

'Suppose so, don't think I'd like that kind of shit at all.'

'Well, come on then tell me about him?'

'Okay, okay, where to start? Well, as we're talking about the U.S., I'll start there. We went down to Mexico for the day while in San Diego. Such a crazy, scary place. We hit Tijuana, decided to go into a strip club for a beer at about two o'clock in the day, as ya do. They had like theses rings hanging from the ceiling traversing the bar, bit like the ones in Gladiators. Well, Phil decided he was going to have a go on them.

About three quarters of the way across he came flying off, he says there was stripper oil or something on the ring, but point is he came off, managed to land on a table full of drinks. The locals sitting at the table didn't look too impressed, so we had to make a hasty exit. Thought they were going to pull out knives or guns. I just grabbed him, and we legged to out the nearest exit. We just pegged it off back for the boarder, trying not to piss ourselves laughing all the way. He had managed to cut his hands on the broken glass, though.'

'Sounds like you two had a lot of fun together?'

'Yeah we did, never a dull moment.'

'Certainly seems that way. What did you get up to at home?'

'We worked at an adventure centre down in Kerry, just went out climbing, canoeing and surfing during our spare time. We were happy just earning enough money to fund our lifestyle. Whenever we were back in Dublin, Phil used to love dragging me out to Dalkey quarry for a spot of climbing. I wasn't a fan of that walk from the train station up the hill, especially with all that heavy climbing gear.'

'Bit lazy, are you? Did neither of you not drive?' By now he knew she was teasing him.

'Na, Phil was all about saving the planet, so it was public transport all the way. I was never that keen on driving either.'

'But you still use public transport now don't you, presume you can afford a car?'

'Just a force of habit now, never got around to learning how to drive.'

'See, he had a good effect on you.'

'Well, yeah, still do quirky little things that he showed me, like turning off the tap while brushing your teeth or switching off the shower while I'm washing myself, leaving it running just waits water. Every little helps he'd say in fighting to save the planet. He used to be like an ad for Tesco!'

'Tell me more about him?'

'Dalkey was his favourite place in the world. Climbing up there, looked like he felt at home, *'at one with the world'* as he would say. He was nearly always first to climb anything. I was stuck sitting at the bottom holding the other end of the rope, just in case he did ever fall. He really was good, made some unbelievably gutsy moves. He'd never climb back down, saying it was never an option. One day we were doing this climb; he was leading as usual. He was about fifteen foot up and had put no protection in yet. So the rope was just going from me straight up to him and was no use to him if he had fallen. Nothing there to catch him.'

'Oh, hang on there, you'll have to explain how this climbing thing works!' Grainne looked perplexed.

'Ah sorry, so you have two people climbing. One ties an end of the rope to himself and starts to climb. As he climbs he has kind of metal wedges, all different sizes that he puts into cracks in the rock and clips the rope into them. The person on the ground holds the other end of the rope and let's it out as he climbs. If the lead climber falls, he drops as far as the last piece of gear he put in and the lad on the ground uses a friction device to stop the rope.'

'Yeah, I've sort of gotten the gist of it now.'

'So he got stuck and his next hold was another three foot above his reach. He just looked down at me and said, *'give us a bit of slack, I'm going for it.'* I was saying don't do it, just come back down, but no he wouldn't. So just had to let some slack out on the line. He leapt for it… lucky enough he made it, then he just scurried off up the rest of the climb without a bother. When I got to the top I called him a *'crazy bastard.'* He just smiled at me pointed out over at the view of Dublin, he really loved it up there. He would sit at the top and just stare out over Dublin Bay, sometimes forgetting I was still at the bottom waiting on his help to climb up. Suppose he really did like to live on the edge.'

He stared to fidget at this point; his iPod was starting to dig into his pelvis from sitting with his legs crossed. He pulled it out along with his earphones, Grainne spotted them and grabbed the iPod off him.

'Oh, what kind of music do you listen to?' She started to flick through his music library.

'Hey, what you doing? How do you know how to use my iPod?'

'Sure I've the same one, you've a hell of a lot music on here?'

'What can I say – I listen to a lot of different stuff and it has shit loads of memory.' Harry said with a cheeky little smile.

'Oh, here's a great song. Very appropriate one for today'

'What is it?'

'Just lie back and look at the sky, I'll play it for you.'

Harry lay back on the grass looking up at the clear blue sky, Grainne lay down too, legs pointing in the opposite direction, heads side by side, putting one earphone in her ear, the other in his ear and pressed play.

Lou Reed, *'Perfect Day'* started to play.

'Oh, I love this song.' Harry expressed with delight.

'Yeah, so do I, now shush and listen.'

They both listened to the song in silence, gazing into the sky basking in the sun. Harry enjoying the comfort of the situation, no pressure to talk.

*****

Chapter 4
Rip Tide
'Velvet Morning' The Verve

Harry and Phil sat on the stony beach looking out into the tranquil sea, each with a few cans of cheap beer. They were in Galway for the weekend, Connemara really was a stunning setting, they both agreed. They were over with a group of friends, Joe, Niamh, Dave, Will and Jim. The plan was to spend one day out in sea kayaks along the coast and the second day Coasteering, (scrambling along the coastal cliffs in a wetsuit).

'This is the life, ain't it?' Harry said as he stretched back on to the grass, can in hand.

'Yeah, so much better than sitting in some office staring at a computer screen,' Phil said still sat upright with his legs crossed, sipping on his own can.

'That really would stifle the life out of ya.'

'You think we could keep doing this for much longer?'

'What? Sitting on the cliff?'

'No, you pleb. Living like this.'

'Sure, why couldn't we?'

'You know, someday we'll meet a girl and settle down, have kids. Can't see us doing this then, we'll have to move into the real world at some stage.'

'Real world? What we living in now?'

'You know what I mean. Growing up, buy a house, start paying bills, all that kind of shite.'

'Jesus man, I never think about that kind of stuff.'

'Ah, I do every once in a while.'

'Jesus Harry. We're a long way off that now, ain't we?'

'Oh yeah, sure we'd need to get a girlfriend first!' Harry said laughing.

'Chance would be a fine thing.' They both laughed as they looked out at the sun glistening off the sea.

The next day as Joe arrived, Harry looked less than impressed with the kayaks he had hired. 'Jesus, Joe. Could you have gotten shittier boats?'

'They'll be fine for what we're doing, now quit moaning.'

'Yeah, Harry quit your bellyaching,' Phil teased.

Harry still didn't look happy but kept setting up his kayak, muttering to himself, 'too bloody long, ain't paddled one of these things since I was a kid.'

They eventually set out on their trip along the coast, they all found the rugged coastline stunning, stopping the odd time just to gaze up at the cliffs. After about an hour of canoeing they arrived at a cove looking in toward a small beach.

'We stop here for some lunch?' Joe asked.

'Yeah, sounds good,' Jim replied from further back with Niamh.

'Yeah, no arguments here.' Will said.

'Yeah, I'm starving,' Dave shouted out.

Harry and Phil were beside Joe, they nodded in agreement with him. 'Hey, Jim and Niamh are looking a little cosy back there, ain't they?' Phil said quietly.

'So they are,' Harry said, peering back.

'Na, not going to happen. He's so not her type,' Joe said quite bluntly.

'She has a type?' Harry said.

'Yeah, I've seen some the lads she's scored. Nothing like Jim at all,' Joe said.

'Hey, look a bit of surf breaking down on the beach. Surf in?' Harry said like a little kid.

'Off ya go,' Phil replied waving him along and off he went.

Phil hated surfing, especially when he capsized, which was all to regular, like sticking your head inside a washing machine.

Harry started to surf the wave and was shooting along having a whale of a time. As he was getting closer to the beach he looked down at the front of his kayak and noticed he could see the sandy bottom. He looked at the nose of the kayak, then the sandy sea floor again, then again. *'My lord'* He thought to himself, *'the nose is going pitch in the sand and I'm going to go face first into the very shallow water get a face full of sand'* This wasn't going to end well. There was no way out of it that he could see, so as he felt the nose of the kayak touch the sand he put his paddle in at the back of the boat, pushed down on it moving the water towards the front, he closed his eyes, fully expecting pain of his face hitting the water with sand to follow.

When it didn't, he opened his eyes slowly to find himself still sitting upright and still in the kayak, much to his surprise. He could hear yelping and cheering from behind him.

'Fuck yeah, that was amazing.' Joe shouted over.

'Woohoo, do it again,' Will shouted.

'That was deadly,' Dave shouted, by this time Phil was up beside him.

'Do what again?' Harry whispered to Phil.

'You don't even know what you've done, do you?'

'Hell no. I just closed my eyes done a reverse sweep stroke and hoped for the best.'

'Well, you managed to spin the boat on its nose, like a spinning top. Looked really cool.'

'Fuck me. I thought I was going to do a face plant into the sand.'

'Don't tell them that, you definitely meant to do it, right?'

'Oh, yeah. Not going to attempt it again though. Thought I was going to lose my nuts when the foot rests shot forward, and the support came towards me.' They both laughed as they got out of the kayaks on the beach. Harry stuck his head inside to fix the foot rests, which had shot down to the front of the kayak.

After their lunch, which the main topic of conversation was Harry's pirouette-like manoeuvre, they set off down the coast, back to towards the campsite. Jim still insisted the move was a fluke and everyone else agreed that if Harry tried it and had succeeded then it was no fluke. On the way Joe spotted that the waves were breaking in between gaps in the rocks jutting out from the cliffs. If timed right then it was possible to get through the gap using the wave, if not then it might hurt a little.

He went first and when he made it through, it looked like fun.

They all started to have a go as they hopped along the coast. It turned out to be great fun and a great way to take the trudge out of the long paddle back, always looking for the next channel to surf through. They had a few close calls, but all made it back to the campsite in one piece to enjoy a few cans around a blazing fire.

Next morning, they set off for their coasteering trip, scrambling along the coast, with a few cliff jumps along the way. Phil loved climbing up high then jumping off the high cliffs.

'Ah Christ!' Will shouted out.

'Gear still wet from yesterday then Will?' Dave said getting out of the van.

'Fuck yeah, never gets any easier.' They were going to have to wear the still cold and damp wetsuits from the day before.

'Hey, we'd better bring a throw rope, buoyancy and first aid kit, just in case. Who wants to carry them?' Joe asked the whole group.

'Here I'll wear the buoyancy and clip the throw rope onto it.' Phil offered, he was feeling a little cold and thought the buoyancy would keep him little warmer if he put it on.

'Here, I'll carry the first aid kit,' Niamh offered.

When they were already they set off, Joe leading the way, Harry and Phil bringing up the rear. They all started to warm up and were jumping from rock to rock. Anywhere where they could get up high, the water was deep enough they jumped in. Some of the climbs were quite high, with only Phil climbing. The rest looked on not knowing if he was gutsy or plain daft. They were coming towards the end, when they stopped at a section where the rocks stretched out about twenty feet.

'Right, I'm going all the way out,' Phil said, and he set off. He made it out to the furthest rock and looked around to the rest of the group smiling.

'Incoming wave!' Harry shouted at him, he peered over the rock and saw a big wave coming his way.

'Shit!' He couldn't avoid it. It was huge and headed straight for him.

'Crouch behind the rock and hold on tight,' Joe shouted at him, Phil got as small as he could behind the rock, held on tight, waited. He felt the wave hit; he closed his eyes and when he opened them he was sitting beside Joe. The wave had managed rip him off the rock and carried him the full twenty feet back. All that had stopped him was the rock that was now at his back.

'Hey Joe, what's the craic?'

'Jesus you're lucky you had that buoyancy on, otherwise that would have hurt,' Joe said looking surprised that he was sitting beside him.

'Yeah.' Phil looked at his hands and they were full of blood. He didn't let go of the rock, the wave had more or less torn him away from it. He had cuts all the way down the palms of his hands.

'Jesus Christ, your hands,' Joe said.

'Yeah, it stings a little.'

'Hospital it is then, far too much blood there.'

They made their way to the van, got changed and drove to the nearest hospital. Phil's hands didn't look as bad now but were still bleeding. It took ages to check in at the hospital as the receptionist, being from Wales, couldn't understand Phil's Dublin accent. He couldn't really write anything down either. They both seemed to be getting frustrated with each other, so Harry came over to sort it out. They moved Phil into a cubicle to wait on a doctor, who came in fairly quickly to assess his injuries. He explained what had happened and the doctor laughed.

'Look the cuts aren't that deep, but I do want to give them a good clean, make sure they don't get infected,' the doctor said calmly.

'What you going to do?' Phil knew it would sting whatever it was.

'The nurse will be in a few minutes to sort you out.' He walked off smiling, leaving Phil to his fate. The nurse came in with a bucket, Phil looked in to see a red liquid. This could only be one thing, Iodine.

'Iodine? No way?' he said to the nurse.

'Yes way.'

'A bucket of it. What do you want me to do?'

'Put your hands in it.'

'Both at the same time?'

'Yes.' He slowly put his hands into the bucket, it took every fibre of his bean to not scream so as the others sitting in the waiting room would hear.

'Your loving this ain't you?' he said to the nurse.

'Look I know it stings, but it's a good thing.'

'It stings? Bit like sticking your hands in a bee hive or a bucket of acid.' She smiled at him, he was still trying not to swear at her and had a face that looked like he was sucking lemons. A few cans of cider later would help kill the pain, well that was if he could hold them. They were heading home the next day anyway.

*****

CHAPTER 5

Riding the wave

'On Melancholy Hill' Gorillaz

Harry opened his eyes, looked around. He was in his own bed, with no hangover again. This was still such an odd feeling to him, he looked at his phone to check the time – eight am. Eight am on a Sunday was usually the time he got home at, he rolled over to go back asleep. Well he did have about two years' worth to catch up on. As he closed his eyes, he thought of the lovely time he had spent the day before with Grainne, the thought of her brown eyes and smile helped him drift back to sleep. He really did like being around her, the way she made him feel, it was like he was himself again. It was different from how Dervila made him feel, she was more a dangerous excitement, he never really knew what was going to happen next with her. Best not go there at the moment, he would never get back to sleep.

He was woken up by his phone. Picking up the phone, it was text from Grainne, he smiled as he opened the message.

'Hey if u r not up to anything, wanna meet up later?'

'Y wot had u in mind?'

'Well, it's nice again, how about a picnic?'

Jesus, he hadn't had a picnic since he was kid, camping at the bottom of a mountain or beside a river didn't really count. It was an opportunity to spend more time with her and that was something he wanted very much.

'Kul, where will I meet ya?'

'I'll drive, where ya living and I'll pick ya up?'

'You never told me you had a car?'

'You never asked.'

'Do I need to bring anything?'

'Na, we can stop along the way.'

'Give us a call when you on the way and I'll give you directions.'

About an hour later Harry was standing, waiting at the entrance of his apartment block, when a BMW M3 pulled up beside him, Grainne smiling out the window. It was red with a gorgeous white leather interior. Travelling is such style was different to what he was used to doing, normally it was in clapped out cars or vans.

'Lovely car.'

'Thanks, only got it last week.'

'Must have cost a bit?'

'Cheeky!'

'Oh, didn't mean it that way.'

'I'm just teasing, my Dad is in the trade, so he picked it up for me.'

'So where are we going then?'

'That's a surprise.'

'Ah, come on, tell me?'

'Oh no, that would spoil it. Come on, get in.'

He sat in the car and sank into the seat. It was so comfortable, it felt like he was melting into it. She had Red Hot Chili Peppers playing, he was impressed.

'Is this on the radio?'

'No, it's my iPod.'

'What else you got on there; I'm liking your taste in music.'

'Yeah, I do like American bands, used to go see a lot of them.

Really love Pearl Jam, got into them at Uni. This lad I worked with got me listening to them.'

'Oh, we used to listen to them all the time. Phil's older brother, Eric, got us into them along with Nirvana and Soundgarden. We were only about eleven or so, but I'll always remember him coming down to us in their parents' sitting room all excited about this band he'd seen on TV during the night before. He'd had to write the name down, pulled a piece of paper out of his pocket and *'Nirvana, Smells Like Teen shirt'* was written on it, this was well before it exploded. He was sort of our hero growing up, he had us listening to all these bands, so we just grew up with them as our soundtrack. Pearl Jam ended up being Phil's favourite band.'

'S*oundgarden'* – I never heard much of them beyond *'Black hole sun.'*

'Oh you should, Chris Cornel is the godfather of grunge. Amazing singer, Eric was, still is, obsessed with him.'

'Oh, I have to try listen to some more.'

'Yeah, I'll lend you a couple of their CD's.'

'Thanks, sure grab my iPod there, wiz through it, stick on whatever you want.'

He picked it up, started to flick through it. He hadn't listened to a lot of these bands since before the funeral, afraid it would open wounds he didn't know how to deal with. But suddenly with Grannie around he felt strong enough to embrace it, she would be supportive.

'Hey, what's your favourite Pearl Jam song?'

'At the mo it's … Wishlist.'

That was one of the songs Harry picked for the funeral, it brought a slight tear to his eye. This really was a test for him? Grainne spotted this.

'Hey, you okay?'

'Yeah, it's just … aw well ya know… it's just that was one of the songs I picked to played at Phil's funeral.'

'Oh, Jesus I didn't know, I'm sorry. Put on something else.'

'Hey, you weren't to know. I'll put it on, it'll be fine. It'll do me good to hear it again.'

He played the song, at the end she said, 'I see why you picked it.'

'Aw, thanks. Helped… it was a song that seemed to fit.'

He was starting to feel a lot better now, the lump was leaving his throat, tears had receded from his eyes.

They stopped at a petrol station, bought some food for their picnic then continued on their merry way. He still had no idea where he was going, vaguely knew they were heading towards Killiney, probably heading to the beach or something. They came over the top of a hill, turned into a car park. He then recognised it, it was the car park of Dalkey Quarry. They had normally walked up from the train station, a route which went nowhere near the car park. She had brought him to Phil's favourite spot. She really was starting to get more and more special by the minute.

'Hey, we're at Dalkey Quarry.'

'Yeah, thought you could show me just how special this place was, show me around Phil's favourite spot?' Again she was smiling, her teeth sparkled in the sunshine.

'It's a bit of a walk now and up a few steps to where he loved to sit and gaze out over the Bay. Hope you don't mind heights or sitting on a ledge?'

'I'm sure you won't put me in any danger, would ya?'

'No I wouldn't, you'll be fine.'

They started to walk into the park, Harry carrying the bag with the food, blanket and glasses in it. Walking through the gorse bushes, Grainne glancing out over Dublin Bay.

'Wow, it really is a gorgeous view up here.'

'Oh wait until you see where we're going, much better view up there.'

He looked up at the upper cliffs, then over to a set of steps.

'No, we're not going up them, are we? That's a hell of a lot of steps.'

'Yeah, we are. It's not that far.' Suddenly he knew how Phil must have felt listening to him moaning about his climbs.

'Well maybe not for you.'

'Come on, it'll be worth it.' He grabbed her by the hand and started to walk.

'It better be.' She winked at him.

'Only one better view I've seen in my life and that was at the top of Yosemite falls and can't really take you there, now can I?' he said, smiling.

'Well, maybe someday.' She held his hand a little tighter.

'Maybe.' He gave her a little wink.

She suddenly she let his hand go, 'Come on then, I'll race ya to the top.' She ran off on him up the steps, she had played him with all the moaning about climbing the steps.

'Hey!' he shouted as he ran after her. There was no way he was going to catch her, so he stopped running and walked.

'What took ya?' She was grinning as he got to the top, he was just shaking his head slowly.

'Okay, you got me.'

'So, which way now?' she asked.

'We're heading over there.' He pointed over to the left, 'the corner of the wall over there.'

They walked over to the wall, Harry stopped at the corner.

'Why you stopping here?' she enquired.

He put the bag on top of the wall jumping up on top after it. He put his hand out, 'come on?' The wall was wide enough for the two of them to sit on comfortably.

'You want me to jump up there!?' She looked shocked.

'Come on it'll be fine; it's not like it's a huge drop on the other side.'

'Are you sure?'

'Yeah, 100%.'

'Okay then.' She put her hand out, he grabbed it to help her up. Sitting on top she could instantly see why he wanted her to come up, the view was amazing. From the corner of the wall there was a narrow piece of land jutting out. She did think it was the side wall of the quarry, but now see saw there was another quarry on the other side. Dublin looked tiny down by the bay and she could see the whole of the city. It was bathed in sunlight, even the water in the bay looked positively warm. She knew how cold the Irish Sea could be from experience.

'You wana just sit here, or jump down and walk out on the ridge?' Harry asked.

'Okay if we just stay here?' She sounded a little nervous.

'That's fine. It's great up here, ain't it?' Harry didn't want to push into anything. Even though out on the ledge was Phil's favoured perch.

'Yeah, I was just thinking that even the water looks warm. Hey, you should come for a sea swim with us some day? No wetsuits though, they're only for wimps.'

'In just shorts, you've got to be joking? Don't think my swimming would be up to your standard.' He raised his eyebrows, he was used to having wetsuits on, even during the summer he would have his '*Shorty Wetsuit*' on.

'I'll give you a few tips,' she teased. 'It'll do ya good.'

'Don't know about that, the little lad ain't a fan of cold water,' Harry said. Grainne laughed, dropping her head quite shyly, blushing a little.

'I'm sure he'll be fine. Don't ya know how to get heat back into him, don't ya?' she finally replied, now it was Harry's turn to blush.

'Hey, see Dún Laoghaire harbour down there?' Harry said trying to change the topic of conversation.

'Yeah, what about it?'

'Well, this is where they mined the rock to build it.'

'No way, I didn't know that.'

'You see the bore holes in the rock.' He pointed one out.

'Yeah.'

'That's where they put the dynamite to break the rock off. Then haul it off all the way down there.'

'Yeah, it's a long way, ain't it?'

'To right it is, I wouldn't fancy lugging that down there.'

They were suddenly interrupted by a couple of tourists walking along the path, with map in hand.

'Could you give us directions back down to Dalkey, we seem to be a little lost,' they enquired.

'Yeah, sure,' Harry replied, 'just follow the wall back to the steps and walk down them. At the bottom walk straight on along the track and down the hill. Go through the gap in the wall, take a left, then the first right down the lane. When you hit the road follow it straight down and Dalkey is at the bottom.'

'You can drop into Bono for a cup of tea on the way down, he's always there.' Grainne chipped in.

'Really? Bono lives around here, it's the Irish version of Monte Carlo. Doubt you'd get past the gate though. She's only kidding.' Harry explained shaking his head at Grainne.

'Hey, thanks for that, much appreciated we might have a look on the way down.' They then moved off on their way.

'Canadians! They'll believe you if you tell them shit like that,' Harry said.

'Ah, I thought it was funny. So how'd you know that, I would have said they were Yanks?'

'There's a difference, I can tell 'cause we spent three months living over there.'

'That sounds great, you two got to travel a lot then. What did you get up to over there?'

'We got jobs working in a climbing centre, it was a great couple of months. That's how we met the lads that organised the trip to California. Really was a great place to live, so clean and everyone so polite. The climbing centre was ten times better than anything over here, we even got to go climbing outdoors too. Their climbs have bolts drilled into the rock, so you only have to clip into them. Makes the cliff so much easier to climb.'

'So, what kind of shit did you get up to? I know you did!'

'Think you know me too well already. We did do a bridge swing, tied a rope in the middle of a bridge, climbed out to the edge and dropped off. Like the swings we used to make on trees, just a little higher.'

'Was that not illegal?'

'Oh yeah, we only figured that out when the cops showed up as we were packing the gear away. Don't know how we got away, but we did. It was far too close for my liking.'

'What would they have done if they caught you?'

'Deportation at the least, one of the lads said we'd broken a whole load of state and federal laws.'

'That's crazy, what's it like going out drinking over there?'

'We had a great laugh going out with all the lads we worked with, some great pubs. Drinking pitchers of beer worked out cheaper. Though, we found this great little pub around the corner from our apartment, twenty cent Buffalo wings and free post cards home. On our second last night there I ended up chatting to this lad, thought nothing of it until he asked me to go home with him. I was like *'Oh no, that's not going to happen!'* He was a little pushy, giving me the whole you'll never know unless you try thing, think that's where I learned the whole no means nothing! Anyway, I looked over at Phil and he was just pissing himself laughing. Then this lad dropped the bombshell that the pub was a gay bar.'

'You were drinking in a gay bar the whole time and never noticed, that's hilarious.'

'Twenty cent buffalo wings, though. We knew we were close to the gay area, but didn't think it was that close. This lad was far too in your face about it, very pushy, freaked me out a little.'

'You two must have been so naive, would have loved to see your face when he said that.'

'Well we were only nineteen and it was our first time away, lucky the girls we were seeing at the time showed up to save us.'

'So ye had girlfriends over there then?'

'Yeah, we met a couple of girls and hung out with them, nothing serious.'

'Probably never had a real serious relationship, have you?'

'Well, I was with Dervila for about two years.'

'Sounds like ye just went out drinking; did ye ever go out and not drink?'

'Eh… I don't think so, only really saw her at the weekends. Seemed like the perfect kind of relationship. You know, all the fun and none of the soppy stuff.' He gave her a wink and a smile.

'Hey, there's more to a relationship than having fun!'

'Oh, like other lads that spend most of their time trying to get out to have some fun? Then when they are out they are trying to score other girls. I'd rather wait for a girl I want to spend the rest of my life with, than just settle for one and end up being miserable. Until then no harm in having some fun.'

'Ah, you've put some thought into this. But how will you know it's the right girl?' Harry was looking down at his feet.

'I'll know; trust me I'll know. Don't want to get old and bitter, projecting all my misery in a jealous rage on the young, who are doing things with their life I wanted to do.'

'Jesus, never would have picked you for a deep thinker.' She reached over and held his hand.

'We're all like onions, with multiple layers, some of us will make you cry,' he looked up at her giving her a smile. She smiled back and thought, *There's much more to him than just this outgoing party boy.* She looked out at the bay and then back across at Harry, he was looking directly at her and their eyes locked, neither looking away.

*****

Chapter 6
Swimming with Wales
'Comfortably Numb' Pink Floyd

'Hey Harry, what ya drinking, usual?'

'Yeh, Heineken?'

Phil arrived back at the table with the two pints. They were on a ferry heading for North Wales on a weekend navigation course. Phil's idea. It would help him fulfil his lifetime dream of becoming a mountain guide in the Pyrenees. A four-day course with one overnight camp. It was being run by an instructor, Mike, ex-special forces or something equally bat shit crazy like that. Phil had met Mike while he was off walking in Scotland, he had the contacts that could land him his dream job. This was sort of a trial for

Phil, Harry was just looking forward to visiting him in the Pyrenees so he could canoe some of their amazing rivers.

'Excited?' Phil asked

'I'd be more excited if I had my kayak with me,' Harry replied.

'Come on, it'll be fun. Told you before Mike is dead sound, he'll look after us.'

'Yeah, those special forces lads are fuckin' nuts. Suppose you do fit right in with them.'

'Yeah and so will you, they like a drink or two.'

'Oh we'll have to take it easy, so?'

'We'll see,' Phil had a large smile on his face; this was never a good sign.

'Ah fuck!' Harry shook his head.

'Drink up, it's your round!' Phil was shaking an empty glass, 'shouldn't be able to see you?' He was holding the glass up to his eye and looking through the bottom at Harry. Harry trudged off up to the bar finishing his pint off along the way, this was going to be a long boat trip and a long night. When he got back to the table there was a group of three girls sitting at the table with Phil, all Harry could think was, *'How does he do it?'* Phil just sat there smiling, Harry sat down with the pints and they both ended up chatting to the girls for the rest of the trip.

When they got off the ferry, they easily found the bed and breakfast they were staying in for the night. Mike was going to give them a lift in the morning. Harry didn't know how Phil had swung a lift from Holyhead, must have made a serious impression on Mike in Scotland. They went out for a few pints that night in the local pubs. Sitting the corner quietly drinking their pints, when a girl and what looked her father came over, sitting down at the table opposite them. Harry looked; Phil looked at Harry. They didn't need to be mind-readers to know what the other was thinking, *What the fuck is going on here?-*

'Heya,' she said smiling, her dad sitting there like she had him on a leash.

'Hi.' Phil said nervously and unsure of what to do.

'You're not from here, are you?'

'No we're just passing through.'

'Oh I like your accent, where you from?'

'We're from Ireland.'

'Oh I love the Irish accent, it's very sexy.' She was now leaning across the table playing with her hair.

'Glad you like it.'

'Oh I really like it, you two up too much later?'

At this point Harry felt like he had to leave the table, 'Excuse me I need to head to the toilet.' He got up, heading off towards the men's room. Phil noticing their pints were getting low sensed his opportunity too. So after a minute or two he said, 'Oh we're low on drinks, I'm just going to head to the bar.' Getting up he headed off to the bar, standing at the end closet to the toilet. Seeing Harry exit he waived him over.

'This place seems a bit odd, doesn't it?'

'Yeah, its bit like the league of gentlemen.'

'Definitely something very Royston Vasey about it.'

'A few cans and back to the B and B?'

'Definitely!'

They quickly retreated back to the relative safety of the bed and breakfast, it felt like a very lucky escape.

They walked out of the bed and breakfast looking a bit blurry eyed. Mike was standing beside an old Landrover Discovery.

'Hey Mike, great to see you.' Phil walked over, giving Mike a big hug. Mike was a big lad, in his forties, about six foot two looking like he kept himself in shape.

'Hey Irish, you have a few drinks last night?'

'What do you think? This is my mate Harry, Harry meet Mike.' Mike was laughing.

'Hey Harry, you like my little jumping leprechaun here?'

'Leprechaun?' Harry looked bemused, nothing like a spot of casual racism he thought.

'Oh, I didn't mean it like that. When I met him in Scotland, he was jumping around on mountains like Spiderman. So hyperactive, never seemed to stop or stay still.'

'Yeah and he's not exactly tall either.' Harry could see Mike was only teasing, he was only using it as a term of endearment.

'Hey hey, less of that now,' Phil jumped in, 'Should we not get going?'

'Yeah, you boys get breakfast in there, or have you only just gotten up?'

'Na, no time for breakfast. You know me too well.'

'Good, I ain't had any either, we'll stop somewhere to get some, I know this great spot.'

They stopped at what can only be described a shack on the side of the road, a supposed truck stop. Mike was indeed right, and it was one of the nicest breakfasts they both had ever had. A proper old style greasy fry up, great for a change from all these healthy options.

They arrived at the lodge where they would be staying. It was a bit basic, but had everything they needed, including a drying room. This was a great thing in a place like North Wales, as it did tend to rain, and it had been raining quite a bit lately. So having somewhere to dry your gear was a bit of luxury. They didn't need much else beside a shower and a bed. Dropping their bags into their room, they headed toward the sitting room, where the group where meeting up. They arrived into a room full of serious looking people with their top of range expensive equipment. It was obvious these people were not short of money and wanted to show it. All kinds of gadgets sat on the table, GPS devices, stoves, head lamps, all looking shiny and expensive. Suddenly Harry and Phil felt a little out of place. All they had was a map and a compass, no fancy equipment. They had to save up to buy their outdoor equipment then make it last years. They got funny looks from a few at the table. Mike called them over into the kitchen.

'Lads, I know you feel a little out of place, but trust me you'll do fine. Phil, I only asked you to come as these are the kind of people you will have to deal with in the Pyrenees. So get used to it.'

'It's cool Mike, we've got it. Just show them what we can do, yeah?' Phil replied.

'Yeah that's it. This is three-day course, day four will just be us having a bit of fun.'

'Sounds good.'

They went back over to the group; introductions were made around the room. There were twelve people in the group with Mike running the course. First up was a map reading introduction, maps were handed out. Mike started to run through things like contours and how you can tell the shape of a slope by them, if it was concave or convex. The spot heights, how to take a grid position, how to find your own position on a map, all kinds of things like this. Harry and Phil were just having a laugh; this was basic stuff to them. One of the students, Sam, decided he knew more than anyone else in the room, started to walk around the room testing people. He came over to Harry and Phil, to interrupt their conversation on who was prettier Scarlet Johansson or Angelina Jolie and who would they rescue first. Sam pointed at two peaks on the map.

'Are these concave or convex?' He sounded quite pushy and like he knew everything. Phil looked up at him, then glanced down at the map.

'Well that one is concave and that's convex.' His reply was quite quick, and he went back to his defence of Angelina.

'You're wrong; its other way around.' Sam was butting in again.

'No, I'm right.' Phil was starting to think this guy was a bit of a dick.

'Mike can you come here for a sec?'

Mike came over to them and stood in between Phil and Sam. 'Hey ain't that concave and convex?' Phil was pointing at the map.

'Yeah,' Mike agreed.

'Oh!' Sam shirked away and sat back down. Phil and Harry continued on with their debate, which would go on all weekend.

After lunch they were going out on a light walk. They all climbed into the minibus and set off. All Mike had shown them was the pub they were going to meet in. He then drove around dropping them off at random points. First, they had to figure out where they were, and then find their way to the pub. Sam and the others had a slight advantage with the gadgets, whereas Harry and Phil only had a compass and map.

'Right, where in hell are we?' Harry asked.

'Hang on, I'll figure it out in a minute,' Phil said with an assured tone.

'Here, give us a look.'

Phil showed the map to Harry and pointed to where he thought they were. 'What ya think?'

'Yeah, looks about right,' Harry replied after looking at the map for a half a minute.

'So, we're agreed?"

'Yeah, definitely where we are.'

'So we're here and we need to be here. Best way to get there?'

'As straight a line as possible. We'll start walking in the direction of the pub and see how we do.'

'Just what I was thinking, shortest distance between two points is a straight line.' Phil set a bearing on his compass and the two of them set off. They had until five o'clock to get there. They set off down the trail and were making good time, until they hit a road which took a sharp left turn. Phil looked at the map and saw the road would eventually loop back around to line they had been walking on. It would just put extra time onto the journey.

'Follow the road or straight on? Straight on will save us at least half an hour,' Phil stated.

'Straight on then,' Harry agreed.

They set off across the field, no trail to follow, but it was okay so long as they stuck to the compass baring. They hit a set of trees, but pushed on through, until they met a stream.

'Man, what do we do? How did you not spot this on the map?' Harry complained

'Shit missed it. We can jump it, it's not that far.'

'Walk down a little, see if there's an easier crossing?'

'Here's fine, look we have to be back first, show the yuppie crew what we can do. What's the worst that can happen? You get wet feet.'

Phil threw his rucksack across the stream and took a few steps back. He ran and jumped over the stream making it.

'Ah shit,' Harry said as he threw his bag across. He too jumping across, just about making it.

They carried on walking until they hit a fence.

'Jump over it?' Harry asked

'Fuck yeah,' came the reply.

Jumping over the fence, setting off across the field. On the way they noticed a driveway and thought it was a bit odd, until they got down a little further. There was a house at the end of it.

'Fuck we've wandered into someone's garden!' Harry sounded surprised.

'Shite we have, best get a move on and out of here quick.'

They started to run towards the fence, when they heard some barking coming from the direction of the house. Phil looked over his shoulder and saw a very angry dog running towards them.

'Run faster Harry.'

'I'm running as fast as I can!'

They just made it to and then over the fence, but still kept running to be on the safe side. Eventually they stopped and sat down to catch their breath.

'Wow, that was a bit too close.' Phil sounded relieved

'Yeah, you're telling me?'

'Best get moving then?'

'Yeah, no more shortcuts then?'

'Stick to the roads.' Phil looked at the map. 'The road is just over there, and we can follow it to the pub.'

Harry nodded, they set of for the road.

'Phil?'

'Yeah.'

'You know this new job you're going for?'

'Yeah.'

'Well you do know, you won't be able to do crazy shit like that, don't you? I mean you'll need to stick to clearly marked trails?'

'Yeah, I know I'll have to be more 'professional' just getting it all outa my system while I'm with you.'

'Man, I'm going to miss you.'

'Stop with that shit, you're going to come over and visit all the time.'

'Yeah, but it won't be the same not having you around all the time.'

'Not the time for this soppy shit, Harry. Change the subject.'

'Okay, okay, so Scarlett is the one we need to save,' Harry said rapidly changing subject.

'Oh no, I thought we settled this, definitely has to Angelina.'

This lively discussion continued as they strolled off down the road, both equally convinced they were right.

When they were about five minutes down the road from the pub, Mike drove by them in the minibus.

'You're late.' He shouted out the window, as he slowed down. They both looked at their watches and it was just 5 pm.

'We're only a few minutes late.' They replied, but Mike had already gone.

'Shit, we're probably going to be last there.' Phil sounded annoyed.

'Ah well, what can we do about it?'

'Nothing.'

When they got to the pub, Mike was sitting outside not looking to happy.

'Everyone in having a pint, Mike?' Phil asked

'No, you two are the first back. You might as well go in and have a pint, I'll go out and look for the rest. They were supposed to be able to map read! All that fancy shit hasn't done them a tap of good.'

Mike headed off in the minibus, the two lads looked at each other and smiled.

'Pint then?' Harry enquired

'It'd be rude not to.'

'Maybe the barmaid can settle the argument?'

'Can we not let it drop for a while?'

Harry gave him a wry smile as they went into the pub. They were on the third pint by the time the rest of the group were back. Mike still looked less than impressed but couldn't really do anything as they were paying him well to teach them. They headed off back to the lodge.

The next morning, they had a quick spot of classroom work before they left on the two-day trek. Mike then brought them outside, where he measured out what looked like a one-hundred-meter track. Harry gave Phil a nod, Phil nodded back. They both knew were Mike was going with this.

'Okay we're going to work on pacing now. This track is one hundred meters long and we are going to walk it counting our double pacing.' Some of the group looked confused.

'Ah, so you pick one foot, I use my right and I count every time it hits the ground, that's a double pace. This technique is vital for navigating in the dark or low visibility, it could stop you walking over a cliff. We've done working out distance from a map, now you will be able to calculate how many paces to a specific point on a map.'

They spent about ten minutes working on this before they left, each pair carrying all their own food and equipment for the two days. They all set off from the same point in ten minute intervals, each team had to plot their own route. Mike then set off to wait at the camping site, looking like a beaten man.

By the time Harry and Phil arrived, a few others had already set up their tents and were starting to settle in. They hadn't been in a rush to get there; they pitched their tent and started to cook a bite to eat. Mike came over to see how they were settling in.

'So, Mike what's the plan for tonight?' Phil asked.

'I was thinking we'll drive down to the local town and have a few pints,' Mike replied.

'Oh, that sounds good. We could do with a pint, couldn't we Phil?' Harry said

'We'll head about eightish, then?' Mike said.

'Yeah, it's not as if we can go too far away now is it?' Phil replied in a joking tone.

'Now, you two better behave yourselves.'

Both nodded back at Mike with a smile, Mike just shook his head as he walked away.

They got to the pub, Harry headed to the bar, spotting a tap marked Heineken export. *'Oh, stronger than the usual stuff'* he thought to himself, I think we'll be having some of that. Buying two pints he went back over to where Phil was with the rest of the group. Phil was looking a bit bored with the conversation, which was all about the rest of the groups' day job and how much money they earn. People trying to outdo each other with their bragging about status symbols and famous people who are members of their tennis club. Harry glanced across at Phil and they both just shook their heads and sipped away at the pints, the first of many Harry thought to himself. Phil was thinking he would need to change the direction of the conversation and quick, otherwise he would lose his mind. Just sticking in the odd little comment should be enough. He waited on a gap in the conversation.

'So, any of ye got any good climbing or walking stories?' Phil asked the group. He didn't get a response, so he kept going, 'So, me and Harry where walking in the Alps last year. On our way back down the guide briefed us on what to do if we lost control on ice. Some of the group had walking sticks, but not me or Harry though. No one had an ice axe either, which would have been useful. As some of you may know if you start sliding on ice, you roll onto your stomach and use your ice axe as a break. In this case we were told to use walking sticks instead. As we were walking down I heard a shout from behind me and looked around to see one the lads running towards me, pole swinging in the air. I had to duck out of the way as it swung over my head and landed on my back. I started to slide down the hill and thought to myself, what am I supposed to do? Roll onto my front and stick pole in the snow, oh right I don't have a pole! So I just slid on my back and stuck my rucksack hands, elbows, feet, and head in as deep as I could to the snow to slow down. I could see a row of stones at the bottom and was just hoping I stopped in time, just had to close my eyes and hope. If I had hit the rocks it really would have hurt and being up at 2,500 feet getting help would have been hard. Lucky when I opened my eyes I was about two foot away from the rocks.'

He looked up to see if he had managed to lighten the subject and a few of them were smiling. As they had a few more drinks the talk slowly turned to the more humorous side of outdoor life, with recanting all the close scrapes they had had. By the end of the night everyone was quite tipsy and starting to get along well, they had seemed to get beyond the ego-driven bullshit. Harry even managed to trip over one the tent guidelines, ending up falling head first into the tent, which gave everyone in the group a laugh, even Mike.

The next morning, they were all up early for another walk, everyone seemed to be feeling the effects of the night before. Harry and Phil managed to talk Mike into letting them set off last, so they could have more time to recover. That export was taking its full effect. When they finally did set off, clouds were starting to set in. Phil noticed it was coming in over the top of the hill they were heading up.

'Shit, that don't look good.' Phil sounded a little alarmed.

'Yeah, we won't be able to see jack shit in a bit.'

'Look at the map. See the trail we have to hit on the other side?'

'Shit that's not wide at all, could easily miss it.'

By this stage the cloud had come in and they couldn't see very far in front of themselves at all. They stopped walking.

'We're going to have to pace this out,' Phil said, as he looked at the map to plot their route to the next point.

'You got it worked out?' Harry asked

'Yep, just follow me.'

They both made their way to the top first, not much being said as they were both making sure they we're getting the pacing right. Eventually they found the trail they were looking for and it was less than a foot wide. They both knew that if they just followed this now they would make it to the end of the walk with no major problems. As they came towards the end they met Mike on his way up, as usual he was not surprised to see them back before anyone else. Everyone else arrived at least twenty minutes later, they were all still feeling the effects of the night before. Phil had managed to really impress Mike, especially with the way he managed to bond with the group, eventually.

The next day it was just Mike, Phil and Harry out walking. Mike's plan was to really check out Phil's mountaineering skills, throwing everything he could think off at him. He was impressed at the way he was handling everything in a cool, calm manor. Harry was getting a little bored and started to play around a little. They had just come over the top of a hill, Harry noticed the ground was like a wet sponge from the rain over the last few days. He started to jump up and down to test the spring in the ground. He slipped and started to slide, it felt like being on a waterside. When he stopped, he got up and shouted back to Phil, 'Hey, that's great fun!' He then took a few steps and jumped into another slide, this time after about ten foot he started to pick up speed. He thought to himself, *Fuck, I'm going a little fast here!'*

When he looked up and saw a large rock in his path, there was no way he was going to miss it. He knew if he hit it straight on he would more than likely break his coccyx and that would not be fun. He decided to use a little trick had learned from canoeing, he lifted one ass cheek to try steer himself away from the rock. Feeling that if he hit the rock with his gluteus, it would cause less damage than hitting it flush on his coccyx. He hit the rock and jumped about three foot in the air, when he landed he thought, *Fuck, that hurt!'* he looked over to see a cliff a couple of feet away from him, if he had not hit the rock, he would have gone straight over the edge. It looked like it was about a hundred-foot drop, he thought *'Shit I'd never have survived that.'* Suddenly he felt a bit better about the impending burse on his gluteus.

He looked back up the mountain to see how far he had slid, could only see Mike, no Phil anywhere. Mike looking as white as a ghost was jogging toward him. *'Where could Phil be?'* scanning around, he still could not see him. Everything seemed to slow down, Mike seemed to be running in slow motion, he was shouting something Harry wasn't able to hear him. Everything was silent, he felt an awful feeling in the pit of his stomach, this wasn't good. Harry made his was over to the edge of the cliff. As he looked over he could see how far it was down, just then Mike was standing beside him, stopping him form looking over.

'Where's Phil?' Harry asked. The knot tightened in the bottom of his stomach.

'He… he… he saw you sliding… and he… he just took off sliding after you… did you not see him shoot by you?' Mike seemed dumbstruck, a man who had probably witnessed some horrid things, but was still visibly shaken.

Harry suddenly knew at this point Phil had slid over the side of the cliff, he just sat down where he was, numb, numb with fear. There was no way he could look over the edge, he felt like he was going to puke. There was no way anyone could survive a fall like that.

Mike looked over the cliff and just turned away covering his eyes. Eventually he took out his phone and called Mountain Rescue, he knew it would be body retrieval. He then went over, sat down beside Harry, put his arm around him and squeezed him tight. Harry rested his head on Mike's shoulder as they waited in silence on the Mountain Rescue to arrive.

*****

Chapter 7
Tow Back
'Heart-Shaped Box' Nirvana

Harry lay in his bed, didn't feel like doing anything, still couldn't believe Phil was gone. The funeral had been two weeks ago, couldn't even leave his room much during that time. The curtains remained closed, just curled up in bed in the dark watching old films. Couldn't bring himself to doing anything or going anywhere. All he could think was *'If I hadn't had been messing about, Phil would still be here.'* The guilt was just eating away at him. His Mam knocked on the door.

'Hey, how you feeling now? You want something to eat?' She said as she stuck her head the door.

'No thanks,' he replied from under the sheets.

'You have to eat something?'

'Really ain't hungry at all.'

'At least get up and go out for a walk or something. The fresh air will do you good.'

'Might get up in a while.'

'Maybe you'll take the dog for a walk? He'll be good company for you.'

She closed the door, hoping she had gotten through to him; he had spent days in his room. Harry rolled over, pulling the sheets over his head. Like that would help!

About an hour later Harry arrived down into the kitchen dressed, his Mam smiled gently at him.

'Right I'll bring the dog for a walk.' he said still sounding downcast, at least the dog wouldn't ask him if he was okay or ask him to discuss his feelings.

'Have a little something to eat first, will ya?'

'Okay, I'll have a sandwich.'

'Sandwich and a cup of tea on the way. Sit down at the table there.'

He sat at the kitchen table, waiting for his food to be brought over. It really was an effort to try to force it down, the tea helped take the dryness out of his mouth.

Setting out on his walk, the dog seemed happy to be out with him. Making his way along the river, the dog was acting like he hadn't seen him in a while, looking for Harry to play with him all the time. The sound of the flowing water was quite soothing, and the dog was taking his mind off things. This was nice, he really didn't want to talk to anyone, the company this dog was all he required. He didn't seem to care what was going on, not trying to console him, he was happy just to chase after his ball and bring it back. Harry looked up to see someone walking his dog in the opposite direction, he was hoping he could get away just saying hello. As he got closer he realised he recognised them, it was Sam, an old school friend who he had met again at the funeral. There was no way he could dodge this conservation, now he had made eye contact.

'Damn, this is the last thing I need,' he thought to himself.

'Heya Harry,' Sam said as he stopped with his own dog, Harry's dog ran over to him and they started to play together.

'Hey Sam, how's it going?' Harry said trying to keep the chat as short as possible.

'Fine, how have you been coping?'

'Ah, you know… getting there.' This was why he'd stayed inside all the time, the sheer awkwardness of the people he met. Nobody seemed to know what to say to him, or they made clumsy attempts to comfort him.

'At least you're getting out and about?'

'Yeah, the dog is keeping me company.'

'Seems to getting along with mine well.'

'Yeah, he's a playful thing.'

'Takes after you then?' Sam said with a smile.

'You could say so, but not at the moment.' He gave him a wry smile back.

'Hey listen, a few of us are heading into the city centre on Saturday night for a night out. You should come along?'

'No thanks, I'm not great company at the moment.'

'Come on, a few drinks will do ya the world of good.'

'I don't know. Not really feeling up to socialising right now.'

'Seriously man, come on, heading into town will get you away from it all, take your mind off it, even if it's just for an hour or two.'

'Okay, I'll head out for a little while then.' Harry was only saying this to get away from Sam. He had no intention of meeting him.

'Cool, here give us your number and I'll text you on Saturday, let you know what time and where. I promise it'll be a great night.'

They both walked off in their different directions, Harry drifting back off into his own thoughts, throwing the ball every once in a while, for the dog to bounce off and fetch.

Saturday came with Harry received a text from Sam outlining his plans for the night. They were heading out early enough, meeting at about six pm. Harry's Mother encouraged him to go out with Sam, finally she nagged him into going. Harry was hoping people wouldn't try to mollycoddle him, he would be happy enough to not talk about it at all. That was the main reason he was going out, to take his mind off it, so talking about it would only serve to defeat the purpose. For once his Mam was happy to see going out drinking. He had a really long shower, trying to psych himself up, then waded through his wardrobe searching for something to wear. Jesus his choice in clothes was shocking for a night out in town, he was always going out in rural bars and dressed like he did. He had very few shirts and only one pair of shoes. Who was he trying to impress anyway? He ended up putting on an old pair of flat trainers, jeans and a check shirt. It would have to do; he didn't plan to stay out long in any way. Putting in his earphones Harry headed off for the bus into the city centre, maybe a bit of Guns n' Roses would help gee him up a little. *Paradise City'* always seemed to do the trick.

When he got into the pub Sam was the only one of the group he really knew. There were a few others he would have known from school, and a few he didn't know at all well. 'Hey, you made it.' Sam sounded genuinely happy to see him, as he walked over to give him a hug.

'Yeah, hopefully a few drinks will do me good.'

'Come on over, I'll introduce you to the gang.' Harry looked over at the group, he suddenly felt a way to under dressed. The lads all had short clean cut hair, looking neat and tidy, the girls in dresses looking prim, everyone seemed confident and assured. Here was Harry in his trainers, jeans, check shirt feeling like a wet flannel over the room. But he shuffled over to the group, head down not really making eye contact, Sam made the introductions. Looking around the circle, everyone seemed pleasant enough, then a flash of light; this bundle of energy caught his eye, it was a girl across the other side of the circle. She smiled at him, he found himself smiling back, which surprised him no end. She had short blonde hair, with strikingly blue eyes, a short white strapless dress, set off with fuchsia pink high heels and a clutch bag to match. He was quite taken aback by her. She leaned forward towards him.

'Hi, I'm Dervila,' as she kept smiling, moving closer to him.

'Hey, I'm Harry,' he replied as he shook her hand, *Why shake her hand you idiot - was that the right thing to do? Probably not. Aw man!'* She was now stood beside him.

'So, what's your story?'

'What d'ya mean?' Harry shuffled back into himself, putting his hands into his pockets.

'Well, I see some sadness behind your eyes, you don't really look like you fit in here either, or wanna be here, now do you?'

'Well … you're spot on there. I used to go to school with Sam and a couple of the lads. Just back in town a couple of weeks and they asked me to come out for a drink.' Harry didn't want to mention what had just happened, just try put that to the back of his mind for an hour or two. Maybe she could help him do that, she seemed nice.

'Just back from where?'

'Ah nowhere exotic, just was working down in Kerry.'

'Ah, that would explain the dress sense.' Dervila gave him a smile and a wink.

'Hey, it's shabby chic.' Harry replied, he was starting to loosen up now and relax a little. Dervila was a bubbly person and seemed to be good fun.

'Don't know about that, I'd say you would scrub up quite well. First thing we'd need to do is get you a haircut.' She reached over starting to play with his hair.

'Hey!' He was protesting, but he quite liked it.

'So what were you doing over in the wild west then?'

'Hey, it's not that bad, I was teaching canoeing, rock climbing, archery, things like that.'

'Oh so you're a bit of an adventurer then? Exciting.'

'Not so much now, quit my job a couple of weeks ago, back home to live in Dublin now.'

'Ah so you'll be around for a while then?' She gave him a quick nudge on his forearm.

'Yeah, guess so, just need to find a new job.'

'What, you quit without having a new job lined up?'

'Yeah, a bit daft I know. Sure I'll find something somewhere.'

'First thing you need to do is get a haircut and do a spot of shopping, fit back in with the town people, d'ya know?'

'You sound like my Mam there, always at me to cut my hair. Was already thinking of going into town on Monday to do that.' Harry was surprised this came out of his mouth, as he had no plans to anything like that.

'Worry about it then, let's have a little fun tonight.'

'Wasn't planning on staying out long, to be honest.'

'Ah don't spoil my night, we're going to head off clubbing later. You should come?'

'Sure we'll see. Hey, I'm going the bar, fancy a drink?'

'If you're going I'll have a G&T.'

He went to the bar, came back with the two drinks, giving Dervila hers. He was feeling a bit better now, coming out was a good idea. This girl was so bright and lively.

'Thanks,' she said, smiling. It was so intoxicating it was drawing Harry in.

'So, tell me about you. What's your story?'

'Well, I'm not as active as you, pretty much stayed in Dublin my whole life. I just like to go out and have fun.'

Sam came over to stand in between them, eager to see how they were getting along. 'Ye, two seem to be getting along well?' The two nodded, smiling back.

'So now you're back in the big smoke, what are your plans?' Sam asked Harry.

'Haven't really thought about it yet.'

'Well first thing is to get yourself a decent suit and a haircut for interviews. You do have a bit of money put aside, don't ya?'

'Yeah, I have some savings.'

'Get yourself a Monday to Friday 9 to 5 job. It's the only way to go.'

'Really?'

'Yeah, that way you have evenings free and weekend. You don't want to be sitting in work when everyone else is sitting in the pub, especially on a sunny Saturday,' Sam explained

'Oh yeah, nothing worse than that,' Dervila interjected.

Harry nodded in agreement, soaking up all the information provided, while sipping his pint. He would need a new job, as there was no way he was going back to working in the outdoors. He couldn't really show up to job interviews in his Dad's suit either. It was nice to have confirmed what he had already known deep down.

'Oh yeah, we were only just talking about this. I'm going to get onto that Monday, go do a bit of shopping I suppose.'

'Yeah do, you were always quite bright at school, I remember that.' Sam was trying to encourage Harry into doing something constructive.

'I've already told him he'll scrub up well.' Dervila said to Sam.

'Right I'm off to the bar, anyone want a drink?' Sam asked both Harry and Dervila.

'Yeah, sure why not,' Harry replied.

'Hell yeah,' Dervila replied.

'Same again?' They both nodded in reply, before Sam headed off to the bar.

'They're going down well?' Harry asked her.

'Always do.' She said putting down her empty glass. He was going to have to catch up.

'Where did you learn to drink like that?'

'Older brothers. So you going to come the club with us?' She started to dance a little in front of him.

'You're doing a good job of persuading me.'

Outside the nightclub Harry clambered out of the taxi, helping Dervila too, shoes being an issue.

'Jesus, you got a taxi for that distance, it's only down the road!' he said, sounding a little shocked.

'Tell you what, you try walking in these and see how you do?' She was indicating her shoes.

'Suppose, you do have a point there. Really don't know how you manage walk in them, let alone to dance so well.'

'The things we girls do to look good.'

'Well you do a great job at it.'

'Awh thanks,' she said blushing a little.

'They will let me in here, won't they?' He was sounding a little anxious.

'You'll be fine walking up with me.' She linked his arm as they walked towards the door. When they got up the bouncer looked them up and down, more Harry than Dervila. He nodded at them and waving them through into the club, people in the queue shaking their heads as if to say, *'what's she doing with him?'*

Harry had never been to this club before, so it was a completely new experience to him. She led him by the hand into what was essentially a huge hall, with a stage at one end. It reminded him a little of being at a concert. It was packed with people dancing, generally having a good time. She took him over to the bar, ordering drinks for both of them. He was handed a pint of something that looked like cider with ice. He wasn't a massive fan of cider, but, *'What the Hell'* a drink was a drink and he took a sip.

'What on earth is that?' he blurted out, it was like no cider he'd ever tasted.

'It's a double vodka and Lucozade,' she replied laughing.

'It's not that bad actually, once you get over the shock of it not being cider.'

'It'll keep ya going, hate that red bull shit. Has the funkiest taste ever.'

'Yeah and who's idea was it to mix it Jaeger? That's just plain wrong.'

'Couldn't agree more.' She raised her glass and he raised his.

'Where's everyone else?'

'Ah, there on the way.' She didn't seem too bothered. Harry was looking around to see if he knew anyone. Obviously, he didn't, this was not the kind of crowd he'd usually associated with. He was sort of hoping he'd see Sam. As he peered across the crowd, he spotted him, he suddenly felt a little relieved. Dervila was a lovely girl, but he had only met her, she could just leave him to shack up with some other random lad at any stage. Where would that leave him. He waved over to Sam, who waved back and made his way over. He gave Harry a big hug when he arrived.

'Ah, you came along? Good to see you,' Sam said to Harry.

'Yeah, thought I'd come along and check it out.'

'You seem to getting along well with Dervila,' he said, giving him a nudge.

'She's a lovely girl.'

'Single too.' He was still nudging him, egging him along.

'Yeah, I sort of gathered that. You know her well?'

'Not really, she's just a friend of a friend. Get stuck in there my son. Looks like she likes you, too.'

'We'll see, we'll see.'

'What are you two talking about? Hope it's not me.' Dervila had appeared out of nowhere.

'Would we? Na just giving him a little career advice, that's all.' Sam said in defence.

'Yeah, he's in my ear about this and that,' Harry said shaking his head. Dervila just laughed.

'Come on, you're dancing.' She grabbed Harry by the hand, Sam pushed him in the back towards the dance floor. Harry wasn't too sure about what looked like a tropical jungle to him, steam rising from people sweating. The dance floor was huge, packed tight with people. She held his hand as she squirmed her way through to find a spot where they could both dance. Harry was looking around as they were weaving through the crowd and people were throwing some odd shapes, some with hands in the air like trees waving in the wind. He just kept following until she stopped in a small clearing. She turned to face him, starting to dance, taking his both his hands. As he looked into her eyes, it was as if it was just the two of them in the room, she pulled him in tight to her, their lips locked. He felt like he was floating about five feet off the ground – only for the fact that he was holding her hands, he would float away. He really was lost in her, it was like he was sucked into her magical world and he didn't want to come back from wherever this was.

Eventually they had to leave the dance floor. Well, it was time to go home and the club was shutting. They got their coats, left the building, meandering down the road a little, not really knowing which direction they were headed. Dervila's feet were a little sore from the heels so they stopped for a break, sat down on a step for what seemed like a few minutes.

'Come on their, move along.' The two looked up to see a Garda standing over them.

'We're just having a chat, officer.' Harry replied back.

'Well, it's time for you to go home?' Harry glanced at his watch, it was 5.30am, where they really talking for that long.

'We're going now; my feet were a little sore from the heelguard,' Dervila said as she stood up. They both started to walk down the road again.

'You wanna come back to mine? It's not that far and sure I have some beer in the fridge,' Dervila suggested to Harry.

'Sure, why not.' Harry replied after thinking about it for all of five seconds.

Harry sat barefoot on the sofa in Dervila's place, he had taken off his trainers and socks, Dervila had asked him to remove them before they entered the sitting room. He was now trying to figure out how the remote control for the TV worked. Eventually he got the TV switched on and lay back and waited for Dervila to come back with the drinks. She arrived in with two bottles of Corona, sat down beside him, snuggling in. Harry had managed to find some music channel that actually still played music. Harry glanced across at Dervila, she was looking back at him biting the side of her bottom lip. Harry found this quite arousing, for some unknown reason.

'So you have a good night then, adventure boy?'

'Yeah, all the better for meeting you.'

'Hey, don't go getting all corny on me now.'

'Okay, it would have been better if I hadn't then.'

'Very funny.' She put her hand on his leg.

'You really did help me get my mind off something.'

'Sam was saying you needed cheering up alright.'

All Harry could think was *'oh no she's she not going to ruin it now by asking him how he felt and if he wanted to talk about it.'*

Instead she straddled him and gazed deep into his eyes. Her eyes were the bluest Harry had ever seen, like the crystal clear Caribbean Sea. She then leaned forward and whispered into his ear, 'don't worry I'll help you forget all about whatever it is.' She proceeded to nibble on his ear a little, moving down to lightly kiss his neck. Harry suddenly felt all the stresses and strains of the past couple of weeks just melt away.

She then picked her head up and again looked into his eyes, Harry just lay back on the sofa in semi-disbelief at what was happening. She moved her head towards his slowly, gave Harry a quick kiss on the lips and pulled her away again quickly. Harry was tingling with excitement and anticipation. She did this a few times becoming quicker and a little more aggressive each time, until they ended up in a full on embrace. Dervila was running her fingers through Harry's hair and grinding on his lap. Harry could feel his foot knock over the bottle of beer, Dervila picked up her head and said, 'don't worry about that, I'll clean it up in the morning.' She went back to kissing Harry.

When they came up for air ,Dervila said. 'Jesus, this is driving me crazy. Come on.' She stood up, grabbed Harry by the hand and led him into her bedroom. She shut the door behind her and pulled him in close to her. 'Don't want my roommate seeing this!' As they were kissing she started to unbutton his shirt, pulling it down his arms and dropping it on the floor. She pushed him, he ended up back against the wardrobe. She stood and gazed at his body, Harry was actually quite athletic with all the canoeing and climbing. She nodded, walked over and pulled him into an embrace. Harry's heart was beating so fast he was sure she could feel it. She pushed him up against the wardrobe door running her hands up and down his back, nibbling his ear.

It was now Harry's turn to try to unzip her dress, but he couldn't seem to get a grasp on the zipper and he just ended up fumbling about with it. 'Don't worry about that,' she said to him as she pulled him out, spun him around and pushed him back onto the bed. She proceeded to give Harry his own slow private striptease. He already knew how well she could dance from the night club, but now she took it to a whole new level. Dervila removed her dress slowly and it dropped on the floor, she turned away while she removed her fuchsia pink underwear. All Harry could think as turned to face him was, *'Oh my god she's the most amazing thing I've ever seen.'*

Harry was lying back on the bed, just his feet hanging over the edge. She approached him and proceeded to open the fly on his jeans, pulling them off along with his boxers. Dervila crawled slowly over his body until she was straddling him. She then grabbed his wrists, held them above his head, lowering herself down to lightly kiss him on the lips and on to his neck, then down to his chest. This was definitely taking his mind off everything.

Harry arrived home the next morning feeling very tired, but somehow had a bit of a spring in his step. He decided to head straight to bed, as he was getting changed he could feel his back tingling a bit. Taking off his top, went over to his mirror peered over his shoulder to try see his back as best he could. As he glanced over at his back, he could see scratch marks down his back. *'My Lord, what has she done to me? She even managed to draw blood!'* Harry wouldn't be walking around the house shirtless for a while. He climbed into bed, smiling for what seemed like the first time since that fateful day on that mountain in North Wales.

*****

CHAPTER 8
In the green room
'Wonderful Tonight' Eric Clapton

Harry got out of the shower, he was bouncing around like Richard Simmons, now he had to decide what to wear for his date with Grainne. They had a great day together the week before; he had suggested going out for a meal and a few drinks, the following week. Harry had been looking forward to this all week, he even had a little surprise planned. He opened his wardrobe, started to flick through his clothes – to dress casual or put on a shirt was the question. He really wasn't a fan of wearing dress shirts at the weekend; having them on all week was enough for him. A t-shirt would probably be little too casual, so he settled on a causal shirt, jeans and his favourite boots. His boots always gave him that little bit more height, he would need it tonight, as Grainne was about the same height as him. If she had high heels on he would look short compared to her. He was nervous with a kind of knot in his stomach, he hadn't felt that in a while. To be honest he hadn't felt much emotion in the last two years, so a change from the numbness that had been with him since that day in North Wales was a good thing. All he was thinking was, *'Don't fuck this up, by saying something stupid or eating like an animal.'*

Now he was ready. Checking his watch, he needed to early, but not too early. Definitely didn't want to be late. Why was he so obsessed with being early, certainly wasn't the norm for being Irish? He set off butterfly's flapping away in his tummy again; he could get used to feeling this way.

While waiting for her outside Bewelys, he couldn't stand still. He spotted her walking down towards him, all he could think was, *'Oh, my lord. I'm about to spend the evening with her.'* She had on a black dress, short, but not too short It clung to her toned body, her high heels seemed to make her legs look twice as long. Again she didn't have any fake tan on and very little makeup – she didn't need it. He liked this about her.

'Ah, you wore high heels!' Harry said putting his hands out to the side of this head, now she had few inches on him. In their bare feet they'd be around the same height.

'Sorry, had to, couldn't really wear flats with this dress, now could I?'

'Yeah, you're right. Come on let's go. We've got lots to do.'

'Where are we going?' she asked.

'Dinner is not until eight, so I've planned a little something to do first.'

'We going for a drink?'

'Well, in a way.'

He grabbed her hand, they started to walk up to the top of St. Stephens Green, Harry leading her towards one the horse and carriages waiting. – both were white.

'No, you didn't?' she asked.

'Oh, yes I did.'

When they climbed into the carriage there was a bottle of wine waiting for them. Sitting down, he opened the bottle, pouring them both a glass. They set off on a trip around the city, with the sun still shining but quite low in the spring sky. During the trip, they both laughed and joked. It was a very different way to see a city they had both grown up in. The sun was starting to set and created some stunning silhouettes of buildings. It was the last thing Grainne expected from him, but she enjoyed it. 'I could get used to this.'

Harry seemed to know his stuff about Dublin, all about the history, told it with a sense of humour too. She enjoyed listening to him talk about it and it made her smile. That was one thing she missed while away, the Irish sense of humour. After the carriage ride they went to this small but quiet restaurant, which didn't look cheap, and it turned out it wasn't. Tonight was not the night to worry about money; this was about enjoying each other's company. It was the perfect relaxed atmosphere.

'So, how do you know so much about history, Harry?' Grainne asked.

'Ah, you know, one of the few subjects I liked at school. It just sort of sank in and stuck,' Harry replied quite shyly.

'You're really a smarty pants, ain't you?'

'Wouldn't say that, just remember things.'

'But you don't let people know just how smart you are?'

'No point, people just think what they want anyway. You can't really change their perception, can you?'

'Well, you can try.'

'I just let them think what they want and if I manage to change what they think, well that's good, if not then, so be it.'

'Interesting outlook on life, so you really don't care what people think? That's much easier said than done.'

'Ah, well there are a few people I do care what they think, but not many of them.'

'Jesus, you really were hurt?'

'Yeah, Phil's death did hit me hard. I've only really been able to talk about it since I met you. Just didn't feel comfortable talking about it with others.' Again he had his head down looking at the table.

Grainne smiled at him, he glanced up make sure she was still there and saw her smile?

'It's good you're opening up now, bottling that up will make you end up doing something silly.'

If only she knew, he'd spent the last two years acting silly. Actively encouraged by Dervila, but a willing participant in the craziness.

'The people I have being hanging around with wouldn't really talk about anything serious. They always seemed to just want to talk about the next drink or party.'

'What about this girl you were seeing?'

'Dervila. Oh, she always, somehow knew where the next party was, seemed to know everyone.'

'She sounds like a bit of wild one.'

'Oh it was a wild ride with her all right, never a dull moment. I'm better off without her, though.'

'Sounds a little that way, like that twit I was seeing.'

'Hey, let's make a deal and not talk about exes for the rest of the night?' Harry said as he raised his glass.

'Deal,' she said as they tapped glasses, smiling.

After dinner they headed for a drink in a nearby pub, Harry let Grainne pick which bar. It was quite loud, but they did find a nice spot to sit down with their drinks. Again he let her pick the first drink, he now found himself sitting with a Cosmopolitan. He was slipping away, not looking too impressed, while she was just laughing.

'Why, oh why?' he said sounding a touch exasperated.

'Ah, because it's funny.'

'What you trying to make me look like?'

'Ah, just wanted to see if you would drink it. Test your theory on what others think of you?'

'Ah, aren't you a clever one…'

'Oh yeah, be careful what you tell me.'

'Modest, too.'

'Well, you are a little concerned people will think you're gay?'

'No, I'm worried someone will come over and try to chat me up!'

'Who's being a little confident now?'

He gave her a wry smile, 'Okay, it's my round and my choice.'

Harry arrived back with two Jack Daniels, neat with ice and put them on the table with a smile.

'Now you are a fucker,' she said.

'I was going to get you a Guinness, but just not in a bar like this.'

'My lord, you could have got a mixer with it?'

'No, no, no. That just drowns the bourbon.'

'Since when did you become a whiskey cynosure?'

'Ah, dad drinks it and when I put coke or anything in it, he always gives out,' he replied, giving her a wink and a smile. 'Now drink up.'

'Holly shit!' she said after she took her first sip. Harry just laughed.

After a few more drinks, of their own choice this time, she looked at him and said, 'You wanna go for a dance?'

'Are you ready for some killer dance moves?' he said as he led her to the dance floor.

'What have I let myself in for?' She looked towards the ceiling.

On the dance floor, he was quite clearly dancing in an idiotic way to make her feel uncomfortable. She just stood there shaking her head as he slid by ... she just grabbed him by the arm.

'Come on dance with me, not like a crazy idiot.'

'Okay, I'll dance with you.'

They moved in a little closer. As she got near he took her hand, held it in the air and spun her around pirouette-like, which got him a glare, then a smile. She was now in front of him with her back to him, she reached back and took his hands moving them onto her hips. As a result, he moved in closer to her back. She looked back over her shoulder at him.

'See, this is better than you running around the floor like a five-year-old.'

'Ah yeah, much better.'

After a while she decided to turn around to face him, now his hands were now on her lower back. They gazed into each other's eyes, *'Oh my god,'* he thought to himself, *'this really is going to happen.'* She now had her hands on his shoulders as they moved in time to the music, their heads moved closer and closer together until finally their lips were just about to touch. The world melted into nothingness, it was just the two of them. When their lips did touch Harry could taste her lip balm, *'cherry'* he thought to himself. He knew he didn't want it to stop, hopefully neither did she. He liked the way she had made him wait, it was worth it. Eventually they stopped giving each other a tender look.

'Time for a drink?' she said, holding his hand and heading for the bar.

'So, what you having now?'

'Oh, I'll have a Kopparberg, mixed fruit.'

'Could I get two, Kopparberg mixed fruit please?' he asked at the bar. They found two high stools to sit at, she sat with her legs slightly apart and his legs were together. They sat very close teasing each other. It was like there was nobody else in the room, he could barely even notice the music. Eventually the bar staff came over and told them it was time to leave, when they looked up the place was empty. They left quite sheepishly.

'Hey, I'll drop you off in a taxi. Make sure you get home okay,' he offered .

'Yeah, that sounds good.'

Hailing a taxi, they both got in and sat in the back. She rested her head on his shoulder as they moved off.

'You'd better not go to sleep, 'cause I don't really know where your house is.'

'I won't,' she said.

She just lay there resting on him giving the driver the odd direction.

'Hey, you wanna come in?' she enquired when they got to her house.

'You sure?'

'Yeah, I'm sure I can find you a drink somewhere.'

He paid the driver, got out of the taxi and they went into her house. Harry sat on the sofa while Grainne went off to get a drink. 'I only have bottles of Bud, is that okay?'

'Yeah, that'll be fine.' She got out two bottles, brought them out handing one to Harry while she went over to her iMac, to put on some music.

'What you thinking of putting on?' he asked

'Well, how about I stick on some Red Hot Chili Peppers?'

'Yeah, sounds good.' She put on *'Scar Tissue'* and came over to sit down beside him.

'You like that song?'

'Yeah, it's a good tune. Is it a playlist you've got on?'

'No, I've just put it on random play.'

'A bit of song Russian Roulette?'

'Makes it more interesting, no?'

'Depends, have you any shit songs in there?'

'No!'

'Come on everyone has guilty pleasures, you have to have some?'

'Okay, I do have a thing for eighties music. Duran Duran, Spandau Ballet, Human League, you know?' It was her turn to be a little embarrassed. Harry just smiled.

'Well, that's not too bad. I can accept that.' She punched him in the arm.

'I'll accept that, come on then what's yours?'

'Ah, a bit of poodle rock, Bon Jovi, Van Halen, Aerosmith.' He put his hands behind his head scrunching his nose and squinting his eyes.

'Right, so we both have a thing for eighties music, me pop and you rock. All big hair and makeup,' she said putting her head back and laughing.

'You got any neon leg warmers knocking around then?'

'How did you guess, they're in my room with curling iron and Afro Comb.' She was still laughing. 'So did Phil have any?'

'Oh, he did. He had this thing about ABBA. If we were at karaoke, he would get up and sign *The winner takes it all* very badly. I never knew where to look. He thought he was the greatest singer ever.'

'Oh my god, I'd say that was hilarious.'

It shuffled onto the next song, Pearl Jam *'Given to fly,'* Harry went silent and started to look a little pale.

'You okay?' She asked

'Yeah … just that Phil loved this song and I haven't heard it in a while; he even took it off my PC and iPod.'

'You want me to skip to the next song?'

'No, no, leave it … was going to have them play it at his funeral, but didn't seem right with the way he died and all.'

'How come?'

'Well, we were messing about sliding down a mountain side … I hit a rock at the end, which stopped me. He shot off over the side, a100-foot drop. See what I mean about the song?' he said with a sigh.

'Fucking hell, I can see why you were so fucked up?'

'Well, yeah it is hard to fathom. It was my fault really; he was only following my lead. If I hadn't been messing about he'd still be here…'

'You can't say that; take it you didn't know there was a drop there?'

'No, I didn't.' She could see tears starting to form in his eyes.

'Hear, put your head down here.' She pointed down at her lap, he put his head down and curled up on the sofa. 'It'll be fine, just let it all out.'

The next song to come on was Cold Play, *'Fix You.'* She sat there stroking his hair, his tears dripping into her lap. Eventually she decided it was time for bed; no way she was sending him home. 'You ready for bed?'

'Yeah, just order me a taxi.'

'No, you're staying here, not letting you go home on your own.'

'Are you sure?'

'Yes, now come on.'

She led him into her bedroom, they both got ready for bed. When they got in, she just cuddled him until he eventually fell asleep, then gave him a kiss on the cheek, then drifted off to sleep herself, all the time hoping he was okay.

When Harry woke up he was not in his own in the bed, as he curled back up in the duvet he could smell Grainne. *'Jesus,'* he thought, *'hope I didn't make an arse of myself last night. She probably thinks I'm some sort of emotionally challenged man child.'* He could smell bacon cooking, time to get up. Getting up he put on his jeans, he was still in quite good shape for someone who hadn't done any exercise in two years. Walking into the kitchen, there she was there standing at the cooker looking radiant in her night dress.

'Hey, sleepy head,' she said.

'Hey, I didn't make an ass of myself last night, did I?' he replied, scratching his head.

'No, you were fine; hope you feel better for it?'

'Yeah I do, thanks.'

'So how do you like your bacon? Crispy?'

'Too right.'

'Bacon sandwich and coffee, all right?'

'Yeah, as long you put ketchup mixed with mayonnaise on it.'

'Oh, Marie Rose sauce, that's lovely.'

'Is it not called pink sauce?'

'Maybe? We called it Marie Rose in England.'

'Definitely called pink sauce over here. You're back in Ireland now, better start talking like it.' He smiled as he said it.

'Ah, ya know, bad habits. Still messed up with the number three. Ya know the way we say tree? People over there used to try get me to say three thousand, three hundred and thirty-three. One of the lads used to play the Smashing Pumpkins *Thirty-three'* to me and laugh.'

'That's hilarious.'

'Maybe the first time, but after three years of it.'

She finished the bacon, made the sandwiches, he made the coffee, then they sat down to eat. It had been a while since Harry had felt this comfortable around anyone.

A couple of days later Grainne was sitting at her desk in work, when she received a call to go down to the main reception. She was quite surprised at this as she was not expecting anyone or anything. She arrived down to find a man standing at the main door with a bunch of flowers. There were what looked like a dozen, mixed between white and pink. She accepted them off the delivery man, heading back to her desk, slightly blushing as she passed by her workmates.

She sat down at her desk putting them proudly on display and took out the card. On it was written:

'Thank you. H.'

She took out her phone and sent a text to Harry.

'Thank u so much. Dey r beautiful xxx'

'Glad u liked dem,' came Harry's reply.

'Such a lovely surprise xxx'

'U deserve them.'

'Don't think so but thank u xxx.'

'Ah u do. Just 4 being der 4 me.'

'Thank u so much again Hun xxx.'

*****

Chapter 9
White Sand
'All Apologies' Nirvana

Harry was just home from work on a Monday, when his phone rang; it was Joe his old canoeing mate he had met by chance a few weeks before.

'Heya Joe, what's the craic?'

'Alright, Harry, how's you? Remember I was chatting to ya the other week about the reunion surfing trip?'

'Ah yeah.'

'Well, myself Dave, Will, Jim and Niamh are heading over to Lahinch on Friday if you're still up for it?'

'Yeah, I'll head over, you know I'll be a bit rusty, yeah?'

'It's cool, I told the lads; they would love to see you again, catch up.'

'Super, what time you heading at?'

'Whenever, what time you home from work at?'

'Well all my kit is at Mam and Dad's, I can get there by about six?'

'That'll be fine, I'll pick you up around six thirty?'

'Grand, sure I'll talk to you then.'

Harry hung up the phone, now he would have to talk to his Mam and Dad. Hadn't talked to them in months, they weren't too happy with the way he had been living his life. They didn't like Dervila at all and where not shy about telling him the last time he was home. It might be okay once they realised he had broken up with Dervila and was actually going off canoeing with his old friends for the weekend. He might even tell them about Grainne, things were going well with her, shit he'd have to tell her he was going away too.

He picked up the phone to ring his parents. 'Heya Dad, how've you been?'

'Jesus Harry, it's been ages since we've seen you. Have you been behaving yourself?'

'Yeah, listen I've broken up with Dervila, so not going out as much now.'

'That's good news; she was a bad egg, that one.'

'Yeah finally figured that out, listen is all my canoeing gear still in the house? Going to do a spot over the weekend.'

'That's good to hear, son. Yeah it's all still here, up in the attic, your boat is out the back. When you coming up to get it?'

'Well, we're going on Friday, one of the lads is going to pick me up from yours about six-thirty. Is that okay?'

'Yeah, I'll get it all out for you and make sure it looks all right.'

'Thanks for that Dad, I'll be up about six.'

'Sure give us a ring when you're leaving work and I'll make you some dinner.'

'Cheers, sure I'll talk to ya then.'

Friday afternoon came, Harry set of for his parents' house with his bag in hand for the weekend. He phoned his Dad to let him know he was on the way, he would have a fry and chips ready for him. This was one of the things he missed most from living at home. Joe sent him a text to make sure he was still going, he replied saying he wouldn't miss it for the world. It would be great seeing all the group again, they always used to have a laugh, he hadn't seen them since in around the time of the funeral.

'Jesus, he thought, hope I can still paddle?' He had checked the surf report in work, it had looked okay, not too big or messy, a nice off shore breeze too. He wondered how he would react the first time he capsized on a wave. Like sticking your head in a washing machine as Phil used to put it. Panicking was the worst thing you could do, but that's easier said than done, when it feels like you've just put your head inside a violent raging torrent. Back when he was canoeing a lot he used to be able to relax, figure out which way was up, place his paddle free of the water onto the top of the wave and use the force of the water to roll back up still surfing the wave. Everything seemed to move in slow-motion back then. Could he still do this, or would he in fact panic and have to swim out? *'Just like riding a bike,'* he told himself, *'you never forget, might be a little rusty, but the cold Atlantic water will help it'll all come back.'*

Arriving at his parents' house, loads of childhood memories came flooding back to him. The places he had played as a child even if most of it had changed now, they seemed to have built houses on every bit of green land. He knocked on the door, his Dad opened it and gave him a big hug.

'Good to have you back, son,' he probably meant that both ways, in coming home and cutting back on his bad behaviour.

'Would ya stop?' Harry said pushing him away.

'Okay, come on in. I'll have your dinner ready in a minute.'

'Thanks Dad.' He walked into the kitchen and sat down at the dining table, it was just as he remembered it. He even sat in the same seat out of habit. He ate his dinner, suddenly it felt like he was never away. His Dad brought him over a cup of tea, he hadn't had one since he left the house. As he started to eat his Mother came into the room.

'Heya, son. It's been a while?' She came over and gave him a hug while he was still sitting down; it was like she was glad to have him back too.

'Heya Mam.' He was squirming a little from the hug, still trying to eat his dinner.

'So you finally got rid of that skank, then?'

'Mam!' He wasn't used to hearing words like that coming from her.

'Well, she wasn't good for you, made you act like a different person.'

'She wasn't all that bad.'

'Now you have your blinkers on there, she was bad news.'

'Well, she's gone now, so real no point talking about her.' Harry really just wanted to forget her.

'Okay, nice to see you're going back canoeing. Who you going with?'

'Ah, Joe and the gang.'

'Oh Joe, he's a nice lad, what made you call him?'

'He phoned one night on my way home from work and he said they were going. He asked if I'd like to go and I said yeah. Speaking of that, did you find all my gear, Dad?'

'Yeah, your bag is there, and your boat is at the back gate.'

'Paddle and helmet?'

'Yes, it's all there; smells a bit but still looks okay.'

'Thanks.'

Harry finished his dinner, checked his bag just to make sure it was all there and none of it had decided to rot. He was glad he always washed and dried his gear before he put it away. Everything looked just like he left it a couple of years ago. Then he went out to the back garden to check his kayak, the dog came rushing over to jump up on him.

'Hey Boy. How are you,' he said to the dog while rubbing is neck, the dog didn't know what to do with himself it had been so long. He ran away to look for his ball, came back, then finally went off to get it, running up to drop it at Harry's feet. They spent a few minutes playing together playing catch and wrestling for control of the ball. Harry only then realised how much he missed the dog.

Shortly he had to open the back gate to take the kayak out whereas Joe was waiting in the car. Managing to free himself from the dog, they put his bags into the boot and tied his kayak beside Joe's on the roof rack.

Harry's parents came out to say hello to Joe and see them off. They smiled, looking contented and waving as they drove off.

'Jesus, they looked happy to see you?' Joe said.

'Yeah, ain't seen them in a while.'

'You did drop off the scene for a few years there.'

'Yeah, got involved with this girl, she sort of took up all my time.'

'She hot?'

'She was a nice girl, not your typical outdoorsy type. More of an indoors person.'

'So you still with her?'

'Na, we broke up a couple of weeks ago.'

'Sorry to hear that dude.'

'Ah, needed to break up with her. Lovely girl, just a little too crazy.'

'Just had you out on the leash all the time then?'

'Yeah, it was great for a while, but it was starting to affect my day job and mess with my head. All for the best really. What you been up to yourself?'

'Ah, a bit here a bit there, being running courses and assessments for the Canoe Union, keeps me going.'

'What about the others?'

'All up to different things now, most have proper jobs now. Sure they'll tell you when we get over there.'

Joe had a local radio station on in the car, which really was not to Harry's taste.

'What kind of shite have ya got on? No way I'm listening to this all the way!'

'Here my iPod is in the glove box, just plug it there and stick something on.'

Harry reached over, got the iPod out of the glove box and started to flick through looking for music he liked.

'Jesus, your taste in music hasn't changed. You ever made beyond the eighties, did ya?'

'No, still loving the old stuff.'

Harry was still flicking through, all could find was the likes of, The Rolling Stones, The Doors, Pink Floyd, David Bowie, Credence Clear Water Revival. He decided just to stick it on random play, see what happened. It was going to be better than the radio with all the manufactured bands on there. First song that came on was The Doors *Roadhouse Blues,'* Harry didn't mind it so much.

'Class song, much better than that crap on the radio.' Joe exclaimed.

'Yeah, better than all these manufactured bands,' Harry replied.

'Don't think bands like these would make it today, with these useless talent shows which are more about making the judges famous.'

'Couldn't agree with you more, there.'

'A lot of these lads wouldn't make it through the auditions these days.'

'Yeah, imagine Kurt Cobain rocking up to one of their auditions.'

They both had a good laugh at the thought of that scene.

'Hey, I'll be running a few level four and five proficiency assessments during the winter. It'd be great if you could tag along, ya know, show these lads how it should be done,' Joe asked.

'I'm a little rusty, Joe. Ain't been out in a couple years.'

'Told ya before, it's just like riding a bike, Harry.'

'Yeah, only thing is you won't drown if you fall off a bike!'

'Come on, you haven't lost your bottle, have you?'

'Honestly don't know, Joe. Guess we'll find out tomorrow?'

'Ah, you'll be fine. That cold salt water will blast the rustiness out of ya quick enough.'

'Yeah, thanks for reminding me.' Harry was worried as the manner of Phil's death had shaken him to the bones. Up until then they both had a belief that neither wouldn't die … well not while been adventurous. They had always joked about near misses, how they were destined to do something special. Now he knew this was not the case, he had found it out in the hardest possible way. The fact that he had come so close to sliding over the edge of the cliff himself, without even knowing the precarious position he put himself in, somehow made it worse. Most of their risks were taken knowingly up to that point, who would have known a playful slide on a wet hill would result in one of them dying? Certainly not him.

'Hey, did I tell ya Jim and Niamh got engaged?' Joe said with a smile, he could sense Harry was drifting back to the accident and needed to change the direction of the conversation.

'No way. When did that happen?'

'Well they've been going out about a year and a half. He only popped the question a month ago.'

'It took them long enough to get together. That was always on the cards.'

'You're telling me, everyone else could see he was crazy about her except for them.'

'What happened?'

'Well, Niamh got herself a boyfriend, Jim was none too happy about, gave the poor lad an awful time. Eventually he admitted to her he liked her, she broke up with the lad and they started to go out.'

'I'll have to give him a little stick over that. Any other gossip I should know of, seen as I've been out of the loop a while?'

'Oh, you can find that out for yourself over a few pints later.'

'Yeah, it's always a laugh with ye lads.'

'Sure you'll have a few tales from the last few years?'

'Well, yeah I did find myself in some odd situations.'

'Save them for later, the lads are really excited to see you.'

'Yeah, looking forward to seeing them myself, even if I do look a little different now.'

'Sure we all do. Think everyone has their hair chopped and is clean shaven now.' Joe said.

'Yeah, shaving is a pain, ain't it?' Harry was rubbing his clean shaven chin.

'Total pain in the arse.'

'Love it when I have a few days off and don't have to shave.'

'Yeah, that's brilliant. Didn't even bring a razor with me for the weekend.'

'Neither did I,' Harry said laughing. Joe joined in.

'Hey, all your gear okay after been sitting in storage for a while?'

'Looks okay, just hope it still fits.'

'Should do, if anything you look a little thinner.'

'Cheers Joe, but you don't have to flatter me like a woman.'

'Didn't think I needed to, but if you're that insecure?'

'Oh seriously, my helmet might be a bit big now I've cut my hair.'

'Yeah, I had to put extra padding in mine for it to fit.'

'Shit, don't want that dropping down over my eyes when I'm sitting on a wave.'

'Oh, that would be comical. But we'll sort something out if it doesn't fit; we always do, don't we?'

'Yeah like that time the wheel flew off the trailer,' Harry recalled.

'Oh I remember that, I was sitting in the back of the minibus and all I saw this wheel come skipping by the window. I thought that's a bit odd.'

'Yeah I was sitting in the front and the look of panic on Dan's face driving, was priceless.'

'He did well to control it, though.'

'Yeah don't know how I would have handled that.'

'Took ages to get the wheel fixed, didn't it?'

'Yeah and all of us there hitchhiking with our kayaks.'

'The looks we were getting off people driving by were gas.'

'Imagine what they were thinking, eight lads standing on the side of the road kayaks in hand thumbs sticking out.'

'How else were we supposed to keep ourselves amused while waiting on the wheel to be fixed?'

'Certainly a day I'll never forget.'

'We still managed to get a little paddle in as well,' Joe said.

'Was that the day I snapped my paddle in two?' Harry asked.

'Jesus, I can't remember. Maybe it was, something's just seem to blur into one and other.'

'That was quite interesting, having to paddle the rest of the river with half a paddle.'

'Oh I'm sure a few more of these beauties will come out over the weekend.'

'Ah yeah, probably loads we've even forgotten.'

Eventually after stopping for petrol and a quick snack they reached Ennistymon, just outside Lahinch. As they drove through they went over a bridge, Harry looked out over at the river. 'You ever shot them falls?' he asked Joe.

'No, can't say I have.'

'You know what they're called?'

'No.'

'Four Fucks Falls.'

'Why on earth are they called that?'

'Well as soon as you go over the top, you just about have enough time to say fuck, fuck, fuck, fuck, before you hit the bottom,' Harry said, laughing.

'That's hilarious, we should do them on the way home.'

'Yeah, shouldn't take too long. Hope there's enough water though.'

'Sure we'll see on the way home.'

*****

Chapter 10
Ferry Glide
'Party Line' **Joey Ramone**

Dervila led Harry into the night club by the hand. It was about twelve o'clock and they had spent the last few hours working their way through the city from pub to pub. She had thought bringing him to Harry's Bar for cocktails was quite amusing. Harry just shook his head, pretending this was something new to him.

As they sat at the bar, he had managed to discover his new favourite cocktail, a whiskey sour. The barman had commented that he had never seen two people look so in love, and it was only their third date! They really only had eyes for each other.

They had stopped on route for some Indian food, Harry ordering one the hottest items on the menu. Dervila laughed at his attempt of trying to finish it. He did not give in trying, despite her telling him it was okay if he didn't finish it.

Now here they were entering the Jungle again, Dervila really did love her dance music, it all really sounded the same and was too thumpy, thumpy for Harry, but wherever she went he was sure to follow. She was that intoxicating. As they weaved through the cacophony, Harry kept as tight to Dervila as he could, he could easily get lost in here.

'Over there.' She pointed over towards a table on the far side, 'there they are.'

'There who are?' Harry replied a little confused, he had thought it would just be the two of them and was quite liking that idea. He didn't want to share her.

'A few heads I know from work.' She weaseled through the crowd and across the dance floor, dragging Harry with her over to the crowd. At the table, she pulled Harry out from behind her, introducing him to the table. There were that many people none of the names registered with him.

'Plonk yourself down there Harry, I'll go get us some drinks, Vodka Lucozade okay?' Harry nodded saying he was happy with her choice as a few in the group squeezed up to let him sit. 'Hi', he said to the lad he sat down beside.

'Hi Harry, so you're going out with Dervila then?'

'Still early days but going well. Sorry, I didn't really catch your name there, she whizzed around the table so fast.'

'Ah no worries, it's Ross. She's a great laugh, always at the heart of everything.'

'She's a real fire cracker, alright.'

'Never a dull moment with her, always up for a party that girl. Her phone is like the party line.'

'I'm starting to realise that. But, I like it.'

Dervila arrived back from the bar with the two pint glasses, handing one to Harry. There was just enough room on the edge for her to sit down beside him. 'I see you've met Ross, don't mind anything he says, he's a joker.'

'Who, me?' Ross protested. Dervila winked at Harry as she took a sip of her drink.

Putting her drink down, she announced to the group, 'Hey, who's coming dancing?' She really loved her dancing. Most of the group seemed eager to hit the dance floor with her, Harry just followed.

After a few minutes, there seemed to be a call to gather into a circle around one lad. Harry just went with the flow, not really knowing what was going on.

'What are we up to?' Harry asked Dervila.

'You'll see, just watch Barry there.' She nodded towards the lad at the centre of the circle, who was messing about with what looked like his legs.

'What the hell is he up to?'

'He has two prosthetic legs and he's making them face the wrong way. When he does it, you have to make like nothing's wrong.'

Harry looked down to see Barry's legs facing the wrong way, 'That's crazy,' he said laughing.

'Remember, just act natural once the circle breaks.'

'Got it.'

The circle broke up, with them all going back to their groups, intermingling with each other. Dervila brought Harry over to dance with Barry. As they were dancing away they could see the confused looks on people's faces when they saw Barry's feet. They all found it really hard to keep a straight face, pretending everything was normal, especially Barry. After a few minutes, he decided he'd had his fun, putting his legs back on the right way around. The group started to drift off the dance floor, suddenly Harry found himself on his own. He didn't really mind as he was starting to enjoy himself, even starting to like some of the songs. So he moved off on his own through the crowd.

As he meandered through the crowd he spotted what looked like a girl being hassled by a bloke. He didn't like this, so he moved towards them. She made eye contact with him. Had she just summoned him towards her? He was drawn towards her; she was definitely giving him the eyes looking for his help. He got closer and closer, she moved towards him. She started to dance beside him, what does he do now? Talk to her, confront the bloke hassling her? Suddenly he looked up to see this burly bloke with all his massive friends in a circle around him. *'Holy Fuck, this was a bad idea! I'm gonna die here.'* Then just as quick a hand pulled him out from the danger zone and to safety.

'Come on let's head back to the table.' It was Ross

'What the fuck was that?'

'Russians! Now come on James Bond, time to move before they come looking for you.'

'Huh, James Bond?'

'Yeah, saves the girl from the nasty Russians.'

'Ah, I get it now.'

They got back to the safety of the table. Dervila got up to let Harry sit down between her and Barry.

'Fuck sake Dervila, you might want to watch your boyfriend a bit closer. He's nearly after getting the shit kicked outa him by a group of Russians.'

Dervila turned to Harry, 'What happened Harry?'

'I thought some lad was hassling a girl and thought she was calling me over to help her.'

'Harry, first off. What the fuck, you have me!' She stood up, she was right, she did look stunning in her tight red dress.

'Uh … em… I was only trying to… em… help her.'

'I know Harry; I'm just messing with you. Seriously though stay away from them, just looking for a fight, they are.'

'Yeah, I've seen them do that before.' Ross chipped in, 'that girl is his girlfriend and she's in on it. Draws saps like you in. Then it's the whole, you trying to score my girlfriend thing. Never ends well.'

'Oh shit!' Harry seemed shocked at this, he had spent far too long out west, where nothing like this would happen. What had happened to his city while he had been away?

'Not to worry Harry, you're okay and in one piece, that's all that matters.' Dervila said sensing Harry's unease, 'I'll get you a shot, help steady your nerves.' She headed off towards the bar, not even giving him a chance to reply.

Ross sat down in the seat she had just vacated. 'Seriously, Harry you okay? You look a little rattled.'

'I'm fine, just didn't think people would do stuff like that? Thanks for saving my ass there, Ross.'

'It's cool man, yeah a bit of a pisser that good looking girls can sucker you like that. Just stick with Dervila, she'll do you no wrong.'

'Good advice, Ross. Thanks, be doing that from here on.'

'Causing trouble there, Harry?' Barry asked.

'Apparently so, Barry.'

'All good … they're a group of assholes, they've sort of taken over that corner of the dance floor. I just stay away from it now. It's not worth the hassle, it'll end up getting nasty. Just looking for a fight.'

'Fuck them. So you work with Dervila too?'

'Yeah, she's a lovely girl. Don't know where she gets all her energy though, always on the go.'

Dervila came back to the table, putting two shots down.

'What are they?' Harry asked.

'Ah, stop being a ninny and drink it.' She picked it up, 'Come on.' Harry picked it up, they clinked glasses, and both downed the shots.

'Ugh! Sambuca.' Harry said, squirming and banging the table.

'Come on we're going dancing,' she said bouncing about.

'Might leave this one out.' Harry said, 'Foot is a bit sore.'

'Okay, honey you take it easy. Anyone else?' A few others went leaving Harry, Barry and Ross at the table chatting away.

'So what's up with your foot then Harry?' Barry enquired.

'Ah, I had an ingrowing toenail a few weeks ago. Ended up getting infected, needed a course of antibiotics. Very sore, you ever had one?'

Ross butted in with, 'Did you just ask him if he ever had an ingrowing toenail?'

'Yeah?'

Ross put his hand to head, 'He has two prosthetic legs, you just saw that about twenty minutes ago!'

'Oh, yeah.' Harry's face reddened a bit, 'sorry Barry, I wasn't thinking.'

'It's fine Harry, no need to walk on eggshells around me. I'm used to stuff like that slipping out of people's mouths.'

'Ah, thanks Barry. Here I'm heading the bar, buy you a drink?'

'Yeah, sure why not. Thanks.'

'You too Ross?'

'Cheers man.'

He woke up the next morning in Dervila's bed with the mother of all hangovers. Rolling over, she was still out cold, face down in the pillow. *'Good,'* he thought, *'I can go back to sleep now, moving would just hurt.'* He rolled back over, closing his eyes. When he opened them again he could feel her pressed up against his back, cuddling him.

'Moring lover,' she said. 'How's the head?'

'Moring honey, feel like shit. Moving my head hurts.'

'Oh me, too.'

'You, hangover. Never thought you suffered from them.'

'I am human. I do get them too, every once in a while.'

'Good to know,' he said, rolling over so they were now face to face.

'Pub for a nice greasy fry up, that'll sort us both out.'

'Sounds like a plan. You having a shower first?'

'Yeah.' She hopped out bed heading into towards the bathroom, leaving Harry lying on the bed thinking, *How in the hell can she move that fast? My head hurts if I lift it off the pillow.*'

A while later they arrived at the pub closest to Dervila's house, found a table and sat down waiting on the server to come over. As they studied the menu, she arrived over. 'Hey, how are you this morning?'

'Supper thanks,' Harry said lying through his teeth.

'What can I get you?'

'Two full Irish breakfasts, please.' He looked at Dervila, who nodded in agreement. 'Do you do a Bloody Mary?'

'Yeah, we can make one for you. For you ma'am?' She glanced over towards Dervila.

'Oh, I'll have a gin and tonic.'

'Super, I'll have your drinks over in a sec and your food will be about ten minutes.'

'Thanks.' They both said together as she left the table.

'A bloody Mary? Where did you get that idea from?'

'Great for a hangover. Discovered it when I was over in San Francisco.'

'Oh, look at you mister well-travelled, importing your fancy drinks from America,' she said giving him a wink and a little kick under the table.

'Hey, it's not that fancy.' Her smile was already helping him feel better.

'So, what d'ya wanna do after this?'

'Oh, I don't know.'

'Head back to mine and bed for a bit?' Her smile suddenly became sexier, bringing Harry to life.

'Now, I'm likening your thinking.'

The server arrived back with their drinks, they toasted to the rest of the day. Their food couldn't come quick enough now. Neither could think of any other place or person they'd be with in the world.

*****

Chapter 11
Bongo-slide
'Force of Nature' **Pearl Jam**

Harry and Joe arrived at the Bed and Breakfast in Lahinch dropping their bags up into the room. Everyone else was already there waiting on them in the living room. Arriving into the room, everyone got up to come over to greet him all giving him a hug. Harry felt good to be back in the old gang, it was just a shame one was missing.

'Right, pub? Don't know about ye, but I could do with a nice cold pint.' Joe was trying to hurry the rest out the door.

'Right, keep your hair on, we'll be off in a minute.' Will responded as Joe was trying to push him out the door.

'Yeah Joe, it's not like its last orders.' Dave said sticking his two pence in. They left the house and headed off down the road to the local pub. When they walked into the bar, the barman looked over in their direction pointing. Harry pointed at himself. 'Me,' he mouthed.

'Yes you. Behave yourself tonight,' the barman replied. Harry looked a little confused at first, then he suddenly remembered why.

'Okay, will do,' he replied as he walked over to a seat, sitting down.

'Pint?' Joe asked Harry.

'Yeah, please.'

'You can tell me what that's all about when I get back.'

Joe arrived back with the drinks. He asked, 'Well, go on then, spill.'

'I was in here with Phil one night, we were chatting to these two girls. While they were in the toilet Phil made a bet with me that I couldn't get one of them to dance on the bar with me. So I said yeah as soon as the next good song comes on. So, the girls came back, and we started chatting away to them again. We were getting along well, eventually a good song came on, can't remember which one. I stood up tried to get her to climb up on the bar, eventually I just picked her up and sat her on the bar. I jumped up, started to dance and grabbed her by the hand. She stood up and started to dance beside me. We were having a great laugh until she nudged me in the ribs, I tripped over one of the taps, ended up on the floor in behind the bar. Phil said I looked like a Meer Kat when my head popped up from behind the bar, looked around and darted for the end of the bar. We sort of had to bolt for the door, trying not fall over laughing along the way …' The group laughed.

'What about the girls?' Dave asked.

'Well they were with us; we ended getting a few cans from the office and sat on the beach with them, having a laugh.'

'Ah should have known with you two,' Dave replied.

'We really do miss Phil ya know, but it's good to have you back; thought we'd lost you too for a while,' Niamh said.

'Well it's good to be back, I know I did lose my way there for a while. Now less of that kind of talk now, we're all here to have a good time.'

Harry raised his glass. 'To Phil,' he said, and everyone tapped glasses.

'Right so what craziness have you lined up for tonight then Harry?' Will enquired.

'What have ye being doing over the last two years? If ya need me for a bit of fun.'

'Having boring nights in?' Will said smiling.

'Yeah, so boring that even these two hooked up.' Harry looked at Jim and Niamh.

'Yeah, it was that boring,' Jim replied quite sarcastically.

'It took ye long enough to figure it out between you.' Harry gave them a wink.

'Ah well, least we're here and couldn't be happier,' Niamh butted in.

Harry smiled at the two of them. 'Congratulations to the two of ya. When's the big day?' Harry asked.

'Well, it'll be about two years; we need to start saving,' Niamh replied.

'You going to have it here in Ireland or go away?'

'We're going to have it here; you know I'm the only girl in my family. Mam and Dad want us to have a big family day out.'

'So Jim, you decided on your best man yet?'

'I'll probably be my brother, definitely won't be you.'

'Ah why not Jim?'

'Stop teasing, he's right. Let you plan the stag party!?' Niamh cut in.

'It'd be fun.'

'Well I want a groom for the wedding. Not him stuck on an island in the middle of nowhere.'

'Ah, you know me too well.'

'Right you fuckers, time for shots, everyone to the bar!'

'Oh no!' said Niamh.

'It's a bit early, no?' said Will.

'Never too early for shots,' said Joe.

'Right come on everyone to the bar, Tequila all round,' Dave said as he marched off to the bar. Everyone followed in dribs and drabs. Harry knew this would be the start of a long, long night.

'Come on, get up, you lazy fecker.' Joe was shaking Harry, trying to wake him up.

'Jesus, what time is it?' Harry replied as he opened his eyes.

'Time to get up.'

'6.30!' Harry said as he looked at his watch.

'Come on, tides are just right, let's go.' Joe was trying to hurry him up. He gingerly got out of bed, started to get dressed. He had forgotten that tides don't really know or care if you have a hangover, or what time of day it is.

'Big waves?' Harry asked, hoping the answer was no.

'Surf report says about 5 foot, nice offshore breeze.' Joe seemed excited.

Harry was starting to get a little nervous now, what if he fell out as soon as he got on the water. What if he bottled it as soon he tried to *'catch'* the first wave? Self-doubt was a fairly new experience to him and he wasn't liking it. Time to get on with it, suck it up and get stuck in.

They arrived at the cars to see everyone there, some looking a bit ropey, it had been a late night and there had been a fair bit of drink consumed. Nothing had been unpacked from the trip down, so they all jumped into the cars and drove down to the beach. The plan was to surf the kayaks for a while, go have a quick shower then off to get some breakfast. They had nothing planned for the afternoon but were going to take the kayaks back out in the evening when the tides were right again.

When they parked at the beach, took the kayaks off the roof racks and put them at the entrance to the beach. They then all changed into their canoeing gear, carried the boats down on to the edge of the water. There were only a few other people on the beach, mostly people with surfboards. It was a beautiful morning, the offshore breeze made for nice waves. The waves themselves were coming in nice steady sets, with decent gaps between them. This made Harry happy and the others looked impressed with the conditions as well. Harry was one of the last onto the water as he had been fiddling with his gear to make sure it fitted properly and that his kayak was set up to his liking. Joe had commented that this was unlike Harry, as he was usually the first on the water.

He sat in the kayak, set to go. The helmet was the most annoying piece of equipment to sort out. Wriggling in the kayak to make sure he was comfortable, he put his hands into the water to shuffle the canoe along until it reached water deep enough for him to paddle. He started to paddle out through the breaking waves, the wind at his back, trying all the way to keep himself perpendicular to the waves, getting sideways was a big no-no, as it always led to a capsize. The first big wave he paddled up caught him flush in the face, *'Wow, that woke me up,'* he thought to himself. It was quite refreshing to say the least. The skills were now slowly coming back, the paddle strokes and controlling the kayak with his hips. Confidence was starting to return, now to make his way out beyond the breaking waves and really test himself by surfing a wave back in.

Sitting out beyond the breaking waves looking in at the shore, he'd always liked this view, bobbing up and down looking in towards the shore. The calm before the storm. Now to wait for the wave that felt right to surf in. He was watching a few of the other lads getting trashed by waves. No way he was going to bottle it today, he knew he was just as good if not better than them. He was just going to have to go for it, the longer he took the harder it would be. *'Okay here's a good looking wave, time to go.'* The wave was approaching as he looked over his shoulder, he started to paddle, as the back of his boat lifted, he started to paddle faster and faster, trying to match the speed of the wave. When he felt the wave fully take the boat, he stopped paddling, placing the blade of paddle in at the rear of the boat, to use it like a rudder steering the kayak. He switched between paddling and steering to keep himself perpendicular to the racing wave. *Just like riding a bike,'* he thought to himself, it was such an adrenaline rush he felt amazing. At this point he managed to get the boat a little sideways; whoosh he was upside down. *'Shit,'* was all that went through his head. He could not remember how to roll back up. The power of the water rushing around his head, he knew this was all about feel and not panicking. *Just relax,'* he thought to himself. He knew which way he had gone over and pushed his paddle up towards the surface to the side from which the force of the water was coming. He was hoping to use the breaking wave to roll back up, when he felt the paddle break the surface, he braced it on the top of the wave, flicked his hips and was sitting upright still surfing the wave. This all happened in a split second. He was chuffed with himself and surfed the wave into the shore, where Joe was waiting for him.

'You haven't lost it at all,' Joe said as he walked over to Harry.

'Bit of luck though rolling back up, just went on instinct.'

'Well, it looked pretty impressive from here.'

'Thanks, next time I won't capsize.'

'We go back out and have a little fun on the breaking waves?'

'What you got in mind?'

'Just follow my lead.'

Joe climbed back into his kayak and paddled out to where the waves were breaking, Harry followed him wondering what he was going to do. As the wave came in, instead of paddling up and over it he started to paddle backwards. This caused the front of the kayak to come back over his head and capsize. The kayak was doing a sort of back loop, which looked to be great fun, so Harry gave it a go. The two boys had a good laugh doing this for a while, until it was time to go back for a wash and a bit of breakfast.

As they all sat in the cafe having a bite to eat talk, turned to what they would do during the day while they waited on the tides. Jim and Niamh decided to go for a walk around the Burren. The rest thought that was a little boring, as nothing grew there and there wouldn't be much to see. All you could ever find there where old fossils. Jim would fit right in Harry thought to himself.

'You fancy coming for a spot of climbing Harry?' Dave had turned to face him. Harry was not sure about going, whatever about canoeing but climbing was a different story. He had only ever gone climbing with Phil and even then, it was an effort.

'I don't know Dave; sure I don't even have any gear with me.'

'I have spare gear with me. Come on, none of these lads ever come climbing with me.'

Harry was giving it some thought, there wasn't much else to do for the day except maybe go to the pub.

'Two questions, one - are you going up any hard climbs and two, is it a long walk in?' Everyone knew Harry really hated walking long distances into climbs.

'No and no, I'll take it easy on ya.'

'Right, go on I'll go with ya.'

'Good lad.'

Harry and Dave walked back to Dave's car, then drove out to the climbing spot. Harry was glad to see the rock face was beside the road; it didn't look like it was too difficult either. They got all the equipment out of the car and over to the bottom the first climb. Dave took out a guide book as Harry was setting up the equipment.

'Have you not climbed this before?' Harry asked.

'No, not this one,' Dave replied as he gazed up towards the top and then back at the guide book, trying to plan the route in his head.

'You know which way you're going?'

'Yeah, yeah,' he replied as he motioned with both hands, as to how he was going to climb. They both now had all their gear on.

'Ready to go?' Harry asked.

'Yep,' Dave said as he was tying himself on to the end of the rope. He started to climb stopping to place his protective equipment into cracks along the way, he was going up quickly and making it look easy. Harry was relaxed at the bottom sitting down on a rock, steadily letting the rope out as Dave ascended, contemplating what he'd have for dinner. As Dave got to the top Harry heard a scratching sound followed by a yelp of, 'Shit!'

Harry sprung to life, pulling in on the rope as he had a bad feeling.

'Below!' Dave shouted down, Harry knew not to look up this always meant something, probably rocks, was on the way down. He kept the rope as tight as he could, with his head down. He could hear rocks falling and the scratching scrambling sound of Dave sliding down the rock face. The rope jerked as Dave reached his first piece of protection, which promptly popped out. Harry now heard another, 'Shit!' coming from Dave as he slid down to the next piece. Harry kept his head down, the last thing he wanted to do was to look up and have a rock hit him square in the face, which would do neither of them any good. All he could was wait and hope one of the pieces of protection Dave had inserted would hold, then he could lower him down. He felt the next pop on the rope, followed by another and another. All this accompanied by the scratching, scraping of Dave trying to cling on to something, while effing and blinding. Eventually things went quiet, there was slack on the rope. He slowly glanced sideways, to Dave two feet off the ground, still looking like he was trying to cling on to the rock.

'Dave!' He shouted at him, Dave opened his eyes and looked across at him with a slight look of astonishment.

'Harry!' He sounded a little surprised at where he had stopped falling.

'Did everything you put in just pop out and you slide all the way down the face?'

'Looks that way!'

They both looked at each other and broke out laughing, so hard that their stomachs started to hurt, and they had to sit down.

'So is that our climbing done for the day then?' Harry asked

'Oh yeah, think we've used up all our luck for one day.'

'For the year more like.' They were both still laughing.

'It was a bit hairy sliding down the face of the rock.'

'The noise of it, the scratching and sliding, I'd say you could hear it miles away. Lucky there was no overhang or anything. What happened anyway?'

'Blessed, I was. Got to top, put my hand up to pull myself up and over. The bloody rock I was holding onto came away in my hand, just started to slide down. Lucky I just slid down.'

'Seems like you got a rub of the green from Phil.'

'Yeah, he was a fairly lucky lad.'

'Yeah, I remember one day we were climbing, at about 15 foot up he realised he still had his new watch on, one he'd just gotten for his birthday. He stood on a ledge of no more than a couple of inches, no gear placed in and turned around to face me. He took off his watch, tossed it down to me, so as he wouldn't scratch it. As it left his hand, he promptly followed it down and landed flat on his back. Got up, dusted himself down and shot back up the climb without a bother on him.'

'Jesus anyone else would been shaking after that.'

'Not Phil, nothing seemed to faze him at all.'

Dave and Harry arrived back to find the rest of the group sitting in the beer garden of the pub facing out onto the beach. It had turned into quite a nice day, they each got a drink and joined the group. They described what had happened in graphic detail, everyone had a great laugh about it. They had a couple of drinks and some dinner sitting in the sun, waiting on the tide to come in. There was no way that they were going to walk out to the sea dragging the kayaks. When it did come in a sufficient amount they fetched their kayaking gear and headed into the sea for an hour's fun. They found it quite interesting after a few pints. The cold Atlantic Ocean freshened them up a little.

After their excursion into the sea, they returned back to the beer garden to have a few more social drinks, talk turned to what Harry had been doing over the previous two years.

'So Harry, what have you up to while on your little hiatus?' Will asked.

'I tell ya some other time, ye probably wouldn't like it all,' Harry replied.

'Come on, tell us a little,' Joe cut in, they all seemed very interested now leaning in closer.

'Okay, I met this girl and spent most of my time with her.'

'Yeah, what was her name? What was she like?' Niamh asked.

'Dervila, she's sort of your typical girl you see around town.'

'Blonde, fake tan and Ugg boots?'

'Yeah, something like that. She was a lovely girl, just into different things than you or me.'

'So, what did you do together?' Niamh was interested now

'Mainly drinking, going to nightclubs.'

'Is that all?'

'Well we'd go back to house parties and the like as well.'

'A party girl, was she?' asked Niamh.

'Ah no not really, just always seemed to be on the go and didn't stop. I just sort of went along for the ride.'

'I'd say so!' Will cut in with a little innuendo, the other lads laughed.

'No, we had a great laugh together. Really liked her, just figured out there was more to my life than going out on a Friday and not coming home until Sunday evening.'

'Jesus, she sounds like a perfect girl, you still got her number?' Will asked with very cheeky smile.

'Yeah, she seemed that way, only saw her Friday to Sunday.'

'What no sitting in midweek watching soaps?'

'Yeah, none of that.'

'That sounds like a quite shallow relationship, did you get to know her at all?' said Niamh.

'Suppose she gave me everything I needed at the time. She was so bubbly and infectious, made me feel good about myself just being around her. She always seemed to brighten up a room.'

'Sounds like you're still a little hung up on her?'

'No, no, sure there's no harm in remembering someone fondly. Can't just start to hate someone, just because you break up with them.'

Dave arrived back at the table with a tray full of shots, which put a stop to that conversation. Harry was glad as the breakup was still a little fresh and wounds hadn't really healed as yet. He had Grainne now and that was probably one of the reasons he was taking it easy with her. He really wanted to get to know her as a person and not have a relationship not based on partying and the physical aspect. He wanted it to be real and not just a drunken hazy blur on a Monday morning. They toasted to Dave's very lucky escape earlier in the day and downed their shots.

*****

Chapter 12

Coming up for Air

'Dancing in the Moonlight' **Thin Lizzy**

Harry's phone started to buzz on his desk, only a couple of times as it was a text message. He picked it up to see who it was from; it was Grainne. He gave a little smile, he still got a little excited to see her name come up on his phone.

'Heya, soooo bored in work. How's ur day :o) xxx" Was her text, at least someone else was just as bored as he was.

'Yeah, s.s.d.d,' he replied.

'U up 2 much later? xxx"

'Nothin planned, u?'

'U wana come ovr I'll make u something 2 eat? xxx"

'Yeah, sounds gud. Wot time?'

'Spag Bol ok, Bout 7?'

'Kul, c u den. I'll bring a bottle of wine, red or white.'

'Red.'

He sat his desk deep in thought, this was exactly what Niamh had been talking about, getting to know someone and not just go out on the lash with them. It was seeming a bit shallow now, the whole relationship with Dervila, they never would have had a home cooked meal together. Now to think what kind of wine to buy, he wasn't really a wine drinker, so it could be a bit of a challenge for him. Why couldn't he have just said beer?

She did come across as being a bit more refined than him, the only wine he had every drank was the biggest, cheapest, nastiest bottle they find when they had little or no money, the kind you would have to use lemonade as a mixer, just to take the edge off it. Somehow that would not be good enough for tonight. He was used to living on his own and didn't really eat all that well, not that he couldn't cook a proper dinner, but he couldn't really be bothered.

He walked into the off license and stood in front of the wine rack staring at the bottles of red wine blankly. Did he just go by price? The more expensive the better, he felt a bit of pressure to choose a decent one. As he was staring at the rack, the sales assistant came over to him.

'Need a hand there? You're looking a little lost,' she asked him.

'Oh yeah. I'm looking for a good red wine?' He sounded relieved to have the offer of help.

'Is it to go with a meal?'

'Yeah, spaghetti Bolognese.'

'You want an expensive one or cheap?'

'Well mid-range, you not too cheap but not mad expensive.'

'Here try this one.' She picked one up and handed it to him.

'You sure this is nice?'

'Yeah she'll love it, it's the one I'd pick,' she said to him with a smile.

'Is it that obvious?'

'Yeah, you're putting far too much thought into it.'

'Okay, I'll take it then,' he said laughing to himself, as they walked up to the counter for him to pay.

'Lucky girl,' she said as she took his money.

'Hope she thinks so,' he replied as he left the shop.

He arrived at Grainne's apartment, knocked on the door and waited. Feeling just like a kid again knocking on a girl's door and waiting on her father to answer. It's not as if he had anything to worry about, but he was still on edge. He hoped he had dressed right for the occasion and that she would like the wine he bought. He could hear her approaching the door, he made sure his shirt and hair were fixed right. She opened the door and gave him a kiss on the cheek.

'Heya, come on in.' As she held the door open for him. 'You know where the sofa is, it won't be long now.'

'Hope this is okay,' he said as he handed her the bottle.

'It'll be fine as she looked at it. Did you pick this yourself? Cause it's a really nice bottle.'

'Em… well… I did ask the girl in the off license.' She was laughing as she headed off to the kitchen and he went off to wait on the sofa watching the TV.

'Right it's ready.' She shouted in from the kitchen. He walked into the kitchen, it looked like she had put a lot of effort into the preparation.

'This looks great.'

'Will you open the wine?' She said handing him the bottle and the bottle opener. He opened the bottle, with the cork coming out in one piece, much to his relief and poured them both a glass. She had placed everything in the centre of the table for them both to take whatever they wanted. Sitting down they started to eat.

'This really is lovely.' He really did mean it, it was.

'Thanks. You cook much yourself.'

'Ah a little, when I can be bothered.'

'What would you make then?'

'Must say I do make a kickass chilli. You should come over and try it some time?'

'Really?'

'Yeah, now it won't be anywhere as fancy as this. I don't even have a dining table.'

'Where do you eat then, on the sofa?'

'Well yeah, it is only me there so why not?'

'So, you'd bring me over, have me sit on your sofa, drink beer and eat off a tray?'

'A tray? Who said I have one of them?' He replied laughing.

'You're an awful kidder, ain't ya?'

'I'm not kidding; I eat off a cushion.'

'My lord, we'll have to sort that out.'

'What, buy a tray?'

'Maybe your whole apartment. God knows what it's like?'

'It's not that bad really, sure I'm never really there.'

'Typical man,' she said shaking her head.

'I think you'll be surprised and in a good way.' He gave her a wink.

After the meal they both went to sit in the sitting room and finish the bottle of wine. 'So fill me in a little on your hiatus from family life?'

'Ah so you had a good chat with my Mam then?'

'Yeah, bumped into her when I was visiting Dad and she told she hadn't spoken to you in a while, she was worried about you. Thought you'd gone off the rails a bit.'

'Ah I sort of did, but you know had to figure it out for myself, wouldn't listen to anyone.'

'But, looks like you sorted yourself out, which is good; you could have been lost to everyone.'

'Yeah as I did, my old life just seemed to fall back into place. Lucky I didn't burn too many bridges.'

'Come on, fill me in. You have to have some good stories after being on the piss for all that time?' she said as she snuggled up to him.

'Hey, I wasn't drinking every day! I still had a job and went in.'

'Sorry, but you still have to tell me what you were up to.'

'Okay, okay, it was just after Phil's funeral and I went out for a few drinks with Sam, you remember him from school.'

'Yeah I remember him, nice lad.'

'Yeah he is. So he was the one who pulled me out of my slump and encouraged me to go out and get a job. Also to go shopping for new cloths, hence the current image. Anyway on our night out he introduced me to Dervila and we hit it off.'

'Ah, so this is where you met the famous Dervila?'

'Yeah, you sure you're okay talking about my ex?'

'Well yeah, if it helps you deal with your issues.'

'Issues? What issues?'

'Well, you haven't really dealt with the loss of Phil, have you?'

'I thought I had, you know, with the funeral and that?'

'Takes more than that, you just lost yourself in going out and buried all them emotions. How much did you talk about him in that time?'

'Not much, if at all.'

'How about the guilt of it? You know how he flew over the edge and you didn't.'

'We'll I did think about that quite a bit for the first couple of weeks, then I started to go out and got a job. Didn't think about it too much then.'

'Ah, so you buried all the emotions then?'

'Well yeah, now that you mention it.'

'You cut off anyone and anything that reminded you of him too?'

'Shit yeah I did; activities too.'

'So how do you feel about it then?'

'Obviously I miss him. I wonder why him and not me. It was sort of my fault, 'cause he wouldn't have done it but for me.'

'You sort of have to understand that you can't control other people's actions and can't be responsible for them either. You will go bonkers if you start trying to control everything. It's the way the universe works, it was pure chance you survived and he didn't. He made a conscious choice to slide down the hill after you, it's not like you tied to him to you and dragged him down the hill.'

'Jesus, that's a bit harsh.'

'Maybe, but something you need to hear, you can't mess up your own life because something that was out of your control. You do realise how destructive what you were doing was?'

'Yeah, sort of realised that. Went to the doc 'cause I didn't feel too well and during the chat about my lifestyle he told me to calm down a little, that I was starting to have panic attacks.'

'So, that's what brought you around then?'

'Yeah, I just realised I was on the verge of fucking up my life one day. An epiphany of sorts, you could say.'

'It's good you had the cop on to sort yourself out, many don't and they end up with nothing and no one.'

'Yeah glad I didn't end up a complete dipso. Could have easily ended up like them lads sitting by the canal drinking cans all day.'

'Look, you really are a smart, kinda funny guy.' She gave him a nudge in the ribs.

'Hey!' he said. 'Seriously, it has been good to talk about it, has made me feel a lot better.'

'Good, you really can't be feeling bad about yourself, life is far too short for that.'

'You're right there. So what d'ya wanna do now?'

'How about we stick on a DVD, I have a few over there. Have a look through.'

'They not all chick flicks, are they?'

'No, you should find something you like there.'

He started to flick through the rack of DVD, he picked up one and turned around to face her.

'You have *The Forty-Year-Old Virgin.'* Love that film.'

'Yeah me too, stick it in there.'

'That's a bit rude, ain't it?' he said giving her a wink.

'It's you that has the rudey mind, not me!' She smiled back at him. She snuggled back up to him as the movie started.

After the movie Harry looked at his watch, it was late. Grainne had fallen asleep and he was afraid if he moved he would wake her up. He found the remote and put on the TV, he really did need to go home. He felt Grainne move, she woke up and looked at her watch. 'Jesus look at the time,' she said.

'Yeah, I should probably go home.'

'I'd drop you home, but we've had a bit to drink.'

'It's fine I'll get a taxi.'

'Ah here, sure stay here and I'll drop you off in the morning on my way swimming.'

'What time you going swimming at?'

'I leave here about 6am. Is that okay?'

'Yeah that'll be fine, loads of time to have a shower and get ready for work.'

Grainne led the way to her bedroom, at least this time Harry wasn't an emotional wreck and she wouldn't need to put him to bed this time. Harry was nervous as they entered the room. Grainne went into the bathroom to get ready for bed. He stood in the room waiting, not really knowing what to do, wait there climb into bed? So he sort of shuffled about the room which was only lit but a lamp on the side of, so stripped down to his boxer shorts and managed to stub his toe on the end of the bed. *'Christ that hurt,'* he thought as he progressed to hopping around the end of the bed, which he then duly fell onto, holding his foot, trying not to yelp out in pain.

Grainne entered the room dressed in a short night slip, which really showed off her long athletic legs. The pain in Harry's foot abated, she climbed into bed beside Harry and cuddled up to him. 'You could have got under the covers, you know.' She gave him a tender kiss on the lips and

Harry pulled her in tight. The kiss turned more passionate and he moved his legs in between hers. He could feel her writhing against him and then they rolled over so as Harry was on top of her, with her legs wrapped around his hips. She now had her hands coming up under his arms, running her fingers through his hair. She then flipped him over so as he was lying on his back. Grannie sat up and peeled off her slip, then leaned back in to kiss him again pressing her body against his, putting her hands down to remove Harry's boxer shorts. She hooked her legs in behind his knees and held the back of his head. She reached over and turned off the light.

*****

CHAPTER 13
Pirouette
'At My Most Beautiful' **R.E.M.**

Harry walked out of the building he worked in and took his phone out to check it. It was lunchtime; what better way to spend it than chatting to Grainne sitting in the park. It was a nice early summer day and by the time he got down to St. Stephens green, a lot of other people had the same idea. He found a place to sit and opened his lunch. He phoned Grainne, she answered and luckily was on her lunch too.

'Heya, how's you?' she said.

'All the better for hearing you.'

'Ah, stop being so soppy.'

'Why, you sitting in your staff room?'

'Yeah.'

'Oh, I'm sitting out in the sunshine.'

'Don't be rubbing it in, will ya.'

'But it really is lovely out.'

'Hey, you fancy coming for a swim in the sea at the weekend?'

'What, you'll kick my ass.'

'I'll take it easy on ya. One thing though, you can't wear a wetsuit.'
'No way, it'll be freezing.'
'Ah, I'll lend you a swim hat.'
'A swim hat? Fat lot of good that'll do me.'
'Come on, it'll do you good.'
'Can I not just go watch?'
'You're a wimp, suck it up, come on.'
'Right I'll go and bring my gear just in case.'
'Supper stuff. What you up to later?'
'Not much, you wanna come over to mine, see how I live?' he said laughing
'Yeah, should I bring a tray?'
'No, I have a spare cushion.'
'You going to cook your famous chilli?'
'Just for you. You going to bring some beer?'
'I will yeah, what kind you want?'
'Corona would be nice.'
'I'll be over around 7?'
'Yeah cool, sure give me a call and I'll buzz you in.'
'Yeah, sure I'll talk to you in a bit.'
'Yeah, chat later.'

He hung up the phone and started to eat his lunch. He would have to stop at the supermarket on the way home and then tidy his apartment, make it look some way respectable.

Later they were sitting down to eat on his sofa, he had found a table buried under junk, which they could put their food on.

'This really does look lovely, where do you learn to make it?' Grainne seemed surprised looking at the plate of food Harry had put before her.
'Mexico.'
'Really?'
'No I'm just kidding, just made it one day and it was nice.'
'So this swim at the weekend?'
'Yeah, I told you you'd kick my ass.'
'I remember you being a good swimmer at school. You still can with all your water sports, can't you?'

'Yeah, but that's different. Very rare I swim when I'm canoeing, only when I fall out and that's not very often.'

'Cocky, ain't you?'

'Well I don't!'

'Right, I'll bring you for a swim in the pool on Saturday, see how good you are. Then we go the sea on Sunday?'

'Okay only if you come canoeing with me some day?'

'Deal.'

'Will we stick on a DVD?'

'Yeah, you can choose.'

'You sure, you probably only have loads of bloke films.'

'Na, think you'll be surprised.'

She started to look through.

'You have a lot here, don't ya?' She was browsing through his extensive DVD, CD and Vinyl collection.

'Yeah, I do just buy them, have a lot of old ones.'

'You mind if we watch this one?' She had picked one up and showed it to him.

'Oh, '*Into the wild*' ain't seen that in a while.'

'It's a good film.'

'Yeah, Phil made me watch it one night. His parents gave me a lot of his stuff and that was with it.'

'Jesus, I seem to like a lot of the same stuff as him?'

'Maybe that's why I like you.' He winked at her.

'You trying to say I'm like a bloke.'

'No no no.' Harry was now panicking inside as he was thinking he had upset her, but when he glanced over she was smiling at him.

'Got ya! So Phil liked this film then.' Harry now felt relieved, he must really like her.

'Probably because Eddie Vedder sang the soundtrack, he did – it was a very thought provoking film. Mirrored his beliefs in how selfish and obsession orientated we've become.'

'He was right. First time I saw it, it made me think.'

'Hey, you do know you're not going to able to drive home?'

'Well, I hope you have clean sheets on your bed?' she said, smiling at him.

'Yeah, I do.' He had just changed them that day, just in case.

Saturday came, Harry was looking for a pair of shorts to wear going swimming. He couldn't remember the last time he was in a swimming pool. Probably when he was learning how to do an Eskimo roll in his kayak, that didn't count really. He picked up a pair and held them up, they would have to do. He put them in his bag with a towel. He then went to sit and wait for his lift. He listened to a bit of music while he was waiting, a bit of The Offspring *'want you bad,'* a band he had just gotten back into lately. She rang him to come down right in the middle of a good song, *'Shit,'* he thought, guess this will be the first song he plays in the car as he was quite enjoying it.

'Come on hurry up, I'm on double yellow's here.' He shouted out the car window at him.

'Hang on, I'm on the way.'

'You're going to have to learn how to drive, you can give me a lift then.'

'You going to teach me?'

'Not in this!'

'You wouldn't let me drive your car?'

'Not a chance while you're learning.'

He was sitting in the passenger seat by now and plugged in his iPod. 'You don't mind do ya? I was in the middle of listening to this song when you rang.'

'You didn't give me much choice did ya? What song is it?'

'The Offspring, *Want you Bad*'

'Ah good song. Here you got a swim hat and goggles?'

'Em… no?'

'You have to wear a hat in the pool. It's okay I've a spare hat and goggles I'll lend you.'

'Ah, thanks. No real need for them on the river or in the sea. Although I have seen lads wear goggles canoeing, bloody wimps; nose clips too, another joke.'

'I'd say that's looks funny.'

'Especially when you see sweet fuck all under the water anyway, it's a river and all you can see is brown.'

'So they really no use then?'

'About as useful as a chocolate teapot.'

'Suppose the water would look a little chocolaty.'

'That wouldn't be chocolate!'

'No, you're disgusting.' As she made a squirming face, as he just laughed.

Harry was getting ready for the swim and he really did feel silly putting on the latex swim cap, especially the one Grainne had given him, which was a bit girlie. When he came out of the cubical, Grainne was waiting for him.

'What took you?'

'Ah you know, trying to make this swim hat look sexy and not succeeding.'

'It's not the hat you should be worrying about, where did you get them shorts – in the kid's section?'

'What?' He looked a little shocked.

'They a little short, ain't they?'

'Well they are called shorts.'

'Come on, let's just get in and see what you can do.'

There got into the swimming lane in the pool. Grainne started to swim, and Harry just gazed at how she seemed to glide across, when she goes to the side she tumbled at the wall, which looked even more impressive. She came back to the wall and stopped to look at Harry.

'Feck sake, how am I supposed to keep up with you?'

'Go on; let's see how good you are?'

'Okay,' he said as put his goggles on and pushed off the wall. His stroke was a little untidy, but he did have his head down. There was no way he was going to try a tumble at the wall, just touch and turn would do.

'How was that?' He sounded a little out of breath as he got back to the wall.

'Not bad, we'll have to work on your breathing, but you'll be fine tomorrow, picking your head up is what you need to do in the sea anyway so you know which direction you're going.'

'How far are we going to swim?'

'As far as you can. Come on we'll go down the shallow end and I show you a few things, help you swim a little better.'

'You going to show me how to turn like you?'

'No, not yet anyway.'

Harry looked across to the other side of the swimming pool, 'Is he wearing a see through swimming hat?'

'He is yeah.'

'Seriously, it looks like a condom on his head.'

Grainne started to laugh uncontrollably and had to look away, to try not draw attention to herself. 'It …really …does.'

'He's going to see you. Let's move down the other end before you get us in trouble.'

They moved to the opposite end and spent about forty-five minutes practising. Grainne taught him how to improve his stroke as much as she could in the time they had. Harry felt a little like he was back a swimming lessons when he was a child. He did however like the fact that Grainne was in the pool and had a very hands on approach, guiding his arms into position.

They arrived at the sea the next day, it was another cracking day, although there was a bit of a nip in the air and an onshore wind making the sea a bit choppy. Harry wasn't too keen at all about getting in, it was looking a bit on the chilly side.

'You really going to get in, in that?'

'Yeah, it'll be fine, waves aren't that big. Come on,' she said as she started to get changed,

Harry started himself, very slowly. He winced as his bare feet came in contact with the cold ground. This was something he would never get used to, no matter how many times he had done it. They stood at the edge of the water in just their swimming togs, hat and goggles in hand. Grainne was first down the steps, diving in when she got to the bottom and swimming out a little.

'Come on in, it's lovely.'

'Holly shit! It's fucking freezing,' he exclaimed as his feet entered on the first step.

'Get a move on will ya, just making it harder for yourself.'

'Jesus, it's not exactly easy to walk on.'

'Just dive in and don't hold your breath, just relax and take a breath when you come up.'

'Okay, here we go.' He dived in and when he surfaced he did find it hard to relax, but he did.

'See it's not that bad, eh?'

'Not exactly bath water either.'

'Come on try swim a little.' She set off out a bit. Harry put his dead down and started to swim, it didn't seem too hard, that was until he came out of the cove where they had been. He swam up the face of a small enough wave, at the top, he went to take an arm stroke and suddenly there was no water there. He flopped back down on the back of the wave and stopped. He glanced up to see Grainne waiting for him.

'This is completely different to the pool.'

'I told you it would be,' she said, laughing back at him.

They both swam for a little bit more, until Grainne noticed that Harry was getting a bit tired, so she decided to head back to shore. They had spent about fifteen minutes in the water, which was plenty enough for Harry's first time in. They got out and Harry was shaking a little.

'You okay?' She asked

'Yeah just a little cold.'

'Just a little?' She laughed. 'Don't worry I'll warm you up when we get back to mine.'

'Promise?'

'Mind in the gutter again. You can have a warm shower.'

'You getting in too? You save water, the planet and all that.'

'Cheeky.'

*****

Chapter 14
Low Brace
'Under the Bridge' *Red Hot Chili Peppers*

Harry sheepishly arrived into work and sank into his seat. It had been a long weekend and he felt really rough. He just needed to get through the day, go home and climb back into bed. His main goal was to get there without too much interaction with others. He was trying to hide behind his desk partition, when Tom stuck his head over.

'Fuck sake Harry, you look like shit.'

'Fuck off, Tom.'

'Jesus, what were you up to over the weekend?'

'Here I'll tell ya at lunch; need to try sort myself out now.'

'Best part of Monday morning is finding out what you got up to over the weekend,' Tom said sounding a little too excited.

'Should really get a life of your own, Tom.'

'I do, just that all of us can't have a hot girlfriend who seems to let you do as you please. All mine wants to do now is sit in and watch soaps.'

'See, this is what happens when you move in with them.'

'How do you get away with not seeing her during the week?'

'Dervila's not that kind of girl, she's far too social to be sitting in watching soaps.'

'Here I'd better go do some work, talk to you at lunch.'

'Yeah talk to ya then.'

Harry went back to keeping his head down and trying to draw as little attention to himself as possible. This was becoming a bit of a habit on Mondays, but it didn't really bother him, after all he was out having fun at the weekends.

He made it through to lunchtime, headed out to buy himself a sandwich, packet of crisps and a can of coke. He headed back to the staff room where Tom was there waiting, with his packed lunch he had brought in himself.

'I really should start bringing in my own lunch.' Harry said looking at Tom's.

'Yeah you should, save you some money, probably be healthier too.'

'Far too lazy to get up early and make it.'

'So come on fill us in about the weekend.' Tom asked excitedly.

'Ah, met Dervila after I left you on Friday and somehow found myself standing in a phone box in Mayo on Sunday morning.'

'What! That's the other side of the country.'

'Yeah I ended up over in Westport.'

'How on earth do you go out drinking in Dublin on a Friday and wake up two days later in phone box on the other side of the country?'

Harry recanted his weekend. Harry left his work local after a few drinks with his work mates; most had to go home to see their girlfriends or boyfriends. He himself was off to meet Dervila, no chance of a quiet night in with her. She always seemed to know where a house party was on or had somewhere for them to go. He had even taken to leaving some clothes in her place, just so he didn't have to go home to change on a Saturday morning. He could shower and change there before they invariably headed back out.

He arrived at the bar Dervila was in, Sam was there too. He hadn't seen him in a while, since he'd started his current job.

'Hey Harry, long time.'

'Heya Sam.' As he gave him a hug.

'Looking sharp.' He took a step back to look him up and down. He had gotten his hair cut shorter and was in an expensive looking suit.

'Yeah went shopping after our last night out. You see I did listen to your advice.'

'Yeah and some, you dress better than me now.'

'Wouldn't go that far now.'

'Here it's my round, what you drinking?'

'Yeah get us a pint.'

Sam headed off to the bar and Harry felt a set of hands come around his waist.

'Hey you.' Dervila whispered into his ear. He felt her have a little nibble on his ear too. This sent shivers down his spine.

'Well hey back,' he said as he turned around, still in her grasp; she pulled him a little closer.

'You getting a drink?'

'Sam is just getting one for me now.'

'Got a feeling this is going to be a good night.'

'They always are with you.'

'Glad you think so.' She now had a little nip at his lip, just to tease him a bit, as she pulled her head away.

'Would you two cut it out?' Sam had arrived back with the drinks.

'Did you not get me one?' Dervila asked with a grin.

'You weren't here when I asked, so no.'

'I'll get my own then.' She gave a quick spin and headed off to the bar, glancing over her shoulder as she went, giving a look with squinted eyes.

'You two seem to be really getting along?'

'Yeah she's a great girl, we've been spending most weekends together.'

'She seems very playful.'

'Yeah, she's very touchy feely.'

'I'm happy for you, she seems like the kind of person you need at the moment.'

'I am smiling quite a lot lately, which is a good thing.'

'Here she's on her way back, I'll leave you love birds to it.'

'Sure I'll talk to you later.' Sam walked off to mingle with some of his own work mates.

'So what's the plan for later then?' Harry asked Dervila as she arrived back.

'Don't know yet, sure no point in planning things, when plans always change.'

'I'll just follow your lead then.'

'Yeah we'll just go with the flow.'

She turned around and started to dance in front of him, putting her hands up in the air, doing a kind of Axl Rose serpent dance.

'See where we end up hey?'

'Exactly, let's keep it fluid.' She put one hand back and started to play with his hair on the side of his head. She then spun around in one move and they were face to face. She gave him a kiss, slightly biting his lip as she pulled away.

'Oh, I'm going to keep you close all night,' Harry said as he put one hand around her waist.

Harry was starting to get used to the *'jungle'* that was the nightclub scene, he still hadn't got a clue who sang what song. It didn't really matter, as it was not as if he was going to go out and buy them any time soon. They also seemed to change week on week, it really was just a way to lose himself in the rhythm and in Dervila. She did spend most of the night on the dance floor, which suited him. He liked getting lost in the sweatiness of the *'rain forest'* which is what it still seemed like to him. All the bodies jammed together, each moving individually, yet still in unison. Sometimes he would wander off away from Dervila to mingle among the trees. He was always amazed that steam didn't rise off the floor, what with the amount of body heat being produced. He could feel drips coming from the sprinklers and wondered if they would be set off with the heat being produced or the owners would just set them off to cool everyone down. No matter where he wandered he always seemed to end up back with Dervila, which was a good thing.

At the end of the night they got into a taxi and Dervila gave an address to the driver, which was nowhere near her house or his.

'Where are we going?'

'Back to a party, it'll be fun!'

'Cool, how do you find these parties?'

'I just know a lot of people and someone always seems to have one on.'

'Sure you're a long time dead, time to sleep then.'

'Exactly.' She rested her head on his shoulder and snuggled up to him.

They arrived at the house, Harry paid the driver. It was in an older terraced part of Dublin and looked like a student house. As they walked up to the door, they noticed some passed out in the garden. The door opened and Harry hadn't got a clue who he was, but Dervila clearly did. Harry noticed they didn't have any drink with them and he gave her a little nudge to let her know.

'Don't worry, I'll sort us out, you just wait in the sitting room there,' she whispered to him, as she headed off towards the kitchen. Harry walked into the sitting room, where the lads were attempting to play cricket. Cricket, he thought, not exactly the most Irish of sports and to be trying to play it in a sitting room? He looked closer and saw one of them was Ross, met him a couple of months before. Ross gave him a quick wave and a wink. One of the lads swung the bat at the ball which had been bowled at him, he missed by miles and caught the lad standing beside him flush in the shin. *Fuck!* he thought, that had to hurt, fully expecting him to crumple up in a ball on the ground. He stood there, looked at the lad who had just hit him and they both started to laugh. '*Whatever,*' he thought to himself as he headed over for a spare seat, well away from the swinging bat. 'Hey Harry, you want a game?' he said waiving the bat at Harry.

'No thanks, Ross.' He waived his hand from side to side, he was useless at organised sports.

'Come on, give it a go?'

'Really, I'm fine.'

Dervila arrived back in the room with two glasses and headed over to sit beside Harry.

'Hey Dervila, your boyfriend is a bit of a dry-shite!'

'No he's not, now fuck off Ross and play your silly games somewhere else.'

'Calm down.' Ross walked out of the room.

'Don't mind him, he can be a bit of a dick at times, but he's okay,' she said to Harry.

'Wasn't bothering me really.' She sat down on his lap and handed him a drink. 'Here drink this.'

'What is it?'

'How should I know, I only found them on the table.'

'You're insane.'

'Shush and drink your drink.' They both glanced over towards the TV, some music channel was playing, anything could have been playing really, as the sound was quite low and they were both quite drunk at this stage. They both downed the drinks, which tasted god awful.

'Come on, let's go mingle,' she said to him and grabbed him by the hand.

They spent what seemed like a few minutes moving from room to room, chatting and having a laugh. They made it back into the front room and Harry glanced out the window, it was bright out. 'We should go,' he suggested to Dervila.

'Yeah let's head back to mine and we finish this party.'

Later in the morning Harry came out of the shower, to hear Dervila chatting on the phone. They had only been back from the house party a couple of hours and she was talking about heading out again.

'Who you talking to?' he asked as he approached her.

'Ross,' she said as she hung up the phone.

'That lunatic with the cricket bat?'

'Yeah him. Get dressed, we're heading out. He'll be over to pick us up in an hour.'

'Where we going?'

'Road trip.'

'Oh no.'

'Yeah, now I'm going to have a shower and get ready. Grab a bottle of vodka and something to mix it with.'

'We'll bring some glasses too, yeah?'

'Good thinking, Batman.'

'Would that not be Ross? What with him swinging that cricket bat around and all.'

'Yeah, think we'll call him that now,' she said laughing on her way to the shower. Harry really was glad he kept spare cloths at hers, just because stuff like this was always happening.

They both sat in the back of Ross's car, it was only a three door VW Golf. They settled down, Dervila behind the driver's seat and Harry behind the passenger seat. Harry had found two plastic cups, which they were now filling them up with vodka and coke.

'Hey Harry!' Ross said turning around from the driver's seat.

'How's it going Ross? Nice to see, without you swinging a cricket bat.'

'Oh, that? Sorry about that.'

'Where we heading then?'

'Mayo, did she not tell you?'

'She, she has a name, Batman,' Dervila butted in.

'Batman?' Ross was now straining his head around to look at Dervila.

'Yeah Batman, think that's what I'm going to call you now.'

'Good lord. We'd better head, Eddie is waiting.'

'Eddie?' Harry asked Dervila.

'He's the lad he hit with the bat. So he'd be Robin then?'

'So where about in Mayo are we going,' Harry asked again

'Ah, I'm going to meet a friend who moved over to Newport to live with his girlfriend,' Ross replied.

'Where are we going to stay?'

'Sure we'll somewhere to sleep. My mate will sort something out for us.'

'Ah cool.' They set off for Mayo, stopping to pick up Eddie along the way.

On the way down they stopped in a small town, as Eddie wanted to place a bet on a horse race and watch it too. Harry and Dervila used the stop to go to a local pub for some food, while the other two spent it in the bookmakers. As Harry and Dervila sat eating their all day breakfast, Harry couldn't help but wonder how Dervila always managed to look immaculate, no matter how long they had been out drinking. When they arrived back at the car, the other two were waiting, sitting on the bonnet, looking satisfied with themselves.

'You have any winners?' Dervila asked.

'Yeah, just the one,' Ross replied smiling.

'How much did you win?'

'Couldn't tell you that,' he said giving a wink.

'Come on, tell us?'

'Jammy – fecker won about 1,000 euro.' Eddie cut in shaking his head.

'Jammy! The horse was two to one.' Ross looked at Ed, who was looking a little envious.

'Hang on a minute, you put 500 euro on a horse?' Harry asked.

'Yeah,' Ross calmly replied.

'Are you insane?'

'It won, didn't it?'

'But what if it lost?'

'But it didn't.'

'Crazy fucker.'

'Only a bit of fun, now come on, we have to move on.'

They arrived in Westport, parked the car and Ross phoned his friend. They waited in a local pub for him to arrive. Ross bought the first round of drinks, it was the least he could do after winning the money. When his friend arrived Ross made the introductions.

'Simon, this Dervila, Harry and Ed.' As he pointed them out around the table.

'Hi,' he replied as shook hands with each of them. He sat down, and Ross went up to buy him a pint. They all started to chat, and the drink flowed. They moved from pub to pub throughout the evening picking up people along the way.

Next thing Harry knew he was standing outside a bar, where everyone was suddenly leaving. He looked at his watch it was three-thirty am. Looking around he couldn't see any of the group, *'shit,'* he thought to himself. He pulled out his phone and the battery was dead. *'Fuck!'* It was now what he thought, *'what the fuck am I going to do now?'* Harry headed back to the car to see if they were there, but no luck, it was empty. They must have gone back to a house party. *'Fuckers!'* He started to meander down the street, maybe there was a hotel he could stay in. Then he remembered he saw one on the way in, on the outskirts. It was a bit of a walk, but he got there, he looked up and it reminded him of the Bates Motel. He was hoping it would not be a repeat of *'Psycho"* for him. He walked into the reception, he only had a light coat on and it was the middle of December, so he was quite cold. 'Have you got any rooms?'

'Sorry, no,' came the reply from the young lad behind the counter.

'Come on you have to have something, I'm stuck here with nowhere to stay.'

'Sorry, we have no rooms free.'

'Come on, I'll sleep anywhere.'

'Okay, tell you what. There's a hall over there and you can kip on the sofa in there if you want.'

'Over there?' he said pointing.

'Yeah.'

'Cheers mate, I'll be gone early.'

Harry walked over to the hall, it was dark in there. He headed straight for the sofa to lie down. As he lay down he scanned around the room, in the dark he could see figures. *'What the fuck are they?'* He thought to himself. It was like they were doing a play or something and they had left all the props in there. It reminded him of the ballroom in *'The Shinning.'* It seemed a little freaky to him, but where else was he going to sleep? He tried to shut his eyes but couldn't seem to fall asleep. Where the statues moving? Certainly seemed so in his head. Maybe it was the amount of alcohol he'd had, mixed with the association he had made in his mind with horror films. He tried to push it to the back of his mind and get some sleep. All he could do was keep opening his eyes every once in a while, to check nothing was moving. *'Shit, this is useless, there's no way I'll get any sleep in here.'* he thought. The room was big and quite cold as well, so after about a half hour, he decided he couldn't stay there. It really was starting to freak him out. He got up, bolted for the front door and headed back into town not looking back.

He arrived back near where the car was parked and spotted a phone box. Maybe he could just get enough power out of his phone to find Dervila's phone number and call her. He went into the phone box and got some change out of his pocket, as well as his phone. He switched on the phone, it started up, which was good. *'Please god'* he was hoping he could just make it to her number, he started to scroll down to her name. Just as he saw he number the screen went blank. 'Fuck, fuck, fuck!' he screamed. Why hadn't he memorised her number? He sat down on the floor of the phone box, looked like he was stuck there for the night. So he curled up in a ball to try keep a little warmer and tried to get some sleep. At least he had cover if it did start to rain and that was always a possibility in Ireland, especially over on the west coast.

Come about seven am he had an idea, maybe there would be an early bus back to Dublin that he could get. He left the phone box to go find the bus stop, eventually he found one with a timetable attached to it. Looking up the Sunday times and the first bus wasn't until ten-thirty, *'fucking Sunday times!'* He thought as he walked away, back to the relative comfort and safety of his phone box. When he got back, he decided to chance the car. Maybe they left the door open, or something. *'Harry, you're really clutching at straws here,'* he said to himself, as he approached the car. When he got to the window, he looked in to see all three asleep in the car. He was surprised to see them, must not have stayed long in the party. Eddie woke up when he knocked on the window.

'Where the fuck did you get to?' Eddie said as he opened the door.

'Just wandering around.'

'Here get in, you look freezing.' Eddie got out and let Harry into the back, where Dervila was asleep.

He got in and snuggled up to her, she jumped up. 'What the fuck,' he said with surprise. 'Oh it's you.' As she snuggled up to him. 'Thought one of these two were trying their luck.'

'Hug me tight, I'm bloody freezing, been walking around all night.'

'Why did you not ring me you dope?'

'Phone battery went flat.'

'You not know my number off by heart and use a pay phone?'

'Yeah, got to the phone box, but couldn't remember your number.'

'Silly sod. Now come on, let's get some sleep.'

They all eventually woke up around ten am and went to find somewhere open, so they could have some breakfast. Harry was still feeling the cold, even after snuggling up to Dervila in the car. Over breakfast Harry explained to them about his adventure down to the *'Bates Motel.'* and how much it had freaked him out, to the point he had to run out of the place. Once Ross felt a bit better they decided it was time to head back to Dublin and home. Harry got them to drop him off at his place, he gave Dervila a kiss and headed straight to bed for some much needed rest.

'So there you go, that's how I spent my weekend,' Harry said to Tom.

'That's crazy. Can't believe you went drinking in Dublin and woke up two days later in a phone box over in Mayo!' Tom was shaking his head, wondering how on earth Harry had ended in such a situation.

'That's how we roll,' Harry said starting to look a little better and at least managing a smile.

*****

Chapter 15
Lazy River

'Heya Joe, it's Harry.' Harry was on the phone to Joe.
'Heya Harry, what's the craic with ya?'
'I'm good; how you getting along?'
'Yeah, all good here.'

'Can I ask you for a favour?'

'Yeah shoot, I'll see what I can do.'

'Can I get a lend of an open boat?'

'Yeah, I can get my hands one, what you need it for?'

'Ah, you know Grainne?'

'Yeah, you've mentioned her once or twice.'

'Well I want to bring her out for a paddle, I figure I'll stick her in the front of an open boat with a picnic in the middle, we can make a day of it.'

'Yeah, tell ya what. I'll drop you at the top of the river and pick you back up at the bottom.'

'And what do you want in return?'

'Not much, just come out with me on one of the assessments I'm running during the winter. The ones I asked you about ages ago?'

'Oh yeah I remember, why you want me out on that?'

'It's a level five instructor assessment, I want a group of really good paddlers on it.'

'And you just want me to tag along?'

'Yeah just as one of the group.'

'Well yea. if you think I'll be able for it?'

'Oh course you will, you never lose it.'

'Okay, sounds good.'

'Deal then?'

'Yeah and you'll get to meet Grainne, too.'

'Can't wait.'

Grainne arrived at Harry's place, wondering what he had planned for her. It was Friday night, all he had said was to bring a towel, some spare cloths and some old footwear. She had a feeling this was payback for bringing him swimming in the freezing sea. She knew they weren't going until the morning; she had come over as they were going to leave early the next morning. Harry opened the door, grinning from ear to ear.

'Heya.' she said, giving him a slightly worried hug.

'Good evening.' She followed him into the sitting room, knowing he was up to something. 'I have a little video for you to watch,' Harry said. sitting down.

'What is it?' she responded, sitting beside him.

'You'll see in a minute; prep work for tomorrow.' Grainne now looked worried as Harry pressed play on the You-Tube video he had set up.

'A canoeing video!'

'Yeah, this is what we'll be doing tomorrow.'

The video was of some extreme canoeing, with raging torrents flowing over massive waterfalls.

'We are not doing that?!'

'Yeah, you'll be fine, it's easy.'

'Easy, it looks frightening!'

'Na, it's easy.'

'No fucking way I'm doing that.'

'Ah now I went swimming in the sea, now it's your turn to live up to your promise.'

'Jesus Adams, you could kill me.'

'Now, would I?'

'Not so sure now.'

'Ah, to be sure there ain't any rivers *that* big in Ireland.'

'Thanks, but you're still going to strap me into a kayak. I won't be able to come back up like they do there.'

'I'll teach you tomorrow, all part of the service.'

'Yeah, just like I'd be able teach you how drive in the space of a morning…' she added in a sarcastic tone.

'Keep an open mind and you'll see in the morning. Come on let's go to bed, we need to be up really early in the morning.'

'Yeah, I'm going to have real sweet dreams.'

Joe arrived at Harry's the next morning, parked the car and trailer. 'Heya Joe, come on in. You wanna cup a coffee?'

'Yeah, please.' They both walked into the kitchen.

'You bring the two kayaks on the trailer as well, like I asked?'

'Yea, you are bad, bad man.'

'Shush, you'll ruin it. Loads of water around today then Joe?' Harry said the second part pound enough for Grainne to hear him, while Joe was shaking his head.

'Yeah, the river is huge. Biggest I've seen it in years.'

Grainne stuck her head into the kitchen, looking like someone had told her a tidal wave was coming.

'Morning honey, this is Joe. Joe, this is Grainne.'

'Hey Joe, how are you?' She approached him cautiously shaking his hand.

'Heya, so looking forward to your little paddle today?'

'Oh, about as much pulling my teeth out a with rusty pliers.'

'We going to start your lesson in here.' Harry grabbed a mop handing it to Grainne.

'What do you want me to do with this?'

'Okay, sit on the floor and hold the mop in both hands.'

'I'm not going to sit on the floor.'

'How are you ever going to learn if you won't listen to your teacher?'

Grainne sat on the floor holding the mop, Harry stood behind her, putting his hands beside hers on the mop.

'Okay, so this is how we paddle.' He pushed her right hand forward, placed beside her leg, pulled back, while pushing forward with her left hand, in turn dropping that hand down and pulling back.

'This feels silly.'

'Not at all, it's the easiest way to learn. Now, you think you've got the hang of it?' He let go and walked over to Joe who was standing , drinking his cup of coffee.

'Is this right?' she asked looking over at them.

'What do you think, Joe?' He couldn't hold in the laughter any longer.

'You two feckers.' She stood up and headed for them. Harry hid behind Joe.

'Now, now, careful with that mop.'

'What made you think giving her a weapon was a good idea?' Joe was still trying to hold in the laughter, unsuccessfully.

'Adams, I'm going to kill you!' she exclaimed as the launched towards them both, mop still in hand.

Harry hid behind Joe using him as shield, 'Just playing with you, careful now you'll have someone's eye out.'

'Don't think giving her a mop was a good idea, Harry,' Joe said trying to make himself as small a target as possible.

They arrived at the launch point for their river trip.

Harry started to unload the trailer with Joe, while Grainne waited in the car. It was a beautiful autumn day, sun was shining, and it wasn't too cold. Leaves were starting to fall from the trees. Grainne watched on, looking a bit worried. They took down the two kayaks and the open boat from the trailer, Harry pulled the kayaks out preparing them for the trip.

'Hey, Joe you bring a spare spray deck for Grainne?'

'There should be one in the back of the boat.'

'Ah, yeah here it is, I got it.' Harry pulled what looked like a skirt from the kayak.

'What's that?' she said emerging from the car.

'It's a splash deck, covers the gap, helps stop the water getting into the boat.'

'Just one question?'

'Shoot.'

'How do I get out if I capsize?' Harry found the calmness in her tone quite disconcerting.

'Well you …' He looked up to see her raising her eyebrows at him. Oops, he'd pushed it a bit too far.

'Na, now … I was just winding you up. We're both going in this,' Harry replied moving towards the open boat. 'See no strapping in this one.'

'You're a fecker, Adams!'

'See it's an open boat, some people call them Canadian Canoes. I'll be in there with you, so you'll be fine. Me in the back doing all the work, you in the front chilling out.' He was back peddling now as she stalked towards him.

'Oh, now I feel better knowing you're going to be in there with me.' She picked up a paddle, 'We going to be using these then?' She was looking menacing holding the paddle.

'Yeah …oh something else …there's no big drops, it's fairly flat the whole way,' Harry said still backing away. Joe was hiding in the van trying desperately to stay out of it.

'Adams, I'm going to stick this paddle…'

Before she could finish Harry butted in, 'Now now, I have a nice picnic with me, you'd better behave if you want some.' She put the paddle down and smiled at them.

They set off down the river, Harry sitting in the back and Grainne in the front. He spent a little time at the start showing her how to paddle. It wasn't going to be a long trip, but they were in no real hurry and were going to stop for lunch. They really had struck it lucky again with the weather, for once the long range forecast had been correct. Grainne had put on the wetsuit and buoyancy aid Harry had given her.

They had helmets in the canoe, but as it was flat they didn't need to wear them, he brought them just in case they were needed. As they meandered along Harry sat in the seat leaning back, with his feet dangling out over the side of the canoe. Grainne still seemed nervous clinging on to the paddle as tight as she could.

'This really is the way to travel, ain't it?' Harry said.

'Yeah, it's so relaxing. Great way to soak up the countryside, especially on a day like this.'

'We got so lucky with the weather, didn't we?'

'Yeah, it's a beautiful day. How did you manage to sort that out?' She turned to smile at him.

'Ah, I had a word with the big man.'

'You must have some good friends up there.'

'I do, a really good one. Relax a little there, you look tense. You're not going to fall in, trust me on this. Turn around, face me.'

'No, we'll fall in!'

'You won't, trust me. If you get wet, I get wet and I don't want that.'

'You sure?'

'Yeah, 100%. Come on.'

She put the paddle in the canoe and started to turn slowly, making sure she was holding on at all times. Eventually after what felt like an age, she was sitting on the same seat facing him.

'I'm going to show you how safe it is.' He stood up in the canoe.

'No, don't do that.'

'It's fine.' He now stood up on the seat.

'You're going to capsize the boat.'

'I haven't finished yet.' He now moved his stance to the side gunnels of the canoe, starting to paddle, and smiling as Grainne looked on in horror.

'Get down, will ya?'

'Watch.' He now started to rock the canoe a little. 'See, we're fine.'

'Okay, now get down, will ya?' Harry sat back down in the seat.

'You see my point. This is all about chilling out and relaxing, being at one with nature ,if you like.'

'Ah don't start with that will ya.'

'Be quiet for a minute, just listen.' They both stayed silent and Harry kept paddling. 'You hear that?' he asked her after a minute.

'No, all I hear are birds and wildlife.'

'Exactly, you can't even hear my paddle moving through the water, can you?'

'No, actually I can't.'

'This is the way the Native Americans would paddle, trying to be as quiet as possible. That way they wouldn't disturb the wildlife and they could sneak up on their prey. Any nervousness or tension would be picked up by the animals.'

'Since when have you gone all Ray Mears?' Grainne said laughing.

'Ah, it's just stuff I picked up chatting to old timers when I was canoeing all the time; no harm in trying to protect and nurture the outdoors, is there?'

'No, it's a very noble sentiment indeed.'

'Probably too little too late though, unfortunately. Think the damage has been done, just look at the mess we've made of the planet. Ever since the industrial revolution, we managed to speed up the rate at which the planet is warming, pumping carbon dioxide in the atmosphere.'

'Yeah, the freak weather we're getting all over the world.'

'Oh you know about it? How's the weather related to it?'

'Ah it's all down to climate change; all you have to do is look the massive storms we're getting everywhere.'

'Really?'

'Well yeah as the seas get warmer, the warmer water evaporates, generally it's down around the Gulf of Mexico. The warmer the water the more energy it contains, it has to go somewhere, so when the winds are right huge powerful weather systems form which create hurricanes and the like. The Gulf Stream then drags them over to us, dumping all the shit on us.'

'Really?'

'Sure the Gulf Stream sits off our west coast bringing warm water up from the Gulf of Mexico, controls our climate. It keeps our climate quite mild, but some people think it's in the process of switching off. You see the weather systems all over the world are all connected, they have a fine, delicate balance. We humans have come along and are doing our best to mess up the equilibrium. As the seas get warmer and more acidic, it will lead to rising sea levels and all sorts of other scary shit.'

'Rising sea levels? How's that?'

'Well, what happens when you heat something? It expands yeah?' Harry nodded his head. 'So as they expand the sea level rises. But it's the acidity rising that will cause the real problems, killing sea life.'

'Really.'

'Yeah, look at the Great Barrier Reef. It's being bleached and is dying. I don't know if we can act fast enough to reverse it though.'

'You know a lot about this, don't you?'

'Ah, I've picked up a few things along the way myself.'

'After my own heart.'

'Well, we all need to care about something.'

'We do, but enough of this doom and gloom. Over there looks like this is good spot to stop.'

'Stop for what?'

'Just have a little break and some lunch.'

Harry paddled the canoe into the side of the river and let Grainne get out, without getting wet. He then got out and dragged the canoe onto the river bank. In the middle he had a water proof bag, which he took out. He opened the bag, took out a picnic complete with blanket for them to sit on. They both took off their buoyancy aids in the canoe and sat down on the blanket. The sun was quite low but it was a warm day for the time of year. Harry pulled a nice bottle of wine and two glasses out of the bag.

'Hey, you even brought glasses?' she sounded surprised.

'Yeah, you like?'

'I'm impressed; how did you know they wouldn't break?'

'Simple.' He tapped them together; she could hear the clunk of plastic on plastic. They both laughed, while Harry poured the wine.

'So, Mister Adventure, what's your biggest fear in life?'

'Biggest fear, well at the moment probably your Dad,' he said with a smile.

'Seriously?'

'Not something I think about much …if I tell you, you tell a sole? It's not very manly or macho.'

'Well, it's not like anyone else can hear.' she pointed around at the empty, very quiet countryside.

'So I'm sort of quite a bit claustrophobic. I hate being on a packed bus or in clubs, even have to hold my breath in lifts. Don't know why, just do?'

'You are a real outdoor kind of person, so that's not really surprising. You seem so much happier outside in the open air.'

'Really?'

'Yeah just look how content you are now. So when did this all start then, or has it always been there?'

'Only really started a while ago.'

'You've grown up in an outdoor environment. So when you start to put yourself in enclosed positions, like an office job and them dank cramped nightclubs, you probably feel like you were trapped.'

'Oh, you sort of hit the nail on the head there.' Harry was quite surprised at how insightful Grainne was.

'Guess, I know you too well.' She tapped him on the leg.

'So Freud, what's your biggest fear then?' He smiled back at her. 'Oh yeah, think I already know that? Spiders,' he said, laughing.

'Hey.'

'You did make me come all the way over to yours the other day just to get rid of one.'

'It was huge!'

'They're not going to hurt you. You wouldn't even stay in the same room as it.'

'No, they're horrible things.' Harry just laughed.

'I know it's not like an irrational fear or anything. Not like some people who have plain weird phobias, like being tickled by feathers or daft things like that.' Grainne laughed as she looked out at the river, just as a couple of swans drifted by. 'They really are beautiful graceful birds, ain't they?' she said looking over at Harry, he looked horrified.

'No they aren't, bloody nasty things.'

'What?'

'Oh yeah, they're horrible vicious things. They may look like they're all sweetness and light, but they ain't if you have the misfortune to get up close to one of them.'

'You got a phobia about swans then?' she asked, laughing.

'Hey, this ain't funny. The lads pushed me over a weir one day without a paddle and I had done well getting down without capsizing, just using my hands. At the bottom I looked up to see one of them feckers was sitting there, staring at me. I was trying my best to avoid him.' He was demonstrating this quite vigorously. 'As I got near, he spread his wings and this god-awful hiss came from his beak as he launched towards me. I had to jump out of the kayak and swim to the side. Scared the bejesus out of me. The lads still sitting at the top of the weir were pissing themselves laughing. Put it this way, the moral of the story is *don't paddle a white kayak*.'

He looked over to see Grainne lying on her back rolling around laughing. 'Oh stop, it's actually hurting, I'm laughing that much,' she blurted out through the laughter.

They finished their lunch before getting back on the river to complete their trip while there was afternoon sunshine.

As they got further down the river the quietness was interrupted by a low rumble. 'What's that sound?' Grainne asked.

'What sound?' Harry's replied.

'That rumble.' She looked around at him. He looked straight at her with a grin on his face.

'Time for some fun. Right, I need ya to move back into the middle of the boat and keep your paddle inside.'

'Why?'

"Cause there's a set of rapids around the corner; now hurry if you don't want to get wet. Kneel down and rest your ass against the seat,' he said, as he did the same himself.

'You'd better not get me wet!' She now held tightly onto the side gunnels and put her trust in Harry. As they drifted around the corner the roar of the fast water became louder and louder. Harry was enjoying himself, not so much Grainne, whose knuckles were now white from gripping the side so hard. The water was starting to pick up speed and they could now see the drop. It didn't matter how many times Harry had done this, he always felt the nervous excitement of the situation. Especially now as he really didn't want to capsize the canoe with Grainne in it. Time to concentrate and make sure the canoe was lined up correctly to shoot the rapid. This wasn't the biggest drop he'd taken a canoe over; not even close if the truth be known, but he couldn't mess it up. He was working hard the whole time making adjustments to keep the canoe on the correct line.

'You might get a little splashed here,' he shouted up to her as they went through a narrow gap and over the drop. All Grainne could see was the river trying to squeeze itself through a gap, which was less than a third of its width. Harry was still working hard in the back navigating his way through the gap, having a ball doing it. They made it to the bottom, neither getting too wet and Harry guided the canoe into the side.

'How was that?' he asked.

'It was good fun.'

'Wanna do a bit more?'

'What you got in mind?'

'See that standing wave there?' He pointed at a section of the river just below the gap, where it hit a rock at the bottom causing a wave to form.

'Yeah!' She sounded a bit worried.

'We're going to surf it.'

'Surf it?!'

'Yeah, sit tight …here we go.' Harry set off paddling upstream as fast as he could through the slack water behind the rock. When he was approaching the wave he angled the bow of the canoe out from behind the rock and into the fast flowing water behind the wave. He then used the paddle at the back as a rudder to guide the rest of the canoe on to the wave, keeping it perpendicular to the wave, pointing upstream. They surfed across the wave, Harry then switched sides with the paddle and they came back across the wave. They did this a few times before returning back to the slack water. 'You enjoy that?' he asked her.

'Yeah, it was great fun.' She was really excited now.

Something was ringing and they looked at each other.

'Ah it's my phone!'

Harry tucked it inside his buoyancy jacket in a waterproof pouch. He took it out and answered it. 'Hey Joe.'

'Where are you?'

'We're just up at the weir, we'll be down in minute.'

'Cool, see you in a bit.'

A bit further down the river Joe was waiting on the bank to help them out. They got the canoe out and put it up onto the trailer. 'Hey Joe, wait until you see what I brought to save room in my bag.'

'What is it?' Harry pulled out a tiny chammy.

'Deadly ain't it, it can dry as well as a towel and doesn't take nearly as much room up. You just ring it out and it's ready to go again.' He looked excited about it, Joe and Grainne just looked at him. 'Can you not see the hole in your plan?' Joe eventually asked.

'No?'

'You're getting changed on the side of the road …?' Harry stood there and placed the *'towel'* at his midsection, now he realised that he had no way covering his modesty. Joe and Grainne burst into laughter. 'Okay, any chance I could have a lend of your towel Grainne, please?'

'It'll cost ya?'

'What d'ya want?'

'Oh, that can wait.'

*****

Chapter 16
Stopper

'Mr. Brownstone'   Guns 'n Roses

Harry woke up in Dervila's bed, looked around, she was nowhere to be seen. He looked around for his phone, *'Fuck!'* He couldn't find it, where was it gone. Suddenly he could hear it ringing, where was it? Rummaging around in the bed, he finally found it buried under the pillow. *'Thank the fuck for that.'* Now who was ringing him, 'Hugo' came up on the screen of this phone. Hugo was a lad he had met a few times while out.

'Hey Hugo.'

'Hey Harry, how you doing?'

'Bloody hanging, only just woke up.'

'Things will never change with you. Hey, I'm heading up to Belfast for the weekend, wanna tag along?'

'Where ya staying, I'm not sleeping in a phone box this time!' Hugo just laughed on the other end, as people in their circle most had heard about Harry's little 'adventure' in Mayo. It was one Dervila's favourite stories to tell.

'I've booked into a youth hostel, it'll not cost ya that much.'

'Cool, what time you heading?'

'Going to get the 1 o'clock train, meet you at the train station?'

'Yeah, I'll just nip home, get changed and see you there.'

Harry hung up the phone, jumped out of bed and out into the kitchen. No sign of Dervila at all, she must have gone out. Checking his watch, didn't have much time to get home, then back to the train station. He'd have to just text her and see if she wanted to tag along. Rushing out the door heading back to his place, he had a quick shower at home, quickly packed an overnight bag, then he was on his way back out the door.

When Harry reached the train station he was a little bit early, so he dropped into the bar to wait for Hugo. Sitting at the bar drinking a pint and reading a paper, he checked his phone, still no reply from his text to Dervila.

Hugo phoned him to let him know he was there and Harry headed out to meet him. They both boarded the train and found themselves a seat close to the bar carriage.

'You ever been to Belfast before?' Hugo asked.

'Na, been to the north loads, mostly to the Mourne Mountains. You're not going to bring me anywhere dodgy, are you?'

'No, sure I'm from Belfast, my family moved to Dublin when I was fifteen.' Harry knew he was from the north of Ireland but had never been bothered to ask where.

'Ah, so you can show me around then?'

'Yeah, stick me when we get here, don't want ya heading off down the wrong street, now do we?'

'Ah here, I'll be okay, won't I?'

'Yeah, you'll be fine. I'll keep ya in the city centre.'

'Ah, good. Now d'ya want a beer? I'm off to the bar.'

'Yeah, grab us one.'

Harry headed off to the bar and arrived back with two drinks, which in turn led to a couple more.

Arriving in Belfast after having a few more drinks on the train, they walked into the city centre. Hugo pointed out to Harry that the black cabs are more like busses, that they more or less tell you where they are going and squeeze as many people in as they can. Harry found this quite odd, so was happy to walk. It was a little unnerving walking around with his

Catholic upbringing and Dublin accent, all it would take was to bump into the wrong person who still held all the old prejudices. Lucky there weren't many people like that about any more. They stopped in a tiny pub down a side street and both had a pint of Guinness. Hugo had said it served one of the nicest pints around and he wasn't far wrong. By then it was time to move on down to the hostel to check in.

There were two sets of bunk beds in the room and a locker each. Hostels were cheap, but you did run the risk of sharing the room with complete strangers. Harry had stayed in a lot in his life and never had any real issues, finding they were always filled with like-minded people. Got him thinking of his favourite hostel he ever stayed in. It was when he was in Yosemite National Park, the hostel was split into small huts spread out over a hillside. The idea was to have as little impact on the environment, by not being able to notice the building from the roadside. It was fairly basic, but the fact that they felt so close to nature was something that really appealed to him. Thoughts of Phil started to surface. *Jesus. Snap out it now,'* he thought to himself as they entered the room; no way he was letting his mind wander back to think about things like that. Far too much pain involved there. Lucky enough they seemed to have the room to themselves, hopefully it would stay like that.

'What the fuck?' Harry said as he looked out the room window.
'What you on about?' Hugo replied.
'Rangers supporters club!'
'Yeah, that's where we're going for our first pint.'
'You're joking?'
'Yeah I am, that's on Sandy Row. We won't be going down there, your accent will stick out a little.'
'Thank fuck for that. Don't be scaring the shit out of me like that.'
'The look on your face though, was classic.' Hugo was sitting on the side of the bed laughing.
'Ha ha, very funny. I'm going to have a quick wash before we head out.' Hugo was now lying back on the bed still laughing to himself.

The plan for the night was to go to a few pubs around Belfast City centre and end up in a club close to the hostel. They were fairly close to the university so there was no shortage of lively bars. The first one they went into, Harry spotted a pool table in the corner, it was L shaped. Harry really did think he was seeing things and had to look a second time.

'L shaped pool table?' He whispered to Hugo.

'Yeah, you wanna game on it?'

'Yeah sure why not, I'm not much good at pool though.'

'Neither am I, come on – it's free.'

They set up the game and started to play, neither showing any dexterity with a cue. This was going to be a long game, especially when the cue ball ended up around the bend of the L. All the two of them could do was laugh at their own ineptitude. They had both finished two pints by the time Harry eventually won the game more by default than anything else.

After a few more bars they arrived at a bar called Robinson's. Hugo pointed at the hotel across the road.

'That's the Europa Hotel, the most bombed hotel in Europe.'

'Strange claim to fame.'

'Yeah, Bill Clinton stayed there as well, they say he took up over a hundred rooms.'

'That's crazy shit, who needs that many rooms?'

'One for each mistress, I suppose.' They laughed as they entered the bar and bought a pint each. There was band playing in the back, so they went over to listen. As they walked towards a free spot over in the corner the lead singer waved at Hugo.

'You know him?' Harry asked.

'Ah yeah, used to be in my class at school,' he said as he waved back.

'Small place?'

'You'd be surprised.'

'They're quite good, aren't they?' The band were playing old rock songs, of which he was big fan.

'Yeah, I've seen them play before.' They both stood listening a few songs nodding away. As Harry looked over at Hugo he noticed he had that cheeky grin, which always seemed to lead to mischief.

'Hey, think they'd let me sing?' Hugo leaned in putting the idea out there.

'Jesus, I don't know. This ain't karaoke or the X factor.'

'Feck it, he's my buddy – I'm going to ask?'

'They don't seem like that kind of band.'

'You sure? Crazy fucker.'

'Right, during the next break, I'm heading up.'

At the end of the song Hugo went up to the stage and started to chat to the lead singer. Harry waited smiling, nodding not really knowing what to think or do.

He came back over to Harry smiling and shaking his head.

'He said yeah, just wanted to know what song?'

'You better not make a show of me now!'

'Don't worry, it'll be good. I'll go up and tell them, keep it a surprise.' Hugo bounced off up to the stage and started to chat to the singer, who seemed to be laughing. He turned to the rest of the band, looked like he was checking if they knew the song. Hugo then headed off to the bar and came back with what looked like a pint of orange cordial.

Jumping up onto the stage, he took the mike. The lead singer went over to the side of the stage and sat down drinking his pint which was sitting there. The band started to play and most in the room recognised the song, Hugo launching into *Wild Thing* in his best gravelly voice. At one stage he started to stomp around the stage, he had picked up his pint by this stage. The band were struggling to keep the laughter in, Harry really couldn't tell if he was acting like he was really drunk or was really drunk. Eventually Hugo put his pint down, stopped stamping around and finished the song. The crowd was cheering when he finished and the lead singer came over to shake his hand. Harry walked back down to a laughing Hugo.

'That was classic. How did you come up with it?'

'Ah, it's Ollie Reed. He did it on a talk show one night, absolutely pissed he was and sang with a pint of vodka and orange in hand.'

'Brilliant, can't say I've ever seen it. Deserves a pint that does, same again?'

'Yeah, you trying to get me as drunk as he was.'

Harry headed off to the bar still laughing to himself.

When the band had their next break the lead singer came down to Harry and Hugo. 'Hi, I'm Seamus,' he said introducing himself to Harry.

'Hi, I'm Harry.'

'That was some act there, Hugo. How did you come up with it? Don't remember you being like that at school.'

'It just popped into my head when I was watching you.'

'Just popped into your head?'

'Yeah, I've never done it before.'

'So, you boys out for the night?'

'Yeah.'

'You want to head out with us after we finish our set?'

Harry looked at Hugo and they both nodded.

'Cool, sure I'll give Hugo a call when we're on the way out.'

'Yeah do, sure we won't be too far anyway.' Seamus laughed as he was walking back up to re-join the band.

'Shall we move on?' Hugo asked Harry.

'Sure why not. Where too?'

'There's a nice little bar next door; we'll head in there?'

'Yeah, sounds good, let's go.'

They both headed off to the next bar and were soon joined by the band. Hugo started chatting to Seamus about old times, while Harry was just sipping at his pint. The bass player of the band came over towards him.

'Aye about ya? I'm Billy.'

'How's it going? I'm Harry.'

'That was some laugh you boys gave us back there.'

'Hugo does have his moments.'

'You good mates with Hugo then? He's a good lad, Seamus doesn't have a bad word to say about him.'

'I bumped into him a while back on a night out and we go out on the lash every once in a while now. He's a sound lad alright.' They continued chatting for a while, they were all getting along like a house on fire. Hugo and Seamus joined in to the conversation. Everyone was having a great laugh and the drink was flowing. They all moved on to a night club, where they were joined a group of the bands' friends. Seamus led the group down in a corner of the room, where he had reserved an area. A brown-haired girl sat down in between Harry and Hugo, she was quite pretty. Another lad sat on the other side of Hugo, he started to chat away to Hugo. The girl started chatting to Harry. 'Heya, I'm Mandy, she said in a very cheery tone.

'Hi, I'm Harry.'

'How do you know the band then?'

'Ah I know Hugo, there.' He pointed towards Hugo. 'He's mates with Seamus; how do you know the lads?'

'Me and Stew there.' She pointed at the lad chatting to Hugo. 'We grew up near Billy.'

'Good stuff, you at the gig tonight?'

'Na, we had to go somewhere else.'

'Is he your boyfriend then?'

'No he's not!' she said with a little horror in her tone.

'Hey, just asking.'

'Why you ask, anyway?' She now moved closer to him, Harry didn't know what to think or do. Dervila wasn't here and she was a really lovely girl, but he couldn't do that on Dervila. Suddenly he was jolted back to sobriety by Stew standing up out of his seat and coming towards him.

'Mandy, what are you doing with that Taig?' He looked at Hugo and nodded, 'You with me?' Hugo stood up with an empty glass in hand and started to tap it on the side of the table.

'I'm not. You should leave,' Hugo pointed at the door.

'Yeah, I can talk to whoever I like,' Mandy said to him, while Harry sat there numb with shock.

'Wow, what's going on here?' Billy shot over to see what was happening. 'Well, I think your friend here is just about to leave,' Hugo said to Billy.

Stew just stood still, looking like he didn't know what to do, he knew he was on his own. Only question now was he just going to leave or start a fight?

'Okay Stew, think it is time for you to go home,' Billy said to him quite calmly, but in a stern voice.

He glared at Hugo, then Harry and finally at Billy, then walked off shaking his head.

'Really sorry about that lads, he's never done anything like that before,' Billy said apologising for his 'friends' behaviour.

'It's okay really, at least were all in one piece,' Harry replied sounding very relieved.

'Hate arseholes like that,' Hugo said sitting down.

'Here look I'll buy you a pint.' Billy said as headed back to the bar. He made sure he sat close to Harry and Mandy for the remainder of the night. Hugo was off chatting to Seamus, who didn't look too happy with what had happened and kept shaking his head. Billy knew he would need to explain it all to him later.

'What was that all about?' he asked Mandy.

'I don't know; he's never been like that before. All we were doing was chatting.'

'Ah, there ya go. I'd say he's jealous. Must still have a thing for you.'

'Ah he knows that's never going to happen.'

'Em, I do have a girlfriend,' she said looking at Harry.

'Well… yeah I do.'

'Shame, take it you won't cheat on her?' Mandy said to Harry, who again looked shocked.

'Em, no. Wouldn't do that on her.'

'Ah that's probably why I like you. You're a decent sort.'

'Thanks, I think.'

They all continued to have a great laugh, even Hugo and Seamus came back over to join in. Billy explained all to Seamus and he seemed okay with it. At closing time, they all headed outside, Harry and Hugo were about to head back to the hostel, when a car pulled up.

'Hey, you lads fancy coming back to mine for a beer?' It was Billy shouting at them from the car.

'What d'ya think?' Harry asked Hugo.

'Well at least we know he's not going to ambush us.'

'Well?'

'Hey Seamus, you heading back?' he shouted in Seamus's direction.

'Yeah I'm going for a while,' Seamus answered.

Harry and Hugo looked at each other, smiled, then headed off for the car. It was Billy's girlfriend driving, they all squeezed into the back.

Back at the house they all sat around the sitting room, Billy had a tray of beer and a bottle of vodka, which he brought out. The stereo was on low in the corner and they were all having a good chat. Again Billy and Harry were getting along really well, with Billy's girlfriend even commenting on it. Eventually Harry needed to use the toilet, on the way back he bumped into Billy in the hall.

'Come here I wanna show ya something.' Billy led the way into one of the rooms, Harry followed tentatively, not sure what to expect. 'Right I'm going to show you something, don't tell the other two now, I'm trusting you?'

'Yeah.' Harry said agreeing with him, as Billy walked over to a set of drawers and opened them. Harry didn't know what he was going to pull out, he was hoping it wouldn't be a weapon of any kind. When he turned around he was holding a sash, an Orange Order sash to be specific. It was the last thing Harry expected to see. From his upbringing he assumed all members of the Orange Order hated Catholics and Southerners. Now here he was standing in a room with one, who had saved him from getting in a fight earlier in the night. This night was just getting stranger and stranger.

'You see, we're not all bigots. Some of us think we can all get along and live together on this island.'

'I've never really thought of it, ya know. But, I do think we can all get along. I'm not much different to you.'

'What are you two up to in there?' Billy's girlfriend shouted.

'Em, nothing. Just showing Harry my vinyl collection,' Billy shouted back. 'We'll be out now.'

'Shush now, sometimes it doesn't go down too well,' he whispered to Harry.

'Yeah, it's cool, I won't say a word.'

They both arrived back in the living room, where the other two were starting to look a bit worse for wear.

'Think it's time for ye to head?' Billy's girlfriend said.

'Yeah maybe,' Billy replied.

'Come on I'll drop them back to the hostel. Throw Seamus into the spare room. Can't have Harry wandering around here looking for a cab.'

'What does she mean?'

'Oh yeah, we're just off the Shankill Road.'

'What!'

'It's okay, you're fine. I'd be in more danger if some people found out you were here. Seamus stays here all the time.'

They got a lift back to the hostel, clambered into their beds for a few hours' rest. When they got to the door they could hear voices inside the room. They entered the room to find two girls sitting there drinking a bottle of vodka.

'Heya,' the two girls said sounding very cheery in their American accents.

'Well, hi there,' Hugo said back, Harry could sense he was making his move. Hugo walked straight over to one of the girls and sat down beside her. She offered him a drink, which he accepted gladly.

'Hey, you wanna sit down here?' the other girl said to Harry, patting the bed beside her. Harry really was tired and did just want to go to bed, but then he would be spoiling Hugo's chances with the other girl. So he went over and sat down beside the girl, who also offered him a drink, which he accepted.

'Heya.' He said smiling at her. He glanced over at Hugo who was now kissing the other girl.

'Jesus,' he thought, *'he's a quick worker.'*

'So em… you want to make out as well?'

Harry looked at her, *'twice in one night, this wouldn't happen if I was single, bloody typical!'* This was all he could think. Suddenly he felt his phone buzz in his pocket. He pulled it out and looked at it, it was a text from Dervila.

'WHERE THE FUCK ARE YOU? I'VE BEEN RINGING YOU ALL DAY.' Harry now checked his phone which he had on silent and could see 9 missed calls from her, *'Fuck'* he thought.

'Hey sorry, I just got to go make a quick call, be back in a sec,' he said to the girl as he left for the door to phone Dervila, which was now a matter of urgency.

'Heya Hun, sorry my phone was on silent all day,' he said pulling the phone away from his ear, expecting the barrage.

'So you are still alive then?' she said.

'Yeah really sorry about not getting back, really didn't see your calls.'

'So where are ya then? Belfast?'

'Yeah, Belfast. You got my text this morning then?'

'Yeah, how the fuck did you end up in Belfast?'

'You know Hugo?'

'Yeah.'

'He gave me a call this morning and asked me to come up. His mate had pulled out.'

'So you just went off up there with him, like a gobshite?'

'Sure I had nothing else to do. You were gone out as well.'

'Gone out? I went out to buy us breakfast, I come back to a message from you telling me you're gone to Belfast!'

'Oh, I didn't realise that, so sorry. I'll make it up to you when I get back.'

'I'll bloody strangle you when you get back.'

'Hey look, I really am sorry, hun.'

'Don't hun me. Look, do don't have to go running off just 'cause someone says so. Hey, I'm off back to bed, I'll talk to ya when you get back.'

'Yeah will do, sorry again and sweet dreams.'

'Don't push it, see you tomorrow.'

Harry hung up the phone knowing he was in so much trouble when he got home tomorrow, suddenly a three-hour train journey didn't seem long enough. He walked back into the room to find the girl he had been talking to was now crashed out on the bed and sound asleep. *'Good'* he thought, *'one less problem for him to deal with.'* Hugo and the other girl were now under the sheets, up to no good as far as he could hear and see. He pulled a blanket up over the girl sleeping, then climbed into the top bunk to try get some sleep himself. He couldn't see how this would be possible with the noises coming from under the sheets on the other side of the room. Gave him a bit of time to figure out how to make it up to Dervila, seemed okay once he was talking to her, she was probably just worried about him. How had he not looked at his phone all day, anyway time to try get some sleep. Maybe if I wrap the pillow around my ears it might work.

He left Hugo with the American girls the next morning, so he could get the first train back to Dublin in the morning. Maybe he could catch up on the sleep there he didn't get the night before. Putting his head against the window, he closed his eyes, hopefully he could sleep the whole way.

When Harry got off the train he decided to head straight to Dervila's place, try to smooth things over with her. He stopped along the way to buy her flowers. It was a Sunday afternoon, so he didn't have much choice. He found the nicest bunch he could, also picking up biggest bag of peanut M&M's he could find, she really loved these. She opened the door to find Harry standing there with the flowers and chocolates and gave him a little smile. 'This doesn't get you off the hook, you know?'

'I know, I know. But it's a start hey?'

'Come on in then.'

*****

CHAPTER 17
Deep breath
'Angel' Aerosmith

'Wake up Grainne, wake up.'

She opened her eyes to see a smiling Harry with a tray filled with breakfast. 'What no cushion?'

'I went out and bought this especially for you; look it even has little legs that fold out so you eat breakfast in bed.'

'Ah thanks Harry, you're so thoughtful.'

'Anything for you, my angel.'

'Less of that soppy shit now.'

'Well you've saved me. So I'm allowed every once in a while. You want to do anything today?'

'Think we saved each other. You mind if we have a lazy Sunday?'

'Well it's your day so yeah, why not.'

'Good, PJ's on the sofa then watching some TV.'

'Sounds good, a slob day then maybe a takeaway later?'

'Now, you're getting the hang of it.'

'Come on, sit up; eat it before this gets cold.'

Harry lay down on the bed beside her resting his head on the pillow, while Grainne polished off the breakfast he had lovingly prepared. The speed at which she finished surprised him.

'Jaysus, that was quick.'

'What I was hungry, it was delish, too. So you coming back under the sheets?' she said while putting the tray down onto the floor.

'We going down to watch some TV?'

'We're not in any major hurry, are we? Anyway I need to thank you for the breakfast, burn off some of them calories too.' Harry caught her drift really quick, he didn't need to be asked twice, he was under the sheets snuggling up to her in a flash.

Eventually, they made it down to the sofa for their chill out session. 'So what will we watch then?' Grainne asked.

'Maybe a box set?'

'Sounds good.'

'I've loads over there; sure you can pick.'

'Okay then, let's see what ya have,' she said walking over to Harry's bookshelves which were filled with DVD's, CD's and his Vinyl record collection. 'You really do have some collection here; we'll have to listen to some of your Vinyl records soon.'

'Oh we will do. I've picked them up over time, see I don't watch much live TV, it's all reality shite these days. So nearly always find something there to keep me amused.'

'Em …so what we going to watch then?' she mused as she started shuffling through the box sets. 'Something from the 80's maybe?'

'Good choice, love trashy eighties stuff.'

'Miami Vice? …Na. Colombo? … Na. Ah the A-Team 'What you talking about?' Harry started to laugh at this out loud and just because of the voice she had put on. 'What?' Grainne said, looking towards him knowing the voice wasn't that funny.

'Wrong show. That was Arnold from different strokes, the Little Kid? BA was in the A-Team, Mr T?'

'Ah, so he was my bad,' she said laughing at her mistake, 'I ain't getting on no Plane, fool!'

This made Harry laugh even harder. 'Yeah, that's the one.'

'Okay, we're not watching it though. Um ….How about MacGyver? Bet you loved to watch that?'

'Ah I like the A-Team, the way they could make a tank out of a car and all the scrap metal they just had lying around in the shed they were locked up in. Ah MacGyver another one who could make a hand glider from a paperclip and a roll of gaffer tape; just don't fancy watching it right now.'

'You know what I don't see here?'

'What, I think my collection is pretty complete.'

'Ah not really, I don't see Murder She Wrote.'

'Ah, Jessica Fletcher. The grim reaper herself.'

'What d'ya mean?'

'Sure, wherever she went anywhere someone would drop dead! Cabot Cove is probably the dangerous place in the world to live.'

Grainne started laughing, 'You're right there, I never noticed that. Alright then, so what are we going to watch then? Oh here we go, we're definitely watching this.' She picked one out, setting off towards the TV.

'What is it?'

'Oh you'll have to wait and see, my dear,' she said, putting the DVD in, while hiding the box behind the TV.

'Your teasing me now!'

'Would have thought you'd be used to that by now,' she said sitting down beside him, curling her legs up onto the sofa. Harry then rested his head on her chest, as they both waited on the programme to start.

'Oh, it's Magnum PI!' Harry had finally realised what they would be watching, sounding pleased. 'Love this show.'

'Oh me too, love a bit of Tom Selleck.'

'Like a bit Tom do ya now? I think it's cool as fuck, too.'

'Bit of a man crush there, have ya Harry?'

'Well he is cool. Has to be with his moustache and those eyebrows. There's even a Facebook page called Tom Selleck's moustache.'

'No way?'

'Yeah, I found it one day; it's hilarious.'

'Oh, I'll have to look that one up.'

'Do.' The opening credits rolled. 'That car too helps.'

'Harry, stop drooling over the car.'

'Oh, I could say the same about you and Tom.'

After an hour or two snuggled up watching Magnum rush around Hawaii in his flashy red Ferrari, some always getting himself into and out of some crazy situations, always getting the girl and the better of Higgins to boot. Harry picked his head up from resting on Grainne's chest to look up at her, 'So, Pammy.'

'Hey, less of that now.'

Harry laughed. 'So when you were lifeguarding, did you ever have to jump in to save someone?'

'You do know it's not like Baywatch, don't ya? It's not all tight swim suits and big hair.'

'Ah, don't go spoiling my fantasies now.'

'Well you did ask. The uniforms are a lot frumpier, t-shirt and shorts. Actually I only had to jump in once and that was sort of my fault. We always had poles or aids we could throw in to someone in trouble, so you could pull them into the side. Jumping in is always the last option, just putting yourself in danger.'

'Really? Come on, you have to spill the beans on this jumping in thing!'

'Awh, it was something and nothing really. You know someone drowning will do anything to try stay afloat. Remember the two lads that drowned in the canal a few years back?'

'Yeah, that was horribly sad.'

'I was walking down by it shortly after it happened. My Mam always said, 'if you had been there a little earlier, you could have saved them.' I don't think I could have.'

'How's that, you were a lifeguard at the time?'

'Yeah I was. It was the way it happened, one jumped off the lock into the water and ended up getting caught on an old shopping trolley, down at the bottom. His friend jumped in after to help him, he just grabbed onto him to trying get back to the surface, the two of them ended up drowning. That survival instinct just kicks in, don't know if anyone could have saved them, probably would have ended up getting in serious trouble too. It was so sad; still think about it every time I go past the spot.'

'Oh I remember that, it was awful. See why my mam used to go crazy at me if she caught me swimming in there.'

'She was right.'

'That she was, now you have fill me in on this having to jump in.'

'Really, it was nothing.'

'Come on, you can't say that and then leave me hanging.'

'Seriously, it's not my most heroic moment.'

'What, you had to jump in and save someone!'

'Okay, then I'll tell you.' Harry snuggled up closer into her chest, gazing up at her, 'So we went out for a few drinks after work one Saturday night and I ended up staying in one the girl's houses. I wasn't supposed to work the next day, but she did, so I walked down to pool with her. The plan was to head home from there. But, someone phoned in sick, so they talked me into working. I had my trainers on and shorts with my work t-shirt, so no change of clothes. Anyway it was okay, or so I thought, as I sitting on the side I saw a woman getting into trouble in the deep end, no big deal I thought, we had a telescopic rescue pole close. So I thought I'll extend it out and help her into the side. Put the poll out to her, she grabbed it, all good so far. Then I went to pull her in and the poll came apart, she was left holding one end and me the other! I had forgotten to tighten the joint when I extended it out.'

Harry burst out laughing, 'Oh my god, I know it's bad but I can't help laughing. The thought of her just holding the poll and sinking.'

'You're telling me, I didn't know what to do. She sank straight down holding the poll. I had to jump in after her and pull her out. She was okay, I don't know who was more embarrassed me or her.'

'My god, Just the thought of the woman left holding the poll sinking in the middle of the pool, is too much.' Harry was now laughing so much his stomach was hurting.

'It gets better, Then I had to borrow a pair of trainers, shorts and t-shirt from one of the managers to go home in. God knows what I looked like, my friend walked with me to the bus stop, laughing at me the whole way. It was all her fault; I should have just gone home. Not my best moment.'

'Well it's so funny, but at least you did save the woman so that's good. Come on tell me more, must be more?'

'Yeah, there were loads. Okay one more. I was sitting up on the high chair one day, watching the deep end of the pool. We had the swimming lane in, so people could swim lengths. There was this rope surfer making his way up to the deep end.'

'Rope surfer?'

'Oh, a kid who can't really swim. They hold onto the rope, making their way to the deep end. Anyway, he was clinging onto the rope, so I shouted at him, 'Let go of the rope.' He let go and started to sink, I had to move quick down off the chair, shouting, 'Hold onto the rope. Hold on to the rope.' I then had walk beside him all the way down the pool to make sure he got back to the shallow end. People were looking at me like I was crazy!'

Harry was laughing again 'He didn't drown, did he?'

'No.'

'Well then job done then. Come on one more.'

'You've had your fill of me admitting to doing silly stuff for one day Harry.'

'Awh, I was liking it. Being a lifeguard sounds like fun.'

'It's not really all that, it can be boring at times and the heat doesn't help either.'

'I reckon we'd have fun doing it together.'

'I'm sure we would hun. Right, cup of tea and chocolate biscuit before we watch the next episode? And I mean watch it not talk about my lifeguarding career.'

'Awh, you're no fun.'

'So you don't want tea then?'

'Oh yes I do, please.'

When she came back with the tea and biscuits, they snuggled in to watch the rest of season, there wouldn't be much movement from the sofa for the foreseeable future.

*****

Chapter 18
Capsize
'Straight into Darkness' **Tom Petty and The Heartbreakers**

Dervila heard the knock on the door, it was quite loud and persistent. She was in bed. *'Shit he's forgotten his keys again,'* she thought to herself. She had left him in the club to come home early as she had been quite tired.

'I'm going to kill him,' she said out loud as she headed for the door. The knocking had stopped. She opened the door to find Harry slumped on the doorstep, covered in blood.

'What the fuck happened to you?' she exclaimed trying to peel him off the step. He just sort of smiled at her and gurgled.

'What are you mumbling about?'

She just about managed to get him into the sitting room and over to the sofa. He was still incoherent as she went to the kitchen to get something to clean him up.

'I leave you out on your own for a couple of hours and look what happens?'

She started to clean his cuts, which were mostly to his face. Luckily, they weren't as bad as they looked, still they were going to look messy when he had sorted himself out in the morning.

'Harry? Harry! What happened to you?' There was no way she was going get any sense out of him, or who had he been out with. Who was sneaky enough to drop him at the door, knock and run? Had to be Ross, the gutless fucker, now where was her phone? She found it and phoned Ross, but no answer.

'Harry, you think you can make it to bed?' She got another mumble from him, she didn't want to leave him there. After all, she had no idea how he had injured himself or how bad it could be, so she struggled again to get him to the bedroom and into bed. She made sure she had cleaned all his cuts, at least he wasn't bleeding any longer. He was out cold as soon as his head hit the pillow, she didn't get a much sleep herself as she kept checking on him to make sure he was still alive.

Harry woke up in the morning with an awful headache; he looked over to the other side of the bed to see Dervila lying there staring at him. He couldn't decide if she was pissed with him or not. 'Everything okay?' he asked her tentatively

'You tell me, go look at the state of yourself?'

'What?'

'Check out the state of your face? Don't you know what you got up to after I left last night?' Harry got up gingerly heading over to the mirror to check himself out. When he looked, he saw cuts down his nose and the side of his face.

'Holly shit!' he groaned. 'How the fuck did that happen?'

'Jesus, you don't remember?'

'Well, I remember going back to a house and playing cards.'

'Who were you with?'

'Ross.'

'I knew it, fucker left you at the door, knocked and ran away.'

'Afraid of you, I suppose.'

'He'd want to be.'

'Hang on, I'm starting to remember now. We left the house and were heading home. I decided to jump over a wall, it wasn't that high until I stood on top of it. Then I saw the drop on the other side, it was about eight foot. I over-balanced and couldn't stop myself falling over. I must have scraped my face on the way down the wall, don't remember anything after that.'

'Pissed, were ye?'

'Well, yeah, we were drinking with the Captain in the house.'

'Captain Morgan! You feckin git. Did you land head first? You even manage to get your hands up?'

'Don't know.'

'You could have concussed yourself.' She got up out of bed and started to dress.

'What you doing?'

'Come on get dressed, we're going the hospital.'

'Na, don't need that.'

'You don't get a say.' She grabbed some of his clothes out of the wardrobe, throwing them at him.

'Okay then.' Harry was in no humour to argue with her, so reluctantly agreed. When they got outside the sun was quite bright, Harry couldn't stand it, having to shield his eyes from it.

'You're definitely concussed?'

'What, how'd you know that?'

'Brothers who play rugby, so I know the signs of concussion. Now come on.'

They arrived at the hospital, the waiting room was packed. This was going to take hours, Harry just wanted to go home and back to bed, but Dervila insisted they had to stay.

'Hey, are they cuts on your hands?' She picked up his hands and they were covered in cuts, some quite deep.

'Oh yeah, never noticed them.'

'You're a bloody disaster.'

'Keep telling you, I'll be fine.'

'The dirt in them cuts, you'll be lucky if they don't get infected.'

'Seriously, can I just go home to bed?' He rested his head on her shoulder.

'Hey, stay awake, don't go falling asleep now.'

'Okay, okay, I'll stay awake.'

Finally, after about three hours waiting they got to see a doctor. Turned out Dervila was right, he was concussed, also the cuts in his hands were showing signs of starting to get infected. The only reason they would let Harry leave the hospital was if he stayed somewhere where he could be watched. It was decided he would go stay with his Mam and Dad. Dervila phoned them to say they would be coming over, she knew they didn't really approve of her, but there was no other option. She couldn't look after him; she just didn't have the time to watch him 24/7.

The taxi pulled up at Harry's parent's house, Dervila helped him to the front door, where his Mam and Dad waited.

'Come on inside son. What on earth happened to you?' his Mam said as she led him into the house, completely blanking Dervila in the process.

'It's okay love, we'll look after him now,' his dad said to Dervila, who looked a little shell shocked, she couldn't say anything. He shut the door leaving her standing there alone. She had no choice but to go home, talk to him during the week.

They put him up to his old bed, to rest up. It was the first time they'd seen him or heard from him in months. It wasn't the first time they had met Dervila, they saw her as the main reason they did not see or hear from him much. Once he felt better they would have a chat with him about what he had been up to, first they had to make sure he was okay.

Harry came downstairs after two days lying in bed, watching DVDs. He walked into the living room, where his Mam was sitting. 'How are you now? Feeling better?'

'Much better.'

'Sit down there.' She pointed at the armchair. 'Now, what the hell happened to you?'

'Just an accident, went to jump over a wall, just didn't realise there was an eight foot drop on the other side.'

'Drunk, were you?'

'Yeah.'

'Just look at your state. You need to sort yourself out.'

'I'm fine, it was just an accident.'

'Ever since you met that girl, you've been a different person.'

'Her name's Dervila.'

'She's no good for you.'

'She is. She wasn't even out with me when I fell, it's not her fault.'

'I can't tell you how to live your life, but I can try help you, you need to take a long hard look at yourself.'

'Jesus Mam, I took a tumble, it's not like I'm sitting on a street corner shooting up, is it?'

'I don't like the person you're becoming, to be honest.' Tears were starting to well up in her eyes.

'You wonder why you never hear from me, this is why. You just nag.'

'It's for your own good.'

'Here I'm going back up to my room.' Harry left the room and headed back upstairs, leaving his Mam exasperated in the sitting room. She was wondering if she would ever get through to him. While Harry was lying in his room watching an old western movie, his Dad knocked on the door.

'Yeah,' Harry shouted from his bed.

'Can I come in?'

'Yeah, if ya want.'

Harry's Dad opened the door slowly and came in the darkness of the room. 'Oh, you watching a bit of Clint?'

'Yeah, always good when you don't feel well.'

'What happened with you and your mother?'

'Ah, sometimes she just winds me up.'

'You know she only does it because she cares?'

'Doesn't seem that way to me.'

'She does have a point. You do need to sort yourself out.'

'I'm fine. Just out having fun, that's all.'

'Just look at the state of you.'

'It was just an accident, Dad.'

'That girl too. She's no good.'

'You don't even know her.'

'I know you've changed since you met her.'

'I'm fine. She's a lovely girl. You should give her a chance.'

'Look son, we don't get to see or hear from you at all now. You're always off with her.'

'Well maybe that's just part of me growing up.'

Harry rolled over facing away from his father, pulling the duvet up over his head. His Dad left the room closing the door slowly behind him.

Feeling much stronger the next day, he decided to go home to his own place. He left without saying much to his either of his parents, he really felt bad at the way they had treated Dervila as all she was trying to do was help him. He knew it'd be a while before he spoke to his parents again. He would need to try make it up to Dervila as well.

Harry arrived back at his own place, plopping himself down on the sofa. A few more days to rest up would do him the world of good, didn't have to go to work until Monday. He went into his room and took the duvet off his bed, he was just going to vegetate on the sofa watching some DVD's, he had enough just sitting there. Still not feeling great, the fight he had had with his mother didn't help either. As he lay on the sofa watching a film he had probably seen a hundred times before, it didn't really matter as he kept drifting in and out of consciousness. His phone was switched off and he had left it in the kitchen, as there was no way he talking to anybody. A few days on his own would do him good. Eventually after watching a few films, he had lost count, it was time for bed to try get some sleep. On the way he stopped to use the toilet, dropping the duvet in the hall on the way in.

When washing his hands, Harry caught a glimpse of his face in the mirror. His face really did look some state, unshaven and the cuts were really looking ugly. Hopefully they would clear up and be okay by the time he ventured back out into the world and back to work. Looking into the mirror all he could think was *'what on earth did you do to yourself? You've really managed to fuck yourself up this time.'*

Switching off the light in his room, he climbed into his bed, suddenly he found himself in the pitch black staring at the ceiling, not that he could see much. Harry tried to shut his eyes to get some sleep, but it wasn't going to happen, so he just lay there with eyes open, staring into the darkness. His mind started to wander and think about where his life was. What had been up to over the past while, sure he was having fun, but at what cost? Had he changed that much, like his parents seemed to think. He did have to grow up some time, but there was no harm in the way he had re-invented himself. Dervila really helped him feel good about himself and he seemed to have a great social circle, always someone there if he wanted to go out. He was still young and it was not like he was drinking every day, just at the weekends. Okay, enough of this feeling sorry for himself, he would have to give Dervila a call the next day, apologise for how his parents had treated her. He got up out of bed and switched the light on, checked his chest of drawers, finding some sleeping pills Dervila had given him thinking, *'these will do the trick.'*

The next morning he got out of bed, deciding a nice long shower and shave would help him feel better. He headed into the kitchen, started to make some toast and a cup of coffee. Harry picked up his phone, switching it back on, he would sit down with his food, give Dervila a call. As he waited on his toast his phone beeped, it was a text from Dervila.

'Heya how you feelin 2day, hun? xxx'

This made Harry smile, he knew she could always help cheer him up. 'I feelin' a lot better, thanx.'

'Dat's good. Hope u taking it easy xxx'

'Yeah I am. Hey, sorry bout mam & dad the other day.'

'Don't worry about it, it's not ur fault.'

'Thanx, I told them dey shouldn't hav shut d door like dat.'

'It's fine huni. Hey wud u b up to havin Indian on sat?'

'Yeah that wud be lovely.'

'Kul, I giv u a txt sat we'll sort out a time.'

'Thanx huni.'

'No prob, now rest & tke care of urself xxxx.'

*****

Chapter 19
Eddy Hopping
'Summer in Dublin' Bagatelle

Harry sat back in the chair, it was an uncomfortable piece of plastic, he just couldn't sit easy in it. Sipping his coffee watching the pool, he could think of loads of better ways to spend his Saturday morning, like staying in bed. It was far too early to be sitting there watching Grainne swimming. This was going to be a long hour and a half, how they could swim for that long, he didn't know. It was exhausting just watching them. The only reason he had come down was because Grainne wanted to go out straight from training. *'I really need to learn how to drive and get a car,'* he thought to himself while drinking his cheap petrol station coffee, sitting in one of the most uncomfortable chairs and waiting. Just how graceful Grainne looked swimming, there was something mesmerising about it, quite hypnotic really.

The way she moved through the water looked effortless. She had been at him to get in and try, but Harry was not in the business of making himself look foolish. He would be exhausted after swimming two or three lengths, even what looked the slow lane he knew that would be too much for him.

When the session finished Grainne arrived out to the viewing area, Harry was amazed at how quickly she got changed. She still managed to look stunning, but maybe that was just Harry looking at her through his rose-tinted glasses. Now what did she have planned for him?

'Where we off to?' he asked.

'You're worse than a kid.'

'Come on, tell us?'

'We're going into town, to play tourist for the day. How's your American accent?'

'What!'

'We're going to spend the day pretending to be American tourists.'

'That's insane, but I like it. Where we going to go?'

'Trinity College, jump on a tour bus, Guinness hop store, Kilmainham goal, the zoo. See how much we can fit in.'

'We going to buy tacky gifts?'

'Oh yeah, even have my camera with me.'

'This could be a fun day.'

'We've lots to do, so snap to it.'

'What names are we going to use? How about Stella and Jake?'

'Yeah, we'll go with that. Sure we'll find other fun stuff to do along the way.'

'Like can I be a surf dude?' Harry asked in a silly American surfer accent.

'No.' Grainne rolled her eyes up to the sky.

'Ah, well how about a cowboy then, 'Well howdy there, pilgrim.' He now put on his best John Wayne impression.

'Jesus Harry, stop being silly. I want to try pull this off.'

'I'm just joshing with ya.'

They arrived in the city centre to set off on their little adventure, stopping at a really tourist shop first to see what they could pick up.

'Hey, Stella.' Harry shouted across the shop in his best American accent, holding up a small stuff leprechaun toy.

'Yeah, Jake,' she shouted back.

'You think we should buy this?' Grainne walked over to him.

'Yeah, we can bring him along on our adventure.'

'Okay, we'll call him Larry.'

'Play a little game with him, see how many other people's photo's we can get him into.'

'That'll be a great game.' They bought the leprechaun and headed off for their next stop.

There first real stop was the Viking splash tour, an old World War Two amphibious vehicle, which would tour Dublin on both land and water. They both bought their own plastic Viking helmets so they would fit in. Sitting back the two listened to the guide, they even got to shout at a few passers-by something the tour does; getting guests to shout at unsuspecting members of the public. It turned out to be a good laugh getting to see their own city from a different angle. They were trying to get Larry the leprechaun into as many photos as possible, even though they had no way of eventually seeing them.

From here they got a bus down to the Guinness hop store. In the Guinness Hop Store, Grainne didn't like the taste of the Guinness at all, she really wasn't shy about showing it. Harry couldn't stop laughing; she really was playing up to the tourist facade they were putting on. The top of the hop store gave them some great views of Dublin. From here they jumped back on the bus and off down to Kilmainham gaol, where the leaders of the 1916 rising against the English were executed.

Next they took a trip over to the zoo. Harry hadn't been to the zoo since he was a child, but it was fun to walk around pretending to be looking at some animals for the first time, asking people, 'What's that?' Waiting for their confused reaction and to see if they would in fact tell him the truth.

He did hear a few 'stupid Americans' comments, but by in large people were nice. Grainne, or Stella as Harry kept shouting, had to hang back the odd time just to try stop laughing. Her stomach was starting to hurt she was laughing that much. Little Larry was also doing well in his mission; they were sure they even got him in a shot flying across when Harry threw him to Grainne. *Who knew leprechauns could fly?* Grainne loved watching the sea lions as they reminded her of kids playing in the swimming pool, just playing around. She could probably watch them all day.

Next, they got a tram down to O'Connell Street, where they stood looking at the spire, a large spike in the middle of the street. Harry joking it was an effigy to Dublin's drug problem. They headed off down to Henry Street, then around into Moore Street, the fruit market, it wasn't as Harry remembered as a child. It had all changed now, so they crossed the ha'penny bridge, over into Temple Bar, where they strolled around for a while. This really is the tourist centre of Dublin, filled with bars, which played traditional Irish music, offering Irish food and overpriced drinks. It was not modern Ireland, but a glimpse into a certain vision of the past, what people travelling to Ireland wanted to see. Harry always had a great laugh out and about in here. They moved on to Trinity College, again meandered around the campus, paying in to see one page of the book of Kells, was a bit too much for Harry, so they left, headed off towards Grafton Street, stopping at the statue of Molly Malone to get a photo of Larry with her. Harry thought it would be funny to place him sitting between her breasts, as she was sometimes known as the *'tart with the cart.'*

On Grafton Street they took their time, stopping to listen to the buskers, there were all kinds there. From a group playing classical music to a lad playing on a homemade drum kit and everything in between. Grainne was not too impressed with the lads trying to be statues, but one did manage to get pigeons to land on him, which she couldn't decide if it was very clever or unbelievably daft. Harry didn't like pigeons much and would jump out of the way if one came near. 'Bloody disease-ridden flying rats.'

At the top of the street, beside the shopping centre there was always some sort of show on. Today was no different, there was a man balancing on top of a ladder, juggling. Harry really loved the diversity of acts on show. The street had gone through a phase of mostly having kids busking singing, 'Wonderwall.' They were mostly gone now and it was becoming more culturally diverse, which was a reflection on Irish society as a whole. Harry then suggested they head over to the flea market, which was quite near. Harry used to love wandering around here, as he never knew what he would find. It was the kind of place you wouldn't know what you were looking for until you found it. It was located in such a fabulous old building, just full of stalls and small shops. They didn't find much, but that was half the fun, looking.

Grainne then dragged Harry over to the national museum of Ireland. Here they gazed at not only Irish artefacts, but pieces from all over the world. The most famous of which, the Ardagh Chalice. Grainne was always amazed just how much Harry knew about Irish history. She had been joking all day that he should be a tour guide, he seemed to know as much as the guy on the tour bus, if not more. They left the museum, stopping to get a picture of Larry in front of the Dail. After this they took a walk down to Merrion Square where Harry pointed out the colour statue of Oscar Wilde, in the corner of the park. 'Look at him lounging on a rock, with such a cheeky grin.' Harry pointed out that this epitomised his character. They walked towards Grafton Street, it was late in the afternoon, they were both tired.

'Where to now?' Grainne asked.

'I'm shattered, think we should go for a pint and a sit down.'

'We have done a lot today, where'll we go?'

'Here I have an idea, follow me.' Harry grabbed her by the hand and started to walk.

'Where we going?'

'The smallest pub in Ireland.'

'No way.'

'Yeah, it's only over here.' He led her over what was just a red door, didn't look like a pub at all. It really was just a door. They walked in and straight down a set of stairs. At the bottom it opened up into a small room. It was tiny, like having a bar in your sitting room. They got a drink and found a seat to sit down, it wouldn't take many to fill the bar. Grainne thought it was really quaint and intimate. 'You have fun today?' Grainne asked, now without her American accent.

'Yeah, it was a great laugh.'

'Fun playing tourist in your own city, hey?'

'Yeah, we spend so much time giving out about it, we forget how friendly we are and what a lovely little city it is.'

'It really is…'

'Home after this then?'

'If you want, coming back to mine?'

'You cooking?'

'Em no, you are.' She smiled at him.

'Cheers.'

'It's a compliment, you're a good chef.'

'Flattery will get you everywhere.'

'Here we'll have a look at the photos, yeah?' Grainne said as she took the camera out and they both looked through the pictures they had taken, both laughing.

'Looks like little Larry had a great day.'

Larry was now lying on the table.

'Ah, look at him, he's knackered.'

'We need to get him home to bed.' They both laughed and Grainne put him in her bag, he was definitely coming home with them.

*****

CHAPTER 20
Wipe Out
'Old Town'   Phil Lynott

Harry sat in the waiting room of the doctor, it was packed; he didn't like it at all. Made him feel just like he had on the bus the days before, like the walls were closing in on him.

He had been sitting on the bus going home from work; suddenly he didn't feel too well. Sitting beside the window, he felt the need to put his knees up on the seat in front of him, putting his head down resting it against the window. What was up with him, it was more than his normal Monday tiredness. He felt like he needed air, claustrophobic, then it really hit him, a sudden wave of emotion. He felt like he was going to start to cry. *'What on earth is up with me?'* This was freaking him out no end, *'do I need to get off the bus to sort myself out?'*

Peering out the window it was nearly his stop to get off, good he could hang on, hopefully he wouldn't be like a blubbering idiot by the time he got there. It was some relief to make it home, collapse on to the sofa, still not feeling great. His breathing had speeded up, checking his pulse it was racing. Maybe a shower would help to calm him down a little. He stood in the shower saying to himself, *'sort yourself out son.'* After the shower he went straight to bed, time to go see a doctor in the morning.

Things had been steadily getting worse over the last couple of weeks, he was even starting to feel claustrophobic in lifts when too many people were in there, holding his breath as the lift moved. He'd have to phone into work, tell them he'd be a little late, this was a very worrying turn of events.

So here he was now sitting in a packed doctor's waiting room, kids running around making noise. This was making him feel uncomfortable. The walls were closing in again, he found himself wanting to just get up and walk out. He knew he would just have to hang on in there, sitting in a room full of sick people. He noticed two women sitting close to him were talking.

'So, what are you here for?'

'Ah, with Shane, want the doctor to have a look at his foot. It's very sore.' She pointed at her son, who was running around the waiting room, without any hint of irony. *'Good lord.'* Harry thought to himself, as he sunk down putting his head in between his hands resting his elbows on his knees. Closing his eyes, he tried to calm himself down, feeling now like it was getting harder and harder to breath. How was he going to explain this to the doctor? *'I think I'm going crazy.'* He had no idea how he was even going to start to explain it.

Finally, his name was called, he got up and walked towards the door with nervous trepidation. He opened the door slowly not knowing what to expect and sat down in the chair across from the doctor, who smiled. This helped settle him a little.

'So Harry, what can I do for you?'

'Just haven't been feeling quite right lately.'

'In what way?'

'It's just like everything is closing in me, claustrophobic kind of feeling.'

'Anything else?'

'Well, I was doing an exam the other week, I thought I was going to be late. When I got in I looked at the paper ...I couldn't recognise the language ... it looked like hieroglyphics.' All Harry could think while saying this was that he's going to think I'm mad. He is going to commit me.

'It's okay Harry, seems like you're having panic attacks, which we can sort out easily.'

'Really?' The relief in Harry reply was evident.

'We need to have a look at your lifestyle. Find ways to help you relax.'

'So I'm not going crazy then?' The doctor laughed at this.

'So what's your life like then? Work? What do you do in your spare time?'

Harry described his lifestyle. Deciding to tell the truth, not leaving anything out, as most people do.

'Harry, you really do need find ways to relax. You're working all week, then out all weekend. Your body is not getting time to recover. You need to find a hobby or something, look at yoga or something like that. I really don't want to go down the road of medication, so you've got to take a step back and seriously look at your life.'

'Yeah, you have a point there, I used to go outdoors all the time and it seemed relax me. Maybe I'll should look at getting back into canoeing, or something like that.'

'That'd be a good thing, start by cutting back on the going out first, will you?'

'I'll try.'

'Look try to relax a little and see how you feel. Hope I don't need to see you again, okay?'

'Yeah, it's a deal.'

Harry left the surgery feeling relieved, but a lot to contemplate about how he was living his life. He put his earphones in and headed for the bus stop. He decided to listen to Thin Lizzy for some unknown reason. As he sat on the bus thinking about where his life was, when suddenly it hit him that Thin Lizzy always reminded him of Phil, probably because the lead singers name was Phil too. Could that be why he'd picked them to listen to? Was Phil trying to tell him something, what would he think of the person he had become? Peering out the window at the outside world, looking at the people going about their business, he wondered what kind of stresses and strains they were feeling. Maybe he would only go out one night this week. Go out, do something on Sunday, that didn't involve drinking, maybe. He finally got into work, still contemplating his life. One of the older men was in the locker room when he entered. 'Heya,' Harry said.

'You're late, ain't you?' It was 11am.

'Yeah, just a little.'

'Ah your right. If your half an hour late, they'll shout at you. But, if you're this late they're just glad to see you.' Harry smiled at him, as he was hanging his coat up.

'Best get a move on, see you in a bit.'

'See you later, Harry.'

Harry walked out of the locker room, down to his desk, where he found a note from his boss asking him to call to his office when he arrived in. *What now?* he thought to himself, as he trudged towards the office. Knocking on a door with trepidation again, just like the doctors a couple of hours before, this was not a great start to his new relaxed lifestyle.

'Ah, Harry. Come in, sit down.' He was smiling at Harry; it was not very often he done that.

'You were looking for me?'

'Yeah, just want to make sure everything's okay?'

'Yeah, it's fine.'

'You were at the doctor this morning?'

'Yeah, just not feeling myself at the moment.'

'Look Harry, I'm going to be frank with you.'

'Yeah.' Harry was starting to worry now; this wouldn't be the time to point out his wasn't Frank.

'You're a really bright lad and I do like you; you could have a really bright future, change this company for the better. I'm actually worried about you; the state you arrive in here most Monday mornings. You still do a great job, but just imagine how much you could achieve if you arrived in bright and breezy. That's why I'm hard on you, I know you're well able to do a lot more.' Harry just nodded, not really knowing what to think.

'So you're not going to sack me then?' His boss just laughed.

'No I'm not. You just need to sort yourself out.'

'Funny, doctor more or less said the same thing to me his morning.'

'Well, you're a bright lad, I hope your taking this on board.'

'Oh I am, I am thinking about my life a lot at the moment.'

'Nice to hear it, now back to work with you.' He smiled and Harry walked back to his desk.

At lunch Harry went out for a walk to think about things and clear his head. How was he going to sort his life out? What kind of relationship did he have with Dervila anyway? She was great, but they never seemed to do any relationship kind of things. He only ever saw her at the weekend. Maybe he needed more now. Could she provide it for him? Did he even have any proper friends, apart from his drinking buddies, who again he only ever saw when he was out drinking?

He hadn't spent quality time Mam and Dad in what seemed like forever, last time he had he managed fall out with them too. Even hadn't seen or heard from his old canoeing mates in years. It would be hard to reconnect; he probably had burned all his bridges there. What would he think if someone he knew, just called him out of the blue, after maybe two years? Maybe he would just start with his Mam and Dad, only problem was that they didn't like Dervila at all. Her dropping him off at the house a couple of months before, concussed and with infected cuts, for them to look after him didn't help. More bridges he would need to mend there. Thinking about that, he realised he was left more or less on his own that week, none of his so called friends had called or texted him to see if he was okay. He stuck in his earphones, time for some music to take his mind off things. Flicking through his songs he finally found *'Motorcycle Emptiness'* by the Manic Street Preachers, perfect for his current state of mind.

One thing he did know for sure was that it was definitely time for a change.

*****

Chapter 21
Heavy Water
'Universally Speaking'   **Red Hot Chili Peppers**

'Hey guess what?' Grainne sounded excited, even over the phone Harry could tell.

'What?'

'Guess who I got tickets to go see?'

'Who?'

'Go on guess?'

'I can't.'

'Ah you're no fun. It's the Red Hot Chili Peppers.'

'No way?'

'Yes way. You excited?'

'Fuck, yeah.' Harry looked up to see the whole staff room looking at him, 'She got us tickets to see the Chili Peppers,' he whispered holding the mike end of the phone.

'You still there?'

'Yeah yeah,' he said as he put the phone back to his ear. 'I'd better shoot off back to work, talk to you later?'

'Yeah, chat to you in a bit.'

Harry hung up the phone and wondered how in the hell she had got tickets to the concert, which was on that Friday. He was sure it had sold out a long time ago.

Friday came, Harry was bouncing around the office like a kid on Christmas Eve, even his boss commented on how happy he looked, the difference a couple of months could make. Five o'clock came, he bolted out the door like a greyhound. Grainne was in the Foggy Dew waiting on him for a few pre-concert drinks, he really liked drinking in there, especially the way they would play the music of whatever band were playing. He found her perched on a barstool, a pint with his name on it, too.

'You looking forward to this?' she asked.

'Hell yeah, you get standing tickets?'

'Too right I did. Not a fan of sitting at all.'

'Me neither, should be great gig though.'

'Yeah, I've never seen them live.'

'Seen them years ago when they played Slane,' Harry said.

'Any good?'

'Yeah, they were. Better sound though seeing them indoors.'

'No chance of getting drowned either.'

'Oh yeah, our climate is not great for outdoor gigs. Remember me and Phil went to see AC/DC in Punchestown a few years ago. Sun was shining when we got to Naas for a few pints during the day, so I just had my shorts and t-shirt on. Sure by the time we got in to the gig, it was pissing rain. Went to try by a hat or something, but they were sold out. Ended up buying an extra t-shirt and got soaked waiting on them to come on.'

'Jesus, that's mad. You must have been proper soggy.'

'All was forgotten though when they came on, super show. They really are a stadium band, with their massive show, big blow up dolls and all. Didn't worry about being cold and wet once they started to pump out their songs.'

'Can't say I've ever really listened to them.'

'Oh, you really have to, I'll give you some of their stuff.'

'Yeah, do.'

'So what time we going to head down at?'

'Sure no rush, it's not like we're going to try get up to the front or anything.'

'No, you just end up getting all hot and sweaty.'

'Save that for later, hey?' She smiled and gave him a wink.

'Oh, saucy,' he said smiling back.

'Yeah, we'll have one or two more then head down.'

'Sounds like a plan.'

They arrived down at the venue for the concert, headed in and straight to the bar. When they arrived into the main hall, they were just in time for the entrance of the Red Hot Chili Peppers. They stayed at the back, which was just as good as trying to push up to the front, as they could see just as much without being squashed. No difference in the sound either. Nipping out every once in a while to top up their drinks, Harry was tempted to jump into a crowd of lads bouncing off each other at one stage but thought better of it. They would be heading back into town later and he didn't want to be stinking of sweat.

'Where to now?' Grainne asked as they left the concert.

'Grab a taxi back into town?'

'Yeah, no way I'm walking.'

'Coppers for a laugh?'

'Sure ain't been there in ages.'

'Neither have I.'

They jumped into the first taxi they could find, headed off over to Hardcourt Street, where Copperface Jacks was located. Harry could never really understand the attraction of the place, he wasn't a big fan of the low ceilings, never helped with his claustrophobia. For some reason he just thought it would be a good spot for a change. Anyway they weren't really dressed for a night on the town, both just in jeans and t-shirt. They queued up, why was there always a queue for here? It's not like it's an extra special club, Grainne thought they deliberately kept the queue outside to make it look busy. They got in eventually and were walking towards the bar with Harry leading the way. Harry looked up only to see Dervila walking towards him, what on earth was she doing here? He knew this would happen at some stage, Dublin is such a small city. How was this going to play out? Would she even acknowledge him? Did he have time to duck out of the way, or did he even want too? Bit too late for that, she had spotted him and made eye contact. Now he would have to say something and hope Grainne didn't say something nasty to her or vice versa. Dervila came over and gave him a hug, Harry had to hug her back, even though it felt a little uncomfortable, especially with Grainne standing right behind him.

'Heya,' she said. 'What are you doing here?' she asked him.

'Could say the same to you, not your kind of place is it?'

'Na, not really. Just here with a few heads. So, how you been?'

'Yeah, really good. You?'

'Yeah, getting there. Must say you're looking happier now.'

'Feeling it to. Had a few things I needed to sort out.' Grainne was now kicking him in the back of the leg, looking to know what was going on.

'I'm really happy for you, really am.'

'Thanks. I've only realised lately just how messed up I was. Didn't deal with Phil's death at all well.'

'Well, it's good you've sorted yourself out now. You seem a lot more content.'

'Yeah I am, thanks. Hey, look this is Grainne.' He pulled Grainne forward. 'Grainne, this is Dervila.' Harry stood back and didn't know what to expect. They both looked at each other, each checking the other out.

'So you're the famous Dervila then?' Grainne sounded intrigued by her.

'Oh, so he mentioned me then?'

'All good, I must say.'

'Yeah, I still have a lot of time for Harry, too.'

'He never told me just how good looking you were,' she said again giving him a little kick and he just shrugged his shoulders.

'I better head back over to these heads. See you around?' Dervila leant over and gave Harry a kiss on the cheek.

'Yeah, see you around.' They then both headed off in the opposite direction, Grainne moving right up to Harry's side.

'She seems like a lovely girl,' Grainne said to Harry.

'Oh she is, it was just everything else about her, the circles she moves in. She's always out and knows so many different people, there was always something crazy happening.'

'She helped you to hide from things?'

'Yeah, I suppose so.'

'Come on, enough serious talk. Shot?' Grainne said dragging Harry towards the bar.

They left the club feeling a little worse for wear and started to walk down the road. Harry decided to cut down a side lane, on the way he spotted a casino.

'You wanna go in?' he asked Grainne.

'Yeah, could be a laugh.'

They went into the casino and bought some chips to gamble with. Harry went down to play a black jack, Grainne just watched on. He was doing quite well, even up a good bit, but soon got bored. Then he decided he would play a little roulette. Again he was doing alright sticking with red or black, switching to odds or evens at times, always giving himself a fifty-fifty chance. Then he noticed a small oriental lad on the other side of the table. He was putting chips down all over the table, betting on single and multiple numbers. Harry saw this and thought to himself *I'll have a piece of that.* After a minute Grainne was pulling at his arm quite forcefully.

'What?' he said, turning to her.

'What are you doing?'

'Shush, I'm doing what he's doing.'

'Okay, you do realise he's playing with twenty-cent chips, you're playing with twenty-five euro chips?'

'What!!' Harry looked down closer at the table.

'Yeah and you're doing really badly at it too.'

'Okay then …time to go home.' Harry picked up what few chips he had left and cashed out. He had just about broken even and headed out the door, followed by closely by Grainne.

*****

Chapter 22
Breakers
'Pennyroyal Tea' Nirvana

Harry sat in his bedroom, deep in thought, he knew he was going to have to break up with Dervila. It was not that he didn't like her, it was the craziness of the lifestyle surrounding her. It really was starting to quite literally starting to kill him. He wasn't looking forward to it, but it was best for them both – tonight was going to be the night. Now he would just have to find the right moment when they were out. It might not be easy because they always ended up crowed noisy places.

During the night Harry couldn't seem to get Dervila on her own long enough to have a proper chat. He wasn't sure how to act around Dervila, ending up with him not saying much. Finally, when in the night club, he saw his chance, bringing her over into a quiet corner. He had had a little too much to drink for his liking, but it had given him a bit more courage – this had to be done now. There was no point in stringing her along for a few weeks, it would hurt both of them more that way.

'Everything okay, Harry? You seem awfully quiet tonight.'

'Yeah, I just have a bit on my mind.'

'Awh Harry, you know you can talk to me about it.'

'Yeah, well …uh …that's sort of the thing.' Standing face to face he now held her hands, pulling her in closer.

'Oh!' She stopped smiling, knowing he looked serious.

'I think that …em …maybe we should stop seeing each other.' There was no easy way of breaking into it, he just had to go for it, like pulling of a plaster.

'What? …I mean where has this come from, Harry?'

'I need to sort myself out, Dervila. Drinking and partying ain't the answer.'

'I can help you, you know that.'

'I don't think so, Dervila. I really need to completely change my lifestyle.'

'What stop drinking altogether?'

'No, just cut back, need to find ways to relax, all this… This madness is killing me, feel like I'm cracking up.' Harry could feel himself welling up, he could see the same happening to Dervila.

'Come on, I always thought we were having fun? We're good together, aren't we?'

'Yeah, we are, probably too good. I really, really do like you. Just don't want to change who you are just for me, you'll only end up resenting me in the end.' She was starting to hold his hands tighter now.

'Come on, don't do this to me.' He could see tears really welling up in her eyes now, which was making it harder for him to keep his own emotions in check. He thought this was hard, but it was proving to be much harder.

'This just isn't me, that's all.' He was gesturing around him.

'Come on, can we just go outside and talk about this.'

'Okay then.' She led him by the hand outside.

On the way out they bumped into a couple of girls Dervila knew.

'Hey Dervila?'

'Heya.'

'We're heading back to a house party, wanna come?'

'Em, I don't know.'

'Come on.' Dervila looked at Harry, who shrugged. Harry was tired and he just wanted to go to bed, the whole week had been emotionally draining on him. Maybe we can sit down there, talk properly?

'Okay then, we can have a chat there.' She grabbed him by the hand, dragging him towards the car.

They arrived at the house party, only to find people leaving the house. Someone was saying the police had shown up to break up the party, everyone was now heading home. Party was over. 'Shit, it's over,' one of the girls said.

'What'll we do now?' the other one asked.

'I know where there's a party on,' Harry said from the back.

'Where?'

'I'll give you directions.' Dervila looked at him, Harry never knew where a party was. He directed the girls to his place.

'Here?' one of the girls asked.

'Yeah.' As he got out of the car and headed for the gate to his apartment, closely followed by Dervila and the girls. He opened the door to his quiet, empty apartment.

'Not many here then?' One of the girls said sounding confused.

'You can come in if you want?'

'Na you're okay, think we'll head home.'

'Fair enough,' he said, opening the door, really only wanting to go to bed. Dervila was still tagging along as he walked in the door, he couldn't bring himself to tell her to go home.

'Hey, I'm knackered. Going to head to bed,' he said to her.

'Okay, can I stay here?'

'Yeah, come on.' He was far too tired to get back into this now.

He woke up to find Dervila clinging onto him in bed. *'Shit,'* he thought. *'Did we not break up last night?'* Now he was going to have to break up with her all over again. She stirred and woke turning over to look at him.

'Morning,' she said smiling at him.

'Morning.'

'Breakfast?'

'Hey, you know this doesn't change things?'

'Please, don't say it.' She was starting to well up again.

'I know it's hard, but it's best for both of us, really.' He was starting to well up himself.

'No,' she was now crying.

'I know it's hard, but we have to. Like I said this really isn't me and it's slowly tearing me apart. I really, really do like you. We're just not the right fit right now.'

She got up from bed, started to get dressed, still sobbing.

'You thought it was okay just bringing me back here last night, after dumping me. What was I supposed to think?'

'Well, you just sort of came along. Didn't really mean for it to happen this way.'

'Didn't mean for it to happen! So it's okay to dump a girl, then bring her back and sleep with her again?'

'Hey, this is by far the hardest decision I've ever had to make. I really love being around you, you're so much fun. I just like you far too much to try and change you, just when I'm around you I can't help being sort of hooked on you.'

'Hooked on me, so I'm like some sort of addiction or something.'

'No, no, look I'm coming across right here.'

'You can say that again!'

'Hey, I'm sacred here. If I don't sort myself I going to go mad or worse. I think we're just not right for each other at the moment.'

'So now you think if you stay with me you're going to die or something?'

'No, no, no …I'm not saying that at all.' Harry's head was now in his hands, this was not going the way he had planned it in his head, not at all.

'I'll see you around then, I suppose,' she shouted as she walked out slamming the bedroom door. He could hear a few things smashing, then the front door slammed shut. Harry rolled over and curled up into the duvet. Her scent still lingered on them, he would need to change the sheets. Wiping a tear from the corner of his eye, curling up in a ball, time to try to go back to sleep. He knew he had really hurt her, that was the last thing he wanted, but maybe with time she would understand that it was best for both of them.

There was no way he would get out of bed today, well maybe for a cup of tea.

*****

Chapter 23
Beach Bum
'Here comes the Sun' **The Beatles**

Harry was out with Grainne having a cup of coffee in Dublin City Centre. He still found it hard to think he'd being going out with Grainne over three years. She really was the one for him.

'You do like your Mocha, don't ya?' Grainne said to Harry.

'Yeah it's the only way to have coffee.'

Harry's phone rang, it was Joe.

'Ah heya Joe, what's the craic?'

'Hey, listen, you know it's the fifth anniversary of Phil's death on Sunday?'

'Yeah, it had sort of crossed my mind.'

'We're going to do something out in Dalkey to remember him.'

'What you have in mind?'

'You'll see on Sunday; think you'll like it though. You in?'

'Yeah, wouldn't miss it. Can Grainne tag along?'

'Of course, why you even asking.'

'Cool, what time?'

'Meeting about twelve in the car park.'

'Sounds good, see you then.'

He hung up the phone, didn't say much, his head dropped, Grainne could tell he was thinking about something.

'Everything okay?'

'Yeah, didn't realise that Phil will be five years dead on Sunday.'

'Jesus, so what were you planning to do?'

'Heading out to Dalkey for it. Really is the kind of thing I should remember though.'

'Hey, you went through a major trauma, it can be quite normal to block out things.' She leaned over and held his hand.

'Thanks, ya made me feel a lot better.' He looked up and smiled at her.

'Hey, he knows you miss him and that's all that's important. Don't worry about anyone else.'

'Yeah, suppose you're right there.'

'Come on, let's go for a pint.'

'You sure?'

'Yeah, now come on.' She stood up and grabbed her coat, Harry didn't need to be asked twice.

Sunday came, Harry was at Grainne's place, pacing around the sitting room waiting. 'Would you ever sit down?' Grainne was starting to feel on edge as well.

'I'm fine.'

'Just relax, stop fidgeting. We've loads of time yet.'

'You want a cup of coffee? Cause I'm making one.'

'Yeah, if it'll get you out of my hair for a while.' She didn't know why he was so nervous, maybe because he didn't know what they had planned for today, or how he would react to it. Probably worried he'd show some emotion in front of the others. Better not to mention it to him, best off just being there for him.

Harry and Grainne arrived at the car park just after noon. Everyone was on time for once. Joe had a bag, as had Dave, which looked like it was full of climbing gear, Jim and Niamh had a picnic basket and Will had what looked like a bag of cans. They all smiled at the two new arrivals and started to head in, Joe and Dave leading the way. Not much was said on the way in until Joe stopped. It was cloudy but bright autumn day, sun breaking through the clouds, leaves on the ground from the now bare looking trees.

'Right, this will do?' He checked with Dave, who nodded, indicating they were in the right spot. He put his bag down and took out a blanket. Jim and Niamh started to lay out the picnic, which was all of Phil's favourite food. Will took out the cans, which again were Phil's favoured brand of cider. They all sat down in a circle, sharing out the food and a can each. Grainne turned down the offer; Harry thought nothing of it as she was driving.

'This is very thoughtful lads,' Harry said as he sat down.

'There's more to...' Niamh said, smiling.

'What?' Harry asked.

'You'll see in a while.'

'I thought we'd share our best memories of Phil, while drinking his favourite tipple,' Joe said as he raised his can. They all tipped cans and took a sip. 'Jesus!' Jim said, 'Don't know how he drank this stuff.' They all laughed at Jim's reaction and face after he had a mouthful.

'I'll start then,' Dave said, 'My memory of Phil was an insanely talented climber with balls of steel; he never knew fear, well not that I could see anyway. We were climbing one day and he was about half way up when he noticed he was on the wrong climb. He was stuck and couldn't find a way up or back down. Proper stuck he was and I was no help to him. Next thing

I knew he was on the ground beside me, flat on his back. He said he slipped, but I don't know, could well have just jumped off. He jumped up, said *'thank god the ground is soft'* and skipped off back up the correct climb. He was the good kind of crazy.'

'I'm up then,' said Will. 'Jesus, I had so much fun with him, it hard to think one just one story. It would have to be, just him jumping off anything and everything. That gorge walk we did with the centre, every jump and slide we did on that he found. There was the day he was trying a new slide down this small rapid. I was at the top as he slid down, he disappeared under the water at the bottom, when he surfaced he was jumping up and down like he'd hurt himself. *'Don't try that,'* he shouted up. *'Bloody pointy rock at the bottom.'* He was rubbing his tailbone by now, I was trying not to laugh in front of the kids we had out. One thing's for sure he made that so much more fun, think they still use most of the jumps he found.'

'Okay I'll go,' said Niamh. 'Well I've seen a different side to him, the kind and caring side he shows that we didn't get to see enough of. I was sort of seeing this lad, sorry Jim.' She glanced over at him. 'He wasn't good for me at all, bit of a prick to be honest. Out one night and we had a bit of a tiff. Anyway he fecked off and left me on my own with no coat, no money and no way home. Just so happened as I sat outside the pub on the step balling my eyes out, Phil strolled out of the same pub. He never told me what he was doing in there, probably with some girl, but he found me. It was freezing, so he gave me his coat and dropped me off at home in a taxi, must have cost him a fortune, but never took any money off me. Wouldn't take it when I offered it to him, he cut his night short to make sure I was okay.'

'Here my turn.' Joe said, 'As you all know, Phil was never really into canoeing like me and me not into climbing, so always seemed to be doing different things. The time I did spend with him though were some of the best. I loved his sense of humour, so dry, he could poke fun at himself as well. Sometimes you couldn't tell if he was joking or being serious. Lunchtime was always entertaining. Once he came walking back with a large tea pot, asking if anyone wanted some, as he got to the table he tripped, pot came towards us. Everyone thought they'd be scalded by hot tea, but it turned out the pot was empty! Thought he was great with the groups of kids in the centre, always had them laughing and made sure they enjoyed themselves. Maybe because he never did grow up, he could still relate to them on their level. I really did learn a lot from him and am a better person for knowing him.'

'Okay, my go.' Jim said, 'I'll always remember him being a bit of a show off, we had just stared in the centre, we were only about eighteen. He was setting up the climbing wall and I was at the other end of the doing something with a group of girls all in around seventeen. He free climbed the wall to put the abseil rope up, don't know what he was thinking abseiling down, but he let the rope go. When he realised he was picking up speed he grabbed the rope, only for it to start burning his fingers. What did he do? Only let the rope go to blow his burning fingers, he hit the ground with such a thud. Got up walked to the door very slowly, as soon as it shut behind him, he bolted for the toilet to run his hand under the cold tap. One of the funniest things I've ever seen.'

'Jesus, you're asking for my best memory?' Harry said.

'Well, maybe a couple. You would know a lot more,' Niamh said, smiling.

'Okay then. There were so many, I mean we were mates from the day we met in first class. One day at school a few lads were teasing this girl.' He glanced at Grainne and she smiled. 'They took her bag and threw it up on the roof. When we saw this, we ran over to chase the lads away and make sure she was alright. Phil climbed up on to the roof to get her bag, it wasn't an easy climb, but he made it look easy, got the bag and dropped it down to me. I gave it back to the girl who went on her way back to class. Wasn't the last time we helped her out.

As Phil was climbing down we were caught by the school principal, we were late back from lunch and had been up on the roof. Ended up in the office, they wouldn't take our side of the story. Assumed we were trying to bunk off and hide on the roof.'

'Em, yeah,' Grainne butted in, 'that girl was me.'

'No way?' Niamh said.

'That's unbelievable, that you're together now,' Dave said.

'Yeah, crazy stuff,' Will added.

'He had a little bit of a sadistic sense of humour at times. Once we were out canoeing with a group on the canal. We finished the trip at a bridge and I decided I would jump off the bridge into the canal. So, I climbed up and Phil was sitting on the water underneath. I shouted down to ask him if it was deep enough. He put his paddle in the water and said *Yeah.*' So off I went for the twenty-foot drop into the water, turns out it was only about five foot deep. Lucky I didn't break both ankles! Phil thought it was one of the funniest things ever.'

'Okay best get on with why we're really here,' Joe said as he pulled a small plaque out of his bag, Dave stated to get climbing gear out of his bag and a drill.

'What's that?' Harry asked.

'You know what climb we're at the top of, don't ya?' Harry looked over.

'Yeah, Paradise lost. One Phil loved to free climb all the time.'

'Yeah, we going to put this at the top in memory of Phil.' He handed to plaque to Harry. It said:

'Always climbing, always young, always smiling.
Belay on Phil, take in the slack.'

They set up for Dave to drop over the side and drill the plaque into the top of the climb. They then stood back and raised their cans.

'To Phil,' Harry said.

'To Phil and having Harry back,' Joe said.

'Good to be back,' Harry said just as the sun broke through the clouds, they could see the sun's rays breaking through.

'Hey, my used to always say someone was going to heaven when she saw that,' Niamh said.

'Na, Phil's letting us know he's still about.'

They all sat in a circle staring at the sky in dead silence, for a few minutes.

As they were leaving the quarry Grainne hung back a little, holding Harry's hand and slowing down. 'Something wrong?' Harry asked looking a little confused.

'Yeah, everything's fine,' she looked a bit distracted.

'You sure?' Harry could tell something was up.

'Look, I've something to tell you.' Harry really was starting to worry now; this was an odd time to break up with him. Preparing himself for the oncoming bombshell, he knew he would be gutted. They both stopped walking and stood face to face, Grainne holding his hands.

'Go on.'

'Well …um …you know the way I was at the doctor the other day?'

'Yeah, for a check-up?' Now Harry really didn't know where this was going.

'Well …turns out I was a little late …that's why I went.'

'Late?'

'Yeah, late.' She was nodding at him.

'Oh. …Late.' Now the penny suddenly dropped with Harry. 'And?'

'So …I'm …em …pregnant.' She seemed hesitant and didn't know how Harry would react. He smiled at her, pulled her close and gave her a hug.

'That's great news. You happy too?'

'Well yeah, only cause it's with you.'

'Thanks. Hey, guess we'll have to start thinking about names then?'

'I think we both know what it'll be if it's a boy.' She pulled her head back so Harry could see her smile.

'What if it's a girl?'

'Oh, we can't really call her Philomena, can we?'

'No, we couldn't do that.'

'So what could we use then?'

'Well, his surname was Lynott, so how about Lynn?'

'Hey, you two coming or what?' The call came back from Joe with the others.

'Hang on; we've got something to tell you,.' Harry replied as they both skipped up to join up with the group, both as excited as children on Christmas Eve.

*****

CHAPTER 24
Swim for the Surface
'Come Back'   *Pearl Jam*

Harry's parents sat on the two uncomfortable plastic chairs holding hands How long they had been there they were not sure, was it hours, days? They couldn't tell any more, neither liked hospitals, more so having to spend so much time in such a sterile environment. It was the last place they'd expected or wanted to be.

'It'll be okay, Barbara.' Harry's dad said wishfully trying to reassure her.

'I hope so, Bob.' She replied quietly from her position resting on his shoulder.

As they sat there not saying much more, the room door opened. After a few seconds someone sheepishly entered the room slowly. Barbara sprung from the chair heading for her, Bob had to move fast to avoid the imminent clash.

'Dervila! What the fuck are you doing here?'

'I….em… err….came to see Harry…' Gone was the chirpy confidence she had always exuded, avoiding this confrontation had been her hope, but there was no way of doing this now. Dervila was going to have to face the music for her part in what had transpired the week previous. She had waited a week, hoping he would improve and hopefully arrive at a time when his parents weren't there. Now only was her boyfriend dying she now had to deal with his angry parents, she didn't know if she was strong enough to deal with this.

Bob was now holding Barbara back. 'Now Barbara, calm down, this won't do anyone any good.'

'We wouldn't be here if it wasn't for her!' she was not calming down; Bob was now having to put a bit of effort into restraining her from moving towards Dervila. She bowed her head, tears dropping into the flowers she had carried in with her. She really wasn't strong enough to deal with this.

'Could I please see him?'

'See him, you put him in there! Look at him …. He's fighting for his life.' She was starting to screech now, fighting back the tears. 'look what you've done to him. You still haven't told us what happened?'

Dervila looked shell-shocked when she did lift her head. 'I …. I'm not really sure what happened….we went back…. to …. uh …. to a house party ….' she really was trying to fight back the tears, they all were. 'We were having a bit of fun…. next… next thing I knew…. he …. he was laid out on the sofa.'

'Come on, you know what happened? You don't end up on a ventilator with your organs failing from just drinking.'

'Well….' Dervila was struggling to find the words, 'there were…. em … em … some pills being handed around.' Her head went back down in shame, supporting it with her free hand.

'Oh, so now the truth comes out. So you both took these pills?'

'Oh … em …. err … yeah … yeah we did.'

'And he's the only one…. the only one in here?' The screeching had died down now, her legs became week. Bob supported her stopping her from hitting the ground. Dervila didn't know what to say or do.

'Barbara.' Bob said tenderly. 'How about we go get a cup of tea and some fresh air, we've been cooped up in this room for ages. Harry doesn't need to hear this kind of thing either.' He started to walk her towards the door, as they walked by Dervila he let Barbara walk on and stopped very close to her. 'I'm doing this for my wife, not you. You'd better be gone by the time we come back …. don't come back either. I won't be responsible for my actions if I see you again.' Now it was Bob's turn the fight back the tears. They left the room leaving Dervila standing there alone now openly weeping.

She went into Harry's room to see him lying there tubes and machines keeping him alive, 'oh my God, what have we done?' she thought to herself, 'it was just supposed to be a bit off fun.' She walked to his bed side and held his hand as best she could, still holding the flowers in her other hand.

'I'm sorry Harry,' she struggled to say, 'it wasn't meant to be this way, please come back. I need you, can't do this on my own. I promise it'll be different; I'll be more like a real girlfriend. We can go for dinner, picnics in the park, visit the zoo, you can even teach me how to canoe …. Just come back. Your child needs you Harry.' All she heard in reply was the beep of the machine, the wispy breathing of the ventilator keeping him alive. 'Harry, please come back.' She stood in silence for a while, left the flowers beside him on the bed, then slowly exited the room head bowed. 'I'm really sorry, I didn't know. How was I to know, we'd done it so many times before.' This was more for herself than for what was left of Harry laid out on the bed.

Outside the hospital Bob had made sure he put extra sugar in Barbara's tea, as he approached her he saw a cigarette in her hand. 'Barbara, what are you doing?!'

'What does it look like Bob?'

'You haven't smoked in years.'

'Not the time Bob, we've just found out our son is a drug addict!'

'It's okay Bab's, just got a bit of a shock seeing the cigarette in your hand. I'm sure he was just fooling around and got unlucky.'

'I'm sorry Bob, just she …. SHE has gotten to me …. always said she was bad news.'

'We all had our reservations about her, but he wouldn't listen …. Would he? We can't live his life for him.'

'Where did we go wrong Bob?'

'I don't know Barbara.' She stubbed out half of the cigarette, turned to Bob and hugged him as hard as she could.

Grainne parked her car in the hospital car park, pity she couldn't get it any closer to the door, but no bother it was a good day either way. Her Dad was well enough to come home after a long illness. As she approached the front door with a pep in her step, she spotted two familiar faces, 'Where do I know them from?' She thought to herself, then it clicked *It's Mister and Misses Adams, I used to pal around with their son Harry at primary school. Wonder what they are doing here, man they look sad, hope everything is okay. I should go over and say hi.*'

'Hey, Mister Adams.' She said quietly as she got close, Barbara had her head resting on his chest.

'Oh, Hi.' He replied, not sure how she knew who they were. *'Please don't be another one of his party friends! We would be able for that.'*

'Oh sorry, It's Grainne, I used to pal around with your Harry at primary school.'

'Ah Grainne, you've grown. Didn't recognise you there, ditched the glasses I see.'

'Yeah, laser eye surgery. Sorry to intrude, but is everything okay?'

'Oh we'll be fine, thanks for asking though.'

'Sure it'll work out fine whatever it is.'

'Thanks …. Maybe you should know. It's Harry who's not well, it's not looking good either.'

'Oh my god what happed? He was such a lovely kid, never forget how he and Phil stopped the bullies at school picking on me. Always were my knights in shining armour.'

'We're not sure what exactly what happened, think his drink got spiked or something.'

'Dear me, that's horrible. If I get a chance I'll drop in and see him. Tell him I said hi, will ya and send my love. Hope he pulls through. Sorry really have to dash, now already late for picking up Dad.'

'Thanks again Grainne, we'll pass your message on.' She gave them both a hug and headed off through the door.

'Such a lovely girl.' Barbara said lifting her head to look at Bob.

'She really did grow up to be lovely girl alright.'

'Why couldn't have Harry met a girl like her and not the other thing?!'

As Grainne was speeding as quick as she could through the hospital foyer, she accidently bumped into another woman walking in the opposite direction, knocking her phone and bag out of her hand.

'Oh I'm really sorry.' She said bending down to help her pick them up.

'It's okay.' Came the disheartened reply as she looked up.

Grainne could see she had been crying, 'Jesus you okay?'

'Yeah, just my boyfriend is not well.' She replied taking her phone back.

'Hope he's okay, make sure you take care of yourself.'

'Thanks, I'll try.' Dervila put her phone in her bag, trudging off towards the door, leaving Grainne standing looking after her, grateful she was there pick up her Dad so she could bring him home.

Bob and Barbara arrived back at Harry's to find the doctor waiting outside the door for them, he looked sombre. Looking at each other, they both knew what was coming next. It was time to say goodbye to their son.

'Mr and Mrs Adams, this is not easy to say. His organs have failed, the ventilator is all that's keeping him alive at the moment, there really is no chance of him living any kind of life, he won't survive without the ventilator. You're going to have to make a decision I'm afraid.'

'Oh Bob.' Barbara said as she threw herself into Bob's arms.

'I'll give you a few minutes to decide.' The doctor said as he quietly exited the room.

'Well, Bab's what are we going to do?'

'Oh Bob, never thought we'd have to bury our son.'

'I know, nobody should. But … what's best for him?'

'Time to say goodbye to our son? Let him rest?'

'I think so Babs. This is no life for him.'

They stood hand in hand beside his bed, tears welling in their eyes. Bob was unable to express how he felt, so he stood behind Barbara holding her shoulders while she spoke their last words to their only son, Harry.

'We bumped into one of your old friends outside Harry. Grainne, remember her? You Phil and she were nearly inseparable back in primary school. She's grown into a beautiful kind and caring girl, I think you'd really like her. We really do love you son, sleep well.' These were the last words his mam whispered to him, she leaned over and kissed him on the forehead. Not long after the ventilator was switched off and he was gone. .

*****

'I hung my head'   *Johnny Cash*

EPILOGUE
'Everybody Hurts' REM.

'Bob, answer the door will you?' Barbara called from upstairs. 'Bob!' she called again. *'Bloody man is as def as a post,'* she muttered to herself as she hurried down the stairs. As she got to the door she saw Bob coming out of the Kitchen.

'Where were you?'

'Out the back.'

'Should have known, you and that bloody garden.'

She opened the front door to find a coy-looking Dervila standing there along with a pram. Bob was now looking over her shoulder. This was the last thing either had expected.

'Oh … what do you want?' Barbara asked somewhat cuttingly.

'Great,' thought Dervila, *'they still hate me.'* She shuffled a bit. 'Em … I know I'm probably the last person you want to see, but could please we talk? It's important.'

Barbara looked at Bob, who shrugged and nodded as if to say why not. She opened the front door fully, 'Come on in then.'

'Thank you,' Dervila replied somewhat struggling to get the pram through the door. Bob stepped forward to help her navigate her way into the sitting room. She sat down nervously on the edge of the sofa as close to the door as possible, thinking to herself, *'I need a drink.'*

'Cup of tea?' Bob asked with a kind smile.

'Yes please,' she replied.

'Milk and sugar?'

'Just a small bit of milk please.'

Barbara sat down on the armchair across from Dervila, glaring at her. 'So, what have you got to say for yourself?'

'Oh … where do I start?' She said fidgeting on the edge of the sofa, 'like I said, I know you probably never wanted see me again after Harry's funeral.'

'You wouldn't be wrong there.' Barbara interrupted.

Dervila seemed rattled, 'maybe this was a mistake … think I should go.'

Bob arrived in with the cup of tea and a packet of biscuits, putting them down on the coffee table close to her and sitting beside her on the sofa. 'Look, have a sip of tea, then tell us why you're here,' he said with a smile, a gentleness of someone who maybe knew how hard this had been for Dervila to do, how many sleepless nights she'd had working her way towards this moment. 'Barbara, can we just listen to what she has to say?' She nodded in agreement and sank back into the arm chair.

'Okay, so where do I start?'

'Maybe at the part where you killed our son!'

'Barbara.' Bob glared at her.

'Sorry, go on … you were saying,' Barbara sighed, still seemingly unwilling to listen.

Dervila was now finding it hard to fight the tears welling up in her eyes. Why was she making this so hard for her? At this point the baby who had been so well behaved until this point stirred. She peered into the pram checking to see if everything was okay. She glanced up at Barbara, then at Bob, 'Suppose … I'd better start off by introducing you to … your … well … your grandchild. This is Harry junior.'

Barbara looked at Dervila in shock, then at Bob, who too looked stunned. 'But … how … why … why are you only telling us this now?' she finally stumbled out.

By this time Dervila had taken young Harry from the pram and was offering him to his grandmother. 'Well it didn't feel right at the funeral. I wasn't exactly welcome, was I?' she said holding him across the coffee table.

'He's beautiful. Hey Harry, I'm your grandma,' Barbara said taking him and gazing into his eyes, while he smiled. Was she starting to soften? 'He's the spitting image of Harry when he was a child. So … em … why now?'

'Well … I … thought you'd maybe want to be part of his life. Even if you want nothing to do with me.' The tears were now flowing down her cheeks. Bob put his hand on her shoulder, in an effort to comfort her. He lifted the cup of tea from the table and handed it to her. 'Thank you,' she said taking a sip from the cup in an attempt to gather herself.

'Here Bob,' Barbara said offering the baby to him. 'Isn't he beautiful?' She could not help but feel joy at the sight of a grandchild she thought she'd lost the chance to never have.

'Oh, he is. Looks grand and strong,' Bob replied. 'Can't wait to bring him to his first football match. You do know he's a Man United fan, now don't you?' Bob looked at Dervila, who managed a small laugh through the tears. 'Hopefully you like football more than your dad.' Dervila's tears now turned to joy as she glanced at a beaming Bob.

'Thank you so much,' She managed to blurt out. 'I really didn't know how I was going to manage. It's been so hard already trying to do this on my own.'

'What?!' Barbara said in surprise, 'do you not have any family or friends?'

'No,' came the reply sheepishly, 'it's just me. My mam kicked out my Dad when I was five, I only found out just how abusive he had been to both me and mother when I was older. She tried her best for me but died when I was twelve. Moved in with grandmother who raised me until she also died when I was eighteen. I've been on my own since then. Fell into the party scene as a way to feel something … anything, but deal with the pain of losing everyone, everything. I found out the hard way my so-called friends are only interested in partying, I haven't seen or heard anything from them since I told them I was pregnant.' Barbara took a packet of hankies from her pocket and reached across the table to offer them to Dervila. She took them and started to wipe the tears. 'Harry was different … he was the one I felt I could spend the rest of my life with. He … he was just as … as broken as me.'

'Broken?' Bob asked.

'Yeah, he never talked about it, but I'm sure he blamed himself for Phil's death. I should have pushed him to talk about it, but thought he'd talk about it in his own time. Maybe if I'd talked about my childhood it would have encouraged him to open up. We just seemed to help each other avoid our problems keep the darkness away. I know it was wrong and think about how different I should have done things every day. Harry should be here to look after his son and it's my fault he's not.'

'Bob, a quick word in the kitchen?' Barbara wasn't asking. Bob carefully handed Harry back to Dervila, stood up placed his hand reassuringly on her shoulder as he walked by. 'We'll be back in a minute.' Dervila took hold of Harry and held him up towards the celling, pulling his tummy in towards her to blow air into his belly button. Harry was enjoying it and seemed oblivious to the tension and emotion that enveloped the room.

They arrived in the kitchen and stood face to face at the sink looking sternly at each other. 'So Bob, what are we going to do?'

'Well we're going to look after our grandchild, that's for sure.' There was a certain steel in his voice.

'Yeah, but how will we work it with her?'

'One day at a time. We'll do everything we can to help that girl be the best mother she can be.'

'You seem very forgiving. Not sure I can be.'

'Barbara, blaming her isn't going to bring Harry back. I've been thinking about this a lot lately … it's not like she did anything on purpose. They were young and dumb, made some daft decisions, Harry ended up paying the ultimate price. He made his own choice, he could have always said no.' It was Barbara's turn now to break down into tears.

'Oh Bob. I miss our son. Where did we go wrong? How did we not notice he was in so much pain?'

'We raised him as best we could, Babs. He was a good kid, just picked the wrong way to deal with his grief. Look we have a grandchild now. We need to make sure we do right by him. We need to help his mother out as much as we can. I know it'll be hard, but we need to do it. Harry saw something in her, we need to find that too. Small steps Babs, one day at a time.'

'I know you're right Bob, but, it's just hard. It's hard to accept our son done this to himself and she's a reminder of it.'

Bob put his arm around Barbara, 'come on, let's go spend some time with our grandchild.' They walked back in and both sat down on the sofa either side of Dervila.

'So Dervila, what are your plans when you go back to work?' Barbara asked.

'I don't know, I'll need to find childcare. That'll take a huge chunk of my wages, but I'm determined to raise him right. Give him the best childhood I can.'

'Well Bob, what you think of spending a lot more time, like every week day with your grandchild?'

'You don't need to ask me twice,' Bob replied beaming.

Barbara looked at Dervila. 'So, if you want, we'd like to look after Harry when you go back to work?'

'Oh no, you don't have to do that.'

'Please, we'd love to.'

'Really?'

'Yes really.'

'Thank you so much. I'll pay you whatever I can.'

'No, you won't. It'll be our pleasure to look after him.'

'If you ever want to spend time with him, just give me a call I'll drop him over. I want him to know as much about his father and you as possible.'

'That's really nice of you. Likewise, if you ever need a break, let us know and we'll gladly babysit.'

'Listen I was about to bring the dog out for a walk down by the river, fancy coming along?' Bob asked Dervila. She looked at Barbara, who shrugged, then back at Bob to nod in agreement. 'Great, I'll go get the dog, we can stop and get ice-cream along the way.'

They arrived down at the path running alongside the river, stopping to get ice-creams as promised. The sun was getting low in the sky, but it was still a nice evening. Bob let the dog off the lead and he ran off, into the trees. 'Look at him. I know he misses Harry, was a time he would always bring him for a walk down here.' Bob started to reminisce.

'Until I came along.' Dervila said sounding down beat.

'Hey, he couldn't stay living at home all his life.'

'I feel like I took him away from you, though.'

'You were just his excuse.'

'Tell me more about him as a child. He never really spoke much about it when we were together.'

'We're in the right place. He used to love this river, him and Phil. See that tree over there?' He pointed at a high tree. 'Well they used to always climb that as kids and see the old bit of frayed rope hanging from the branch?' Dervila nodded, 'Well that was their swing, where they'd swing out into the river during the summer.'

'Sounds like they really enjoyed themselves down here.'

'Yeah right up until they left to go work over the other side of the country.'

'Phil, he never talked much about him either.'

'Here come up here I want to show you something.' He walked off up the path to a bench close to the river bank which looked out onto a weir on the river. 'Here, see that weir over there?'

'Yeah.'

'That's where they spent most weekends learning to canoe. They'd carry, well drag, their kayak up here and take turns messing about at the bottom of that weir. They'd spend hours there. Here, sit down.' He gestured towards the bench.

They both sat down on the bench, Dervila taking Harry out of the pram, showing him the river. The dog came running back over and sat down at Dervish's feet looking out at the river.

'He likes you. Doesn't like many people.' Bob said about the dog. She handed the baby over to Bob so she could bend down and pat the dog who snuggled up to her leg.

'Hey buster, look at where your daddy used to play. I promise I'll bring you here for a swim once you're old enough.' Bob said to Harry. 'Might even give you your old man's Kayak.'

Dervila looked at Bob and smiled, she thought to herself, *'things might just be okay,'* everything didn't seem so hard now, a weight had been lifted. Bob smiled back as they both sat in silence staring off into the setting sun eating their ice-creams.

*****

'The First Cut is the Deepest' Sheryl Crow

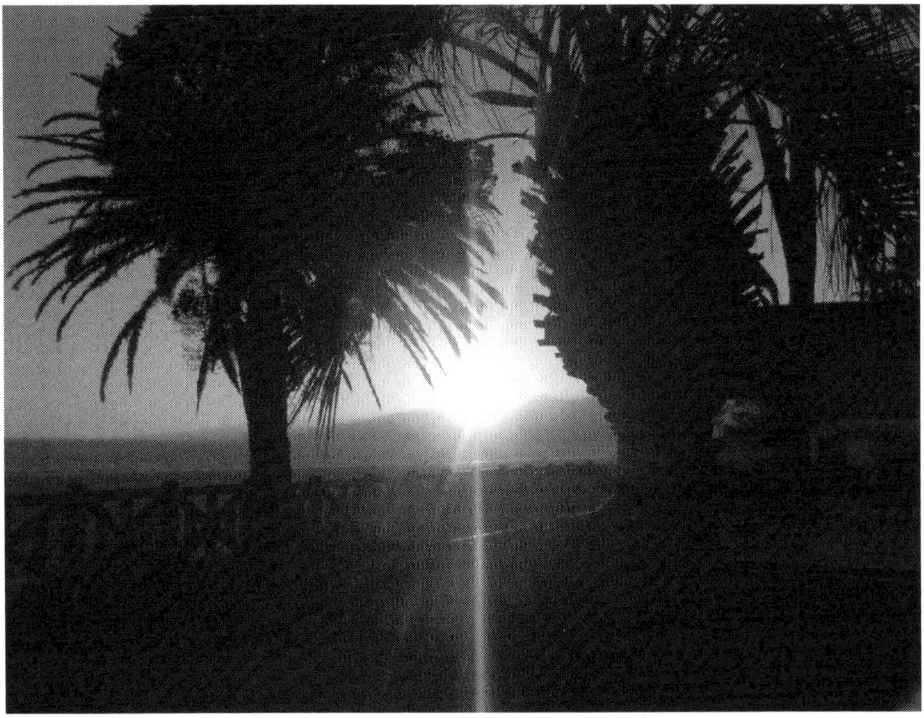

Song List:

'A Design for Life' - Manic Street Preachers
'California Sun' - The Ramones
'Just Like Paradise' - David Lee Roth
'You Stole The Sun From My Heart' – Manic Street Preachers
'You Shook me all night long' – AC/DC
'Cowboy Song' – Thin Lizzy
'Wishlist' – Pearl Jam
'Bonzo Goes To *Bitburg* – The Ramones
'The Boys of Summer' Don Henley
'Perfect Day' Lou Reed
'Velvet Morning' The Verve
'On Melancholy Hill' Gorillaz
'Smells like Teen Spirit' Nirvana
'Black Hole Sun' Soundgarden
'Comfortably Numb' Pink Floyd
'Wonderful tonight' Eric Clapton
'Scar Tissue' Red Hot Chili Peppers
'The Winner Takes it all' ABBA
'Given to Fly' Pearl Jam
'Fix You' Coldplay
'Heart-Shaped Box' Nirvana
'Party Line' Joey Ramone
'Force of Nature' Pearl Jam
'All Apologies' Nirvana
'Road House Blues' The Doors
'Paradise City' Guns n' Roses
'Dancing in the Moonlight' Thin Lizzy
'At My Most Beautiful' R.E.M.
'Want you Bad' The Offspring
'Under the Bridge' Red Hot Chili Peppers
'Society' Eddie Vedder
'Mr. Brownstone' Guns n' Roses
'Angel' Aerosmith
'Straight into darkness' Tom Petty and the Heartbreakers
'Summer in Dublin' Bagatelle
'Old Town' Phil Lynott
'Motorcycle emptiness' Manic Street Preachers
'Universally speaking' Red Hot Chili Peppers
'Pennyroyal Tea' Nirvana
'Here comes the Sub' The Beatles
'Come Back' Pearl Jam
'I Hung My Head' Johnny Cash
'Everybody Hurts' REM
'The First Cut is the Deepest' Sheryl Crow

Printed in Poland
by Amazon Fulfillment
Poland Sp. z o.o., Wrocław